HALF LIFE

Paul H.B. Shin

FIERY SEAS PUBLISHING

Visit our website at www.fieryseaspublishing.com

Half Life

Cover Art by Jess Small

Editing by Michelle Neblett
Interior Design by Merwin Loquias (www.mlgraphicdesigns.tk)

ISBN-13: 978-0-9968943-5-7

Library of Congress Control Number: 2016941582

Printed in the United States of America

First Edition:

10 9 8 7 6 5 4 3 2

Acknowledgements

A special thanks to Chastity Whitaker for believing in the novel and encouraging its completion. I am also indebted to my agent, Mark Gottlieb, for seeing it through to publication.

Dedication

To my late father, C.K., and my mother, K.J., for their
unwavering love and support.

HALF LIFE

A novel

PAUL H.B. SHIN

PART I

Chapter 1

When James Avery opened the window of the SUV, a gush of searing air rushed into the cooled cabin, as though he had opened an oven prepped for baking. He gagged for a moment, and when he caught his breath, there was a faint scent of water lilies drifting in from the Nile.

A black-and-white taxi pulled up alongside the SUV and idled there. No one got in or out. Avery thought about closing the window to let the cabin cool again, but if the taxi passenger was who he was expecting it to be, Avery didn't want the tinted windows to block the view.

It was after business hours and nearing dusk. The water lily petals would be closing soon. The SUV and the taxi were the only vehicles on the block – a manicured street in the Garden City neighborhood of Cairo lined with belle époque estates that had managed to resist the encroaching tangle of new apartment buildings. With groomed hedges and tall gates, the houses had a stately appeal. There was also something out of place about the formality. It evoked a kind of pity, as one feels for a waning beauty dressed in defiance of her age.

A man finally emerged from the taxi wearing a navy wool suit – attire that defied common sense for August here, or any month for that matter if you were concerned with comfort more than declaring your status. It had been a restless weekend of anticipation for Avery. He felt his heart thumping as he opened the SUV door to greet the man.

"Mr. Ambassador," Avery said in Korean. "I'm James Avery from the U.S. State Department. It's good to finally meet you in person."

The man nodded and said, "You're younger than your voice," then climbed into the SUV and sat next to Avery. Heat radiated off the dark fabric of the ambassador's suit. The rear seats had been configured carriage-style, facing one another. A gaunt man with silvery blond hair was sitting across from Avery and the ambassador. He straightened himself when the ambassador climbed in.

Avery introduced the two men. "Ambassador Jang, this is Consul General Walter Cronen."

Cronen offered a handshake, thrusting out his sinewy hand with too much enthusiasm. "Tell Ambassador Jang that the United States government welcomes him into the arms of freedom."

It was an obtuse greeting. Avery found it awkward to interpret verbatim. This welcome that Cronen offered – it was akin to a marriage proposal even before the ink had dried on an acrimonious divorce, and a marriage of convenience at that.

Jang Sung-Gil was North Korea's ambassador to Egypt. He was one of the highest-ranking officials from the Workers' Party ever to defect to the West. That alone would have made this momentous. But it went beyond the treason of single man. He was coordinating his defection simultaneously with his brother, Jang Sung-Ho, a trade attaché in Paris. Both sides of the DMZ would remember the summer of 1997, either as one of infamy or victory.

Jang did not reach for Cronen's offered hand immediately. He waited for Avery to finish translating even though he understood what Cronen had said. And even then, Jang looked at Cronen's hand a moment longer, pondering, it seemed, the consequences – ideological or biological – of pressing flesh with this man. Jang finally clasped it and said, "Thank you."

Cronen nodded to the driver of the SUV through the rearview mirror, and they took off.

Jang had spoken to Avery a number of times on the phone, and seeing him now in person piqued his curiosity about his personal history.

"How do you speak Korean so well?" Jang asked Avery in English, his defection demanding that he try his best to adopt the ways of his new country.

"My parents were Christian missionaries in South Korea. I went to school there until I went to college. My brothers and I grew up playing with neighborhood boys in the alleys near our house in Hannam-dong. My parents still live in that neighborhood."

"How many siblings?" Jang asked.

"Four brothers," Avery said. "And a sister who died when I was very young."

Jang nodded as though in approval of the bounty of siblings, or in sympathy.

"Your parents, still very blessed with many children. Where are your brothers now?"

"Three of them are still in Seoul. One is in the U.S., in North Carolina."

"They do missionary work also?"

"Of one sort or another. Two of them are doctors."

"You are black sheep of your family then? You are only diplomat?"

"Yes. I suppose you could say that." Avery nodded, amused by how Jang dropped the word "the" before "only diplomat," unintentionally suggesting that his was not such a noble line of work when measured against his siblings. It was a common grammatical mistake among Koreans because the language didn't have articles, so the usage of "a" or "the" frequently tripped them up. Jang's unwitting omission hit a sore spot within Avery's family caused by his career choice, or more accurately, by the turn of events that led to his choice.

Avery's father would sometimes ask him as a greeting, "How's the spy business?" It was a wisecrack but Avery still felt the barbs on occasion. "I'm not a spy, dad," Avery would reply, weary from repetition. Having deviated from the family business – saving the bodies or souls of one's fellow man – Avery found himself defending his path at times during holiday gatherings. That in itself he didn't mind, yet in doing so he inevitably came across as strident, and it irked him that his family – mostly his father and brothers – thought of him that way.

"Good to have many brothers. Brothers, like roots of tree," Jang said, using his fingers to simulate the structure. "Roots make tree strong. When you get older, brothers more important, yes?"

"Yes, I agree."

"Now, about *my* brother. Do you have news of him?" Jang switched to Korean for precision.

"He's being transported to a safe-house in Paris. Once we get you and your wife to a secure location, you can speak to him by phone," Avery said.

"Good. I will be relieved to hear his voice," Jang said. "The last time we said goodbye, we didn't know whether we'd see one another alive again."

Cronen grinned as he scanned their faces, trying to appear agreeable even though the last part of their conversation was lost on him. Avery gave him a recap, if only to wipe the expression off his face. Avery had been told a number of times that Americans smile too much. Having lived abroad for so long, he noticed it, too. Rather than giving the impression that they are happy or friendly, it more often than not made them appear naive.

"So why do you consider yourself the black sheep of the family?" Cronen asked at the end of the recap.

Avery didn't feel like sharing his life story with Cronen. He wasn't above sharing personal details or even stories of an indiscretion or two. Even though he had only recently met him, he couldn't quite tell whether Cronen was being friendly or whether he was gathering yarn to ensnare him with later. He had the kind of wide eyes that gave him the aspect of being perpetually startled. With that and the wiry physique of a runner, Avery pegged him as the kind of person who worked out by compulsion rather than for pleasure.

"Let's just say I don't share the missionary zeal of my parents and my brothers anymore," Avery said.

If he and his fiancée had not been such devout Christians, perhaps the fall from grace would not have seemed so precipitous – not that Avery's faith was so simple that he believed his religion immunized him against tragedy, let alone mundane misfortune. Bad things happened to good people all the time. When she died, the world seemed full of indifference, and anger is not fertile ground for faith. He tried to hide it for a while. He felt ashamed, as though he'd abandoned the family business. But you can't fake faith – not to the devout. His father was the first to notice it.

During his fiancée's long illness, Avery would sometimes replay his life in his mind from his earliest memories, in search of some cardinal wrong he had unwittingly committed. He eventually concluded his life had been as unremarkable in sin as it was in accomplishments, so he did not merit being a target of God's attention. Kyunghee's loss cut him so deeply that one day he just stopped in the middle of a prayer and never prayed again.

Avery had made the mistake of thinking that time was promised to him just because his mind could imagine the events to fill it. The moment Avery committed his life to Kyunghee, he pictured their future years together as though they were memories – the past already lived. He remembered their wedding, though the wedding never happened. He remembered their first child, though the child was never conceived. He remembered their strolls on crisp fall mornings as an old couple, though she would never see the landscape of his conjured memories. All these things happened in his mind only, yet to him they happened, and thus were memories, as concrete as any memory of his youth. So when the door to his future with her closed, he felt the loss as one who had shared a lifetime with her.

The way the light through the SUV window caught Ambassador Jang's face reminded Avery of Kyunghee's father in the days leading up to her death. The face, broad; the eyes, narrow; the brows, heavy with the weight of worry. Avery often caught Kyunghee's father staring off into the distance. His daughter lay in a hospital bed, drawing her last labored breaths, drowning in the fluids of her failing body, in defiance of any measure of healing or hope.

"Mr. Avery," the ambassador said. Then, picking up on the little Avery had revealed about himself, he asked, "So you are not a religious man any more?"

Avery looked up at Jang, searching for some clue on his face as to whether his question was spectacularly daft or incredibly wily, whether it arose from an incomplete comprehension of English or a concealed mastery of it.

"I used to be," Avery said.

"It seems then you and I share something in common."

Avery knotted his brow in his effort to decipher what Jang meant.

"We once believed in something very deeply, but no longer," Jang said. "I guess this is why you and I find ourselves here at this moment."

Avery was inclined to think better of him for his betrayal of his country, and at the same time regard him with more caution. It was a mix of fascination and foreboding. He had felt something similar before, as a boy, when the family cat had gingerly laid a bloodied sparrow at his feet one morning. The cat's name was Felix – given such a generic name at the insistence of his father, who believed all animals deserved the utmost kindness but not cloying affection. Until then, Avery had thought of Felix only as a lazy pet that displayed no enterprise beyond finding the warmest ray of sunlight to bask in. Watching the cat groom the dead bird's feathers off its face, Avery realized he had been harboring a beast that was just one kill away from its feral nature.

It occurred to Avery that it might take years for the boys at Langley to decipher everything that Jang would lay at their feet.

"So is this guy the Holy Grail?" Cronen asked Avery after they dropped off the ambassador at a safe-house.

"We definitely landed a big fish," Avery said. "Such a high-level defection is a huge public relations coup."

"Though not the Holy Grail," Cronen said. It was not a question but a declaration.

"No. Not for me, at least," Avery said. "I'm interested in a very specific peek behind the curtain – access to someone who harbors the intimate details of North Korea's nuclear program. Somewhere, he's laboring away anonymously, enabling his country's outsized influence on its neighbors."

"I see," Cronen said. "These things, these quests, they can be quite consuming."

Avery nodded. He had devoted a good deal of his energy lately trying to identify such a person. "I don't know how we could get access to such a person. Is he a Workers' Party loyalist and we have little chance of turning him against his fatherland? Or is he, like Ambassador Jang, someone who considered himself a patriot who could become disillusioned?"

"It's not enough that he become disillusioned, right?" Cronen said. "You have to fall out of favor with the ascendant powers. Isn't that what happened to Ambassador Jang?"

Avery thought it was quite astute.

The famine in North Korea was causing a tectonic upheaval in its political landscape. The question was, is this man, this Holy Grail of nuclear intelligence, going with the flow, or is he being left behind?

Chapter 2

No matter how often he traveled, Han Chol-Soo found the feeling of waking up in an unfamiliar bed disorienting, all the more so because the room he was in now enveloped him in an impenetrable darkness, save for the faint glow from an LED clock that told him he had awoken in those loneliest, deep hours of the night. He found himself gazing into the black reaches of the room for some clue as to where he was, his mind fumbling to reconstruct the hours before he fell asleep.

He groped around for the bedside lamp, and when he turned it on, it was as though the light crystalized his thoughts and he realized he was in a hotel room in Zurich.

Han was sharing the room with a junior consul who was blessed with one of those enviable constitutions that allowed him to sleep soundly whenever he found some place to lean against. He didn't even seem to need a flat surface to lie on. Perhaps it helped that the junior consul had no prescribed responsibilities other than to escort Han on this trip. The Workers' Party preferred its members to travel in pairs while on trips overseas. The soul is weak to temptations in solitude.

Han turned out the light and tried to fall back asleep. It was soon clear to him that he was fully alert from jetlag.

"Lucky bastard," Han muttered to himself and reached for the TV remote control, which Lee, the junior consul, had been playing with all night long before he fell asleep. Lee was still unaccustomed to having so many channels, and presented with so many choices, he could hardly stay tuned to one station for more than a few seconds before he switched again. Han and Lee were two of about a dozen consuls assigned to North Korea's Mission to the United Nations. For Han, it was the latest of many overseas postings. For Lee, New York was his first, and Han simultaneously envied and pitied him for it because he had managed to draw a plum assignment right off the bat. It was all downhill from there

"Just pick one and stay with it," Han had said to him finally when he couldn't stand the incessant channel surfing any more.

Lee looked back at him apologetically. "Sorry. It just feels like I might be missing something better on another channel," he said.

Now it was Han's turn to flip through the kaleidoscope of moving images, with the volume turned all the way down.

And then, something caught his attention on the screen – a flash of something familiar. He doubled back. It was a shot of Kim Il-Sung, the Great Leader, waving from a high balcony. Han turned up the volume a bit, looking over at Lee to see if he was stirred by it.

It was a documentary about North Korea, narrated in German. Han got the gist of it even though it was barely audible. It also showed video supposedly taken from a camera hidden in a bag. One scene showed a street market. The unpaved ground was black, as though soot had been smeared into the dirt. A few children in unkempt clothes milled about in the streets, bouncing from adult to adult with their hands outstretched. Han could tell they were begging. Merchants shooed them away when they got too close to their wares. There was a man supine on the ground in the middle of the market. Passers-by gazed at him incredulously but no one stopped to check whether he was alive or dead. The footage cut to a scene of a cargo ship being loaded with pallets of grain. The sacks were stamped with the American flag.

Han turned off the TV and sat in the darkness for a while, pondering what he had just seen. There was something dreamlike about having one's home described in a foreign language. It didn't seem like the place he knew. Besides, he had seen worse in New York, he told himself, with scores of pedestrians marching by some beggar lying on the sidewalk in busy Midtown, without so much as a glance.

Lee had seen something similar and asked Han one day without any hint of irony, "Do you think the beggar somehow slipped through the perimeter of the city. He's certainly spoiling the case for prosperity, isn't he? Or do you think he was just a shrewd addition to the diorama to enhance the authenticity of the illusion?"

Han recalled chuckling at the time.

It was a little past 3 a.m. In addition to the fact that his roommate had begun to snore rather loudly, he had no desire to be restless in bed, fighting his body clock. He also worried that even if he did manage to fall asleep he would not be alert for his morning rendezvous with the rather elusive Swiss man who had finally agreed to meet him. That was the reason Han was in Zurich.

He turned on the desk lamp and read through some papers, making notes in the margins.

"Is it time to wake up?" Lee said groggily.

"No. Go back to sleep," Han told him.

Lee obediently put his head back down on the pillow and soon was snoring again.

Han's handwriting was bold yet still easily legible. He prided himself on it; attributing his penmanship to the years he practiced calligraphy with an unforgiving brush. The papers he was making notes on contained references to radioactive isotopes – in particular, uranium-235 and plutonium-239. These were the two isotopes used to make fission weapons.

Han had given Lee a crash course last night on nuclear physics after the junior consul kept on trying to make small talk about Han's personal history.

"Were you a math whiz in school?" Lee asked, in all sincerity. The young man seemed a bit smitten with Han, especially after seeing how he navigated the airports and local streets with a working grasp of German. Lee hadn't met any North Koreans before who could speak multiple foreign languages.

"Listen here, Comrade Lee," Han said. "Pay attention and maybe you'll learn something on this trip. You've heard of uranium, right?"

Lee nodded.

"Well, there's more than one kind of uranium. The kind, or the isotope, we want is called uranium-235," Han said, as he began scribbling on a note pad for Lee's benefit. "The problem is it's very, very rare. And it's mixed in with another isotope of uranium that we don't want. So our problem is we have to find a way to sort out uranium-235 from the isotope we don't want."

"And how do we do that?" Lee asked.

"That's what I'm here for. To get the machines that can do that," Han said. "Have you heard of *Little Boy*?"

Lee shook his head.

"That's what the Americans named the atom bomb that they dropped on Hiroshima. That was a uranium-235 bomb."

Lee's face brightened with recognition, and then it darkened again just as quickly with confusion. The young man had a mercurial face. "Don't we make plutonium at our reactors in Yongbyon? I thought we could use that for fuel."

"You're brighter than you look, comrade," Han said with a smirk, and then started scribbling again. "Yes, it's plutonium-239. It doesn't exist in nature like uranium does. It's created in nuclear reactors. The bomb called *Fat Man* that the Americans dropped on Nagasaki was a plutonium-239 bomb."

"*Fat Man*," Lee repeated to himself and chuckled.

It dawned on Han at that moment how young the junior consul really was – to still be amused by fat jokes.

"Whether you use uranium-235 or plutonium-239, both must be highly enriched to create a fissile weapon. There must be enough density for it to sustain the necessary runaway chain reaction."

"*Fat Man*," Lee muttered again quietly, and Han knew that his mind was still stuck back at that point.

He tapped Lee's head with his pen and said, "Pay attention. Radioactive elements like these have a curious property – they spontaneously turn into another element if you just leave them alone. It's almost like gold spontaneously turning into silver," Han said, drawing circles and lines on the notepad. "The time it takes for half of the material to decay into something else is called the half-life. You've heard of that, haven't you?"

"Of course," Lee said. "I studied law. But we had to study physics, too, of course."

"Uranium-235 has a half-life of 704 million years. Plutonium-239 has a half-life of about 24,000 years. That's why plutonium gives off much more radioactivity and that's why it's easier to detect."

It was at this point that Han could feel Lee tuning out, taking furtive glances at the TV remote control. The lesson was over. Han released him to play with the remote.

Some of the pages that Han had scribbled on the evening before, and after he woke up in the middle of the night, he shredded into tiny pieces by hand, placing the confetti-sized debris into a bag. The size of the pieces shrunk by powers of two each time he tore it, so it went relatively quickly. He would later stir the contents and divide it into three separate bags. When he ventured outside of the hotel for whatever reason, he would dump the contents of each bag in three different trashcans on the street, making sure that each was out of sight and sufficiently far away from the others. The process was relatively efficient once one got used to it and necessary in those times when one could not conveniently burn documents or had a cross-shredder handy. Han was meticulous about it and insisted that his subordinates, including Lee, were equally so.

He worked this way in the hotel room until sunlight began to illuminate the edges of the opaque curtains. He did some sit-ups and push-ups. It was his way of maintaining some routine in his life when he was away from home, and for warding off the listlessness and loneliness he felt when he was on the road. When he was done with his routine, he shook Lee awake.

Han looked younger than his age of 39. He had a boyish face – a trait he'd despised in his twenties, when he had wished people would take him more seriously. It was heightened by his natural curiosity. He had grown into it though, that boyishness now translating into an alertness that was absent in many of his contemporaries. Lee had been drawn to it – that youthful fierceness overlaid onto the sense of ease that comes with age.

Before Han got dressed, he lined up all his personal items on the desk – a pen, a wallet, a datebook with a Workers' Party membership card in the back flap, and some loose change. There was also a heavy envelope full of cash that he had fastened with a thick rubber band around the solid midriff like a belt, the envelope wrinkling into tiny pleats. It was a small fortune.

He had been given the money with instructions to buy three Patek Philippe watches – two women's and one men's – that were destined for members of the Dear Leader's family. Han had been given descriptions of the specific models to purchase and the wrist sizes. When Han had checked the amount of money he had been given for the watches, he thought there had been some mistake.

"This is for *three* watches?" he asked his superior incredulously, feeling a bit naïve. The quartz timepiece on his wrist, which he had received as a wedding gift, didn't belong in the same universe of objects as the watches he was being told to buy.

"For that kind of money, they'd better let you travel *back* in time," Han blurted out before he could stop himself.

"You know what the funny thing is?" Han's superior said. "They'll probably just wear them around the house since there's no way they'll wear them in public."

Han imagined them posing with the time pieces next to a Monet or Rembrandt hung on the wall of their living room, reveling in their private opulence that the workers could not be expected to comprehend, let alone appreciate. He tried not to cringe visibly, or otherwise let his face betray his irritation. It didn't even occur to him to be offended by the obscenity of the ruling family's excesses, so commonplace as they were. He was merely annoyed at having to play a part in the latest episode. Han appreciated material comforts, and having traveled widely, he suffered one of the few downsides of such an expanded life – elevated standards for having seen the best of what the world has to offer. Han had grown accustomed to being an ascetic, because he found it best to avoid that constant insecurity of wanting.

After he put on his jacket, he took the items he had laid out on the hotel desk and found a place for each of them on his person, making sure to use an inside pocket for the cash. He found himself repeatedly patting his jacket to make sure it was there, and he felt agitated that he had to run a shopping errand for his superiors in the middle of such circumstances.

"While I'm getting these centrifuges, would you like me to pick up some Louis Vuitton handbags as well? How about some groceries?" Han mumbled to himself.

"Excuse me?" Lee asked.

"Nothing," Han said. "This man I'm meeting is expecting me alone. You can keep yourself occupied for a couple of hours, can't you?"

Lee nodded. "I might take a nap if that's okay with you. I don't think I slept very well last night."

Han smiled and shook his head as he stepped out the hotel room door, taking along with him the three bags of paper that he had hand-shredded.

* * *

Han arrived five minutes early to Lindenhof Square, the meeting location. He had walked the route the day before with Lee and measured the time it took. The square occupied the high ground, not easily photographed from remote locations. It was covered with gravel the size of somewhere between rice and coffee beans. When Han approached the knee-high stone wall on one side of the square, the jade-blue waters of the Limmat emerged over it, and beyond it, street-front buildings, five or six stories high, including the rather run-down Hotel Krone where he was staying, with the Swiss flag hung out front faded by sun and weather to a tired scarlet.

Friedrich Zinner arrived at 9 o'clock sharp. It didn't take long for Han to recognize that he was a bit high strung. He had a habit of looking over his shoulder every couple of minutes. It was distracting and made Han feel nervous. He resisted the urge to look over his own shoulder and instead patted the money in his pocket again.

"Abdul sends his regards," Zinner said.

"How is Dr. Khan?" Han asked in the polite, perfunctory way people ask questions without expecting sincere answers. "He had a very bad cold the last time I saw him in Islamabad."

"Abdul has been busy," Zinner said, casually advertising his familiarity with the father of Pakistan's nuclear program by throwing around his first name repeatedly. Then, in a conspiratorial whisper, he added, "You know, there's a lot of demand for centrifuges."

Han feared it was just the type of thing a salesman would say before jacking up the price.

"Shall we take a walk?" Zinner asked, pointing the way. The two men took a leisurely stroll to nearby St. Peter's Kirche.

"Have you heard the joke about an engineer, a physicist and a mathematician in a room with a fire?" Zinner asked.

"I don't think so."

Zinner cracked a mischievous smile. He knew Han was a physicist by training, and Han knew Zinner was an engineer. It was clear this joke would come at the expense of the mathematician.

"So, an engineer walks into a room where there's a bonfire and a barrel of water with a bucket. He has to solve the problem of putting out the fire, so he tips the barrel over and extinguishes the flames. In the process, the floor is drenched. Are you with me so far?"

Han nodded.

"The physicist walks into the room, sees the fire, sees the water, gets *just* the right amount of water in the bucket, extinguishes the fire *and* all the water turns into steam, leaving the floor perfectly dry."

"Elegant solution," Han said.

"The *mathematician* walks into the room, sees the fire, sees the water, *knows* that a solution exists, and then walks out of the room," Zinner said, peering at Han to see if he understood.

Han smiled and said, "This joke was made by a physicist."

Zinner was older than Han by decades – he looked to be in his early sixties – but Han sensed that Zinner was showing him some deference. Perhaps it was because Han was now his customer. Perhaps it was that Zinner knew of Han's academic credentials. There was no need. Both had veered away from the scholarly path long ago.

"Tell me," Zinner said, "what prompted you to choose your field of study?"

It had not been Han's intention to devote himself to a branch of science that contemplated a method of mass destruction. But ambition, and the resources available to him to fuel that drive, pushed him inexorably towards it. To Zinner, he admitted only, "The Workers' Party paid for my doctorate in Moscow, with a stint in Berlin. The Party does not like for people to chase impractical sciences."

"So, your needs and the Party's needs converged in physics," Zinner said.

Han forced a smile and said, "I am a pragmatist."

"Really?" Zinner said. "I would have pegged you as an idealist. You seem more of the academic type to me."

Han looked into Zinner's eyes a little too long.

"We must all do what we can to fulfill ourselves, right?" Zinner quickly added.

"It is hard to meet Dr. Khan nowadays," Han said, quickly changing the topic. "In the West, he has become – radioactive, if you will."

Zinner appeared to appreciate the pun and patted Han on the shoulder.

"Abdul is merely meeting the demand where it exists," Zinner said, shrugging as if to suggest it was no big thing. "Some may call him names. I think those same people are mad at him for chipping away at their market more than they are of him proliferating nuclear technology."

Zinner stopped walking and lifted up his index finger dramatically and added, "allegedly."

"It is not my place to judge," he continued, once again looking over his shoulder before he started walking again. "You know better than I the opinion that the United States has of North Korea. What they say about your country – does it align with what you know? The same could be said for A.Q. Khan."

Han felt suddenly uneasy. He again touched his jacket, feeling for that wad of cash that he would later use to buy those luxury watches. The amount of treasure needed to purchase centrifuges would not fit into a suitcase, let alone his jacket pocket, but what they had in common was that they were both precision instruments that no one in North Korea would ever see in public.

It wasn't until Han and Zinner were inside the church at St. Peter's, standing before a triptych of stained-glass windows in the rear chamber, that they delved into the details of their business. And even then, Zinner would deftly switch to a discussion of the church's architecture when a wandering tourist came within earshot.

Then, when another tourist approached Han from behind, Zinner leaned over to him and whispered in German, "*Die Vöglein schweigen im Walde.*" He was quoting a famous Goethe poem. *The little birds fall silent in the forest.* Han took the hint and stopped speaking until the man was out of earshot.

The easterly morning light shone through one of the stained-glass windows in the chapel and cast a blue glow on Zinner's face. It resembled the eerie blue pall of Cherenkov radiation emanating from the pool of water surrounding a reactor core.

"I can't remember the last line of that Goethe poem in German," Han said to Zinner, "but from what I remember, it struck me as a bit of a threat, no? Death comes for us all, or something like that?"

Zinner's eyes grew wide. Then he smiled and recited it: "*Warte nur, balde, ruhest du auch.*" *Just wait, soon, you too will be at rest.*

Chapter 3

Jang Sung-Ho, the North Korean trade attaché who had defected together with his brother, was a cautious man by nature. His caution was more of the social variety, well adapted to survival in the upper echelons of the Workers' Party. Climbing the ladder in the Party was unlike corporate advancement in two crucial ways – it was the only game in town and failure was at times lethal. There was no jumping ship. This made every move critical to survival. Having been on the inside for so long, it was a novel experience for Jang Sung-Ho to be a fugitive. He was, accordingly, careful about his personal security, fastidiously following the instructions of his handlers helping him coordinate his defection with his brother. But once he and his wife left the confines of the safe house in Paris and were moved to London, he felt they had escaped the immediate danger of re-capture. His wife in particular began to chafe at the limitations on their movement and the strict prohibitions on their contact with anyone other than Jang's brother, Ambassador Jang Sung-Gil.

August in London was gloriously cool; even more so than Paris. Jang's handlers had put him and his wife up in a squat brick house on a leafy street in Kingston upon Thames. It was modest yet serviceable, and the greatest inconvenience that the Jangs faced was the boredom of being cooped up most of the time, with only one another's company, save for the around-the-clock mute presence of a rotating American agent. The Jangs hadn't spent this much time together even when they were newlyweds.

Prolonged captivity was eroding Jang Sung-Ho's cautious nature, his impulse toward self-preservation. Captivity heightened his sense of time. In his normal life, time was merely a backdrop against which his life unfurled. In captivity he sensed acutely that time was against him. There was too much of it now – a viscous medium impeding gain and hope. The desperate toils of his adulthood, to win, to get ahead, seemed suddenly foolish now that he was here, the gateway where he would be stripped of almost everything that he had worked to build. Captivity was a tomb in which those regrets echoed. Being so, he yearned to escape it.

He felt remorse for not having said a proper goodbye to his elderly mother. Before their defection, his brother had forbidden any contact with their relatives that broke routine, and certainly none that even hinted at their intent. But Jang Sung-Ho could not abide keeping his mother in the dark, especially in light of the hardship that awaited her when the Party learned of her sons' coordinated defection. She grew more easily confused nowadays. That fierce wit of hers that often skewered her hapless peers when he and his brother were boys had faded now into crabbiness when things didn't go her way. He imagined her growing ever more aggravated under interrogation.

Jang Sung-Ho and his wife were waiting for clearance from the Americans to travel to the U.S., and when they complained of cabin fever, the Americans began allowing them short excursions to local parks, shadowed by the State Department agent.

One day, an impossibly crisp and sunny one, Jang Sung-Ho and his wife went for a walk at nearby Hampton Court. In a less-traveled corner of the grounds, plain and somber in contrast with the resplendent gardens that once must have amused King Henry, Jang turned to a wall and wept. What he was lamenting, even he didn't know for sure. He had reached an age when he was burdened with regret more often than he was buoyed by hope. He managed to compose himself before the agent turned the corner of a hedgerow and drew near. It was then that he resolved to contact his mother.

Had James Avery paid a little more attention to Jang Sung-Ho, perhaps he would not have succumbed to the doubts of that dark valley of regret, or remorse, whatever it was. For Avery, getting Jang Sung-Ho to defect with his older brother was just a bonus. His main prize was Jang Sung-Gil, and Avery realized in retrospect that this had made him neglectful when it came to the younger brother's preparation. He had, in essence, underestimated his ambivalence – fatally.

* * *

It was a seasoned North Korean agent, traveling under the diplomatic credentials of a consul, who was dispatched to London to clean up the mess. Cleaning up, in this case, meant terminating the traitors with extreme prejudice. In the end, it wasn't some high-tech tracking device that divulged Jang Sung-Ho's whereabouts, but, as was so often the case in these matters, ordinary human frailty and neglect. By the time Jang Sung-Ho contacted his mother, she had already been carefully coached to ask some key questions that would divulge his whereabouts, with the promise that what remained of the Jang clan in North Korea would not be summarily wiped off the face of the earth.

It was characteristic of this particular agent that he chose daytime for his attack, rather than a covert attempt under cover of night, estimating, correctly, that whoever was the bodyguard for the Jangs would be more vigilant at night. And the nervous vigilance of the agent – a thick-chested man whose close-cropped hair showed signs of premature greying in defiance of his boyish face – infected the Jangs as well.

"What was that?" Mrs. Jang said one evening, bolting up from the bed – for about the fifth time since she and her husband arrived at the Kingston safe-house.

"It's just the refrigerator," Jang said with a hint of annoyance. "Same as last time. And why on earth are you hiding under the sheets? You've got a nightgown on."

Mrs. Jang looked down at herself as though to check that she was indeed clothed, and the startled look on her face changed to one of embarrassment. "So much for the glorious British Empire. They can't even make a fridge that doesn't groan every time it kicks in," she said before lying down again.

Instead of storming the safe-house, the North Korean agent chose the route of patience, at first figuring out their daily routines, then waiting in a van near the house one day until they came out for what he had determined was one of their habitual walks. When the Jangs ambled out of the house, past the rose bush, with the American on their heels, the North Korean agent took measure of them, the American in particular, and he quickly determined the order in which he would attack the trio. He poured a tiny bit of water into the suppressor on his pistol to deaden the sound just a little bit more, even though he was running subsonic ammo. It was, after all, a quiet suburban street.

When all three had stepped onto the sidewalk, the North Korean agent accelerated the van without squealing the tires. He had mass on his side; he would not need much speed. Then he ran into the American agent with his van, pinning him against a brick wall. Quickly, yet without hurrying, he got out of the van and walked up to the stunned husband and wife. He shot them at close range, starting with Jang Sung-Ho. His wife barely had a moment to form a bird-like face of surprise before she, too, crumpled to the ground. She remained conscious just long enough to clutch her stomach, like a woman with child, and to see her husband in repose on the empty road.

"*Yohbo*," she uttered weakly, roughly the equivalent of a word like "honey" that husbands and wives call each other.

The agent fired double-taps into their heads at point-blank range. He then walked back to the American and lingered above him just long enough to satisfy himself that the man was unconscious, his greying hair on one side of his head now slowly turning a savage shade of maroon with blood. Having done so, the agent didn't bother dispatching him. There was no point in incurring the extra risk when there may now be eyes of neighbors upon him. He got in the van, backed up a bit, allowing the American to fold limply onto the sidewalk, and then drove away. He turned a corner without once looking back at the carnage he had left behind, confident that he had accomplished his mission without so much as a wasted breath.

* * *

When Ambassador Jang Sung-Gil heard about the assassination of his brother and sister-in-law, his value as a source diminished greatly. He became less cooperative, as though he harbored a grudge against the Americans for botching the operation. James Avery, to whom the unenviable task of delivering the news had fallen, kept on reliving the moment in his head – the moment the ambassador's face went ashen.

"I don't know what to say, Mr. Ambassador," was all that Avery could manage to say.

Instead of yelling at Avery, Ambassador Jang just stared at him. The room fell silent, and Avery felt the eyes of his colleagues upon him, but he would not look away from Jang's gaze. When the ambassador finally spoke, his words were outwardly without blame. For Avery they were a dagger.

"A man of my years and my past has no tears left to shed, even for my beloved brother," Jang said, then he stood and left the room.

When word spread of the debacle, some people in Foggy Bottom started to avoid Avery, or perhaps worse, were a bit too polite to him. It was the kind of courtesy extended to people you wished to dismiss quickly. Avery knew who his friends were, but the rejection still stung him in the quiet of the night. His great-uncle, an early mentor of his, had told him to beware of the fickle social climbers.

"When you don't have a soul, it's easy to treat people as friends only when they can help you in life," his great-uncle had said. What bothered Avery the most was that he felt he had let down the Jang brothers, as well as his own immediate group of colleagues.

It was a great relief to Avery when he returned to Seoul and his co-worker Dave Baxter greeted him with the words, "Dude, what the fuck?"

Chapter 4

When Ambassador Kim collapsed in the hallway, his underlings first thought the old man had tripped on a loose corner of the carpet. The tattered flooring in the modest quarters of North Korea's Mission to the United Nations in New York was so discolored and uneven in spots that it resembled moss, growing at the mercy of wear and weather. The workers there were constantly getting snagged on it. His tumble would have been almost comical, laughed off as a clumsy lapse of coordination, had it not been for the unnerving way he hit the ground. He made no attempt to grasp for a handhold or to brace himself. He fell face first and he fell hard.

His deputy, who was shadowing the old man back from a meeting at the Secretariat Building, even let out a chuckle. That was before it dawned on him that Ambassador Kim hadn't tripped, but had rather blacked out in mid-stride. That became clear when he landed like a lump of dough. The deputy ambassador later denied ever chuckling. But no one in the office doubted he had. The rumor was that he actually nudged the old man to the ground.

When they rolled Ambassador Kim onto his back, his shirt was already drenched in sweat and he was drooling. His eyes were half open yet unseeing. A tear dribbled from the corner of one eye.

"Ambassador Kim! Can you hear me?" the deputy ambassador said as he shook Kim's face by his chin. The old man's hair was completely silver, and drenched in sweat, it glimmered like pearls.

They called for an ambulance. Even in the commotion, the deputy ambassador insisted that they drag the old man's limp body out into the hallway near the elevator – and it soon became clear that it wasn't to speed the old man's resuscitation, but to get him off the premises of the Mission.

"They can't come in here. The paramedics cannot come in here," Deputy Ambassador Kwon said.

The junior consuls helping to move the ambassador were momentarily confused. It was unclear whether Kwon was stating a diplomatic rule or expressing his own will to prevent them from entering.

"This is the territory of the Democratic People's Republic of Korea," he said, and then added again, "They can't come in here."

Kwon waved his arms as though he were fanning foul air out of a room, motioning toward two of the junior consuls who were dragging the ambassador with his arms slung around their shoulders and a firm grasp on his belt. One of the old man's shoes popped off as they dragged his feet across the threshold. Kwon picked it up and tossed it into the hallway, thereby, at least in *his* mind, forestalling any possible excuse for the paramedics to enter the Mission.

* * *

Ambassador Kim was a diabetic, and he had failed to tell anyone at the office how serious his condition had become. What should have been a simple matter of taking maintenance drugs and following a reasonable diet had deteriorated into a life-threatening lung infection. The last time he'd visited a doctor was some two years ago in Pyongyang, just after his sixtieth birthday and just before he was assigned to New York. The meager budget at the North Korean Mission to the United Nations was such that it did not allow for health insurance for its diplomats – not even the ambassador – let alone new carpeting.

"It's a wonder the ambassador fought it off as long as he did," one doctor had said, barely veiling his condescension as he and his imperious colleagues grilled Deputy Ambassador Kwon as to why this condition had been allowed to fester untreated for so long.

"This is kind of unheard of nowadays," the doctor told Kwon. "We could have easily avoided all this with a medical checkup."

That was just the first in a series of embarrassing encounters that forced the Mission to expose its penury at precisely the time that the nation itself was in the spotlight for its disastrous bouts of famine. Kwon in particular found the public attention intolerable. Even when the hospital found a charity willing to foot Ambassador Kim's hospital bill, Kwon seemed less relieved than annoyed that he and the Mission would somehow be indebted to those nosey do-gooders.

Kwon's preoccupation of late seemed to be with concocting novel ways to enforce a Spartan code of conduct among the Mission's staff. It had grown particularly unbearable in the ambassador's absence. No one actually asked when the old man was coming back from the hospital. Many did inquire about his recovery, which was a veiled way of asking the same question.

Then there were the incessant calls from Pyongyang, demanding to know what was going on, with no regard for time zones. They thought nothing of phoning Kwon at 3 a.m. New York time and grilling him for hours.

"Is Ambassador Kim really ill?" the Workers' Party officials kept asking Kwon, suggesting, without explicitly saying it, that this was a ruse to seek asylum.

The old man had shown some astoundingly poor timing by getting sick when he did. The whole politburo had gone mad with paranoia since Jang Sung-Gil and his brother defected together just weeks before.

One of the young consuls gossiped that he ran into a groggy, sleep-deprived Kwon in the elevator, muttering curses at Ambassador Kim. He said it was as though Kwon wanted the old man to quietly croak and spare him the irritation. And if that wasn't enough, Kwon would also be forced to endure the insult and embarrassment of personally thanking the benefactors footing Ambassador Kim's hospital bills.

* * *

When Han Chol-Soo and Deputy Ambassador Kwon entered the ambassador's hospital room, two men were already at his bedside. Both of them were chuckling politely, seemingly at something the ambassador had said. One of them was Park Jun-Young, Han's fellow consul from the Mission. The other was a man with greying temples whom neither Han nor Kwon had met before. He was seated on a bedside stool, clutching the ambassador's hand draped over the railing of the bed in a gesture of brotherly comfort. The volume on the TV anchored to wall had been turned down. It was showing a re-broadcast of Princess Diana's funeral from a couple of days ago in a split screen with a clip from a news conference by Britain's new prime minister, a rather determined-looking if soft-spoken young man by the name of Tony Blair.

"Ah, deputy ambassador and Dr. Han, we were wondering when you'd arrive," the ambassador said, his voice scratchy and barely above a whisper. His hair, normally combed in awareness of his thinning crown, sat atop his head in a clump. The ambassador's sallow face drooped as though it had become too much for the muscles and flesh to withstand gravity. And he did something that he had never done before – his mouth was agape when he breathed. It was the look of the infirm that Han had seen on some of the elderly in New York, harried by the speed of it all, their eyes confused.

The room had a dampness about it without the smell that sometimes lingers in dank corners. Han found himself sniffing the air, unsettled by the incongruity of moisture and sterility. He had acquired a keen dislike of the smell of hospitals ever since he had been forced to spend nearly a month nursing his wife back to health in a Spartan ward in Pyongyang after the birth of their daughter.

Park motioned to the man sitting at the ambassador's bedside. "This is Mr. Choi Sung-Soo. He's the chairman of the New York Korean-American Grocers Association, which has so graciously offered to help us. Mr. Choi, this is Deputy Ambassador Kwon Woo-Shik."

"So this is the famous President Choi," Kwon said, walking toward him with his hand at the ready for a shake. Kwon used the title "sajang" to address Choi, a title more aptly applied to the president of a largish company. Choi owned a handful of delis, so its usage was more a show of comity. Old habits died hard, including the aristocratic condescension of merchants, no matter how prosperous. "How can we ever thank you for this kindness?" Kwon said.

Choi carefully let go of the ambassador's hand, avoiding a tangle with the IV line, and shook Kwon's hand. "Please, don't mention it. Sorry we had to meet under such circumstances, but I'm happy the Korean community in New York could gather its modest resources to help our brethren from the North. And Mr. Park also tells me you're from South Hamkyong province, deputy ambassador, like myself. That's where I grew up before the war."

"Oh, really? We've come all the way to New York to meet," Kwon said, shaking Kim's hand a bit too vigorously.

Park and Han glanced at one another, both amused by Kwon's enthusiasm. Kwon had a reputation as a pedant and a stickler for paperwork, not to mention prone to bouts of moodiness. None of the traits endeared him to his subordinates. Kim, on the other hand, was liable to cut corners, and gregarious to the point of being almost needy. He hated to dine alone. It was a marvel the two men got along.

As with many educated men who come from humble locales with distinct accents, Han and Park could camouflage their accents to fit the occasion. It was a bit of a generational skill, as men of the deputy ambassador's generation struggled with this and managed instead to sound confused with accents of indeterminate origin.

"Mr. Choi, this is Consul Han Chol-Soo. We were actually classmates at Kim Il-Sung University," Park said. He and Han spoke to one another in an informal tone, absent of honorifics customarily used among people of unequal social stations or age differences of even a few years.

"Dr. Han. I'm so happy to finally meet you. Mr. Park speaks very highly of you. He says you're a man with a bright future," Choi said, shaking Han's hand. The more Choi conversed with these men, the more his childhood inflections emerged through his Seoul-scrubbed accent.

"Comrade Park has a healthy sense of humor," Han said. "Quite the contrary. It's Comrade Park who's the one with the bright future. He always led the way when we were in school, and the only reason I've gotten as far as I have is because I've taxed the limits of my ability trying to keep up with him."

Park smiled. He had an unusually neat row of teeth considering he grew up in a country of privation. At nearly six feet he was also unusually tall compared with many of his peers stunted by lean springs, when the harvest rations began to run out. What his budget suit lacked in upscale material he had managed to compensate with cut by enlisting the services of a skillful tailor, enough so that it spoke of something lithe and athletic underneath. His build befitted his title of security attaché to the ambassador and bespoke of someone who had grown up with a disproportionate share of the country's resources at his disposal.

After the clergyman who arranged the whole thing joined them, Choi took out a white envelope from his inside jacket pocket. "I just wanted to say again on behalf of everyone who responded to our call for action that we are very happy we were able to help our brethren in their time of need," Choi said. "We hope this small gesture will help in its own way to revive the bonds between us as one people."

The ambassador was silent through all this, with a smile across his chapped lips, barely veiling the pain he was in.

"Please accept this as a token of our friendship to you, and with the sincere wishes of the Korean community for the ambassador's speedy and full recovery," Choi said, handing the envelope with both hands to Kwon, who in turn received it with both hands in a show of respect.

Kwon stood there quietly in the middle of the hospital room, looking down at the envelope in his own hands. Han and Park eyed one another, waiting for Kwon to say something. The deputy ambassador just stood there, his head bowing down further and further, as though he had fallen asleep on his feet. Han and Park eyed one another again. An uneasy silence dashed the jovial atmosphere in the room.

Kwon began to say something, but cut himself off, and then again. Han didn't know if he was just at a loss for words or was mumbling to himself. The deputy ambassador had been prickly during the cab ride to the hospital, complaining about how the Mission was losing face by accepting this handout. Han was nervous that the old curmudgeon would blurt out something rude. From the look in Park's eyes, Han could tell he was thinking along similar lines.

Just as Park was about to intervene with a word of thanks, Han heard an almost imperceptible "tap." He turned to Kwon in time to see another tear fall from his downturned face, landing on the envelope clutched in his hand with the sound of a raindrop on a leaf. A few more tears dripped off the end of his nose. No one in the room said a thing. Han and Park looked at one another again, this time in shock rather than in allied mocking.

It was then that Choi stepped forward and clutched Kwon's hands in his own and began to weep himself. "Please, deputy ambassador, don't let us see you so vulnerable," Choi said through sobs. "You're going to make me feel bad for having wounded your pride. You're subordinates are watching. Please."

Choi's words only exasperated matters. The two middle-aged men wept openly, clasping one another's hands.

"Oh, come on, gentlemen. For goodness sake, let's not pour cold water over a happy occasion," the ambassador said in his raspy voice.

Han averted his gaze. He couldn't quite believe what was happening. Moments ago Kwon was ready to pick a fight; now he was sharing a moment of – what was that? Tenderness? With the enemy? Through the window, he scanned the squat skyline of Queens across the East River – its windows, billboards and streetlamps now alert as night fell.

"Of course, Mr. Ambassador. Let's not turn this into such a somber occasion," Choi said as he wiped his eyes with a handkerchief. That accessory dated Choi more than any grey hair. He belonged to a generation that carried handkerchiefs when they wore suits. That, and the ample cut of their jackets, was part of the fashion generation gap among Koreans – even more so than Americans. "It's hard enough as it is for us to have an opportunity to meet. We can't end it in tears like this."

It was then that Choi invited them out for drinks. Even laid up in a hospital bed, hooked up to an IV, Kim was visibly disappointed he couldn't join them. As they shuffled out of his room, the old man demanded to know what exactly they would be drinking.

Choi likened the improbable gathering of North and South Koreans in one room to a mini-summit. He was determined not to let the opportunity pass without some "civilian-level détente," as he put it.

"Who knows when we'll have a chance like this again," the businessman said, egging on both the entourage from the mission and the locals to go out for dinner together.

Round One was soju, with Korean table barbecue. Then, after giving the clergyman in the group the slip, the rest them convened Round Two at a room salon, a venue with private rooms and over-priced liquor served by hostesses, some who excelled in conversation and others who needed to do little more than giggle and sashay in their mini-skirts to win the affections of their clientele.

* * *

It was a blissfully cool early September day in Seoul – the first day of the summer's fever broken; that glorious hint of fall. On his way to work, James Avery saw a group of women huddled next to a gurgling city bus for warmth, caught off guard by the unseasonable chill in their skimpy outfits. Their willowy arms trembled in the wind.

Avery was done with the heat for the year. The dry, noisy heat of Cairo, the swampy heat of Washington, and now this oppressive heat – he'd had enough of it. Unfortunately, a cool day like this was just a teaser. There was plenty of summer left in Seoul. The downside to the autumn chill was that it was bringing on some melancholy in him. He already knew then that as the season deepened and the leaves turned, he would be filled with even more profound regret about what had happened to Jang Sung-Ho.

The daily routine that Avery had settled into after he returned from Egypt and Washington wasn't helping either. These days he spent an inordinate amount of time debriefing North Korean refugees who had recently arrived in Seoul. Invariably they had harrowing tales of escape and hardscrabble lives that had grown ever more unbearable with the deepening famine. When Avery first started meeting with them, he was often mistaken about how old they were – especially the teenagers – because their growth was so stunted by malnutrition compared to their South Korean counterparts. After his interviews with them, he found himself worrying about how they would adapt to life in the South, which had taken such a divergent path from the North that it might as well have been an alien planet. The common language and the modest resettlement stipend doled out by the government did little to ease the culture shock. Sifting through this human misery for potential nuggets of meaningful intelligence was beginning to weigh on him. Avery had dreamed the night before about one particularly skinny 19-year-old who looked like he was maybe 12. The young man was so bewildered by the whole debriefing process that Avery spent more time reassuring him that he had done nothing wrong rather than extracting information from him. Avery awoke abruptly from the dream when the boy's fragile hand snapped like balsa wood in a parting handshake.

These debriefings were the professional equivalent of digging ditches – supremely mundane but necessary. He accepted it without objection as his penance. No matter, he thought, since he would soon enough find himself in New York helping his stateside colleagues prepare for the U.N. General Assembly. Avery took a reprieve from the daily routine by poring through the morning papers. The front pages that day were again plastered with images of Princess Diana, who had died three days ago in a high-speed crash in Paris as her car was being chased by paparazzi through the Pont de l'Alma tunnel. There were photo spreads on inside pages chronicling Diana's all-too-public life, from her sweet post-wedding kiss on the balcony of Buckingham Palace to the depleted sulk after years of battling the Windsors and the merciless British press.

It seemed implausible that she could be alive one moment and gone the next due to something as prosaic as a car accident. Avery half expected it to be exposed as an elaborate hoax staged by her wealthy boyfriend to somehow give the press the slip once and for all and disappear into the sublime anonymity of a well-appointed estate in a Third World country. But then there were the two princes. Could she forsake her sons for the rest of her life or would she periodically summon them to her hideout and risk being found out by stubborn pursuers.

Further into the newspaper, beat reporters carried out the unglamorous meat of the day's journalism. And nestled below the fold on page 32 was an article with a New York dateline that Avery almost missed.

NEW YORK – The Korean immigrant community here is rallying to the aid of North Korea's United Nations envoy, who has been hospitalized since mid-August and unable to pay his mounting medical bills.

Several donors have pledged donations to help Ambassador Kim Young-Hwan, who was admitted to New York University Medical Center due to complications from diabetes, according to a Korean-American clergyman in contact with the envoy.

North Korean diplomats do not have health insurance and the cash-strapped mission was unable to pay the ambassador's hospital costs, which are expected to exceed $40,000, sources said.

Pledges are also pouring in from Korean-American church congregations and business groups, the clergyman said.

Despite a history of tense relations between Pyongyang and Seoul, Ambassador Kim's personal plight seems to have struck a humanitarian chord with the Korean-American community, which has also organized fundraisers in recent months to send food aid to their famine-stricken brethren in North Korea.

Avery sat up in his chair. He had been collecting information on North Korean diplomats assigned abroad but it was hard to come by. The article went on to say that some of the donors had pledged support out of concern that Pyongyang might call Ambassador Kim back immediately, possibly jeopardizing his health. This was a public relations debacle, as if North Korea needed more of them.

"Hey, Baxter. Come take a look at this," Avery said, pointing to the article and waving to his colleague three cubicles down. "Can you believe this?"

"Un-fucking-believable, right?" Baxter said when he walked over. "It's a wonder the paparazzi didn't get her killed before."

"What? What are you looking at?" Avery saw that one of the Princess Diana stories from the front of the paper had jumped above the fold, with a photo of her mangled car, on the same page as the Ambassador Kim story, which ran without a picture.

"I'm talking about *this*," Avery said, tapping the column of text.

Baxter squinted in concentration. "North Korea's ambassador to the U.N. He's in the hospital. They're collecting money." Baxter exhaled and looked at Avery. "I'm still learning the language, man."

"Oh, sorry," Avery said, recalling that Dave Baxter had been re-assigned from Tokyo about four months ago. It was proving to be a good move for him, and he would eventually have another Asian language under his belt – a badge of honor among the itinerant set in the State Department.

Tokyo had until a few years ago been the center for intelligence about North Korea. But the recent famine had created a steady stream of refugees pouring directly into South Korea, bringing with them morsels of information that, taken collectively, began to offer the most comprehensive look ever behind the veil of the secretive country. The volume of intel from Tokyo now paled in comparison.

Avery gave Baxter a recap of the article. "The North Korean Mission to the U.N. can't pay its ambassador's hospital bills. The local Koreans in New York are taking up a collection to help him out."

Baxter picked up the newspaper to read it over again. "The whole country's going down the crapper."

"Well, maybe not just yet," Avery said.

"It must look pretty grim on the inside for all these honchos to jump ship. And now this?"

Grim – that was indeed what Avery was seeing behind the veil.

A few days ago, Avery had debriefed a woman who was sold into prostitution in China after escaping North Korea by wading through a shallow stretch of the Tumen River. She had served out a three-year sentence at a labor camp after she was caught by North Korean soldiers during the latest of her many clandestine trips over the sparsely guarded border.

"In the labor camp, I was given three spoonfuls of corn every day," she told Avery and the two others there to debrief her. One was a colleague in the State Department's Bureau of Intelligence and Research and the other a member of the South Korean Foreign Ministry.

"I counted out the kernels each time. They averaged about 32. On days when I got more than 35, I was ecstatic," she said.

Every refugee had a story of hardship – so relentless, in fact, that Avery began to wonder whether they had been sent by Kim Jong-Il to fool South Korea into complacency. Another refugee told Avery that villagers had begun hiding the graves of their recently deceased.

"What for?" Avery asked him.

The man looked around the room as though seeking permission to speak.

"It's okay. You can tell us."

The man lowered his gaze to the floor. "Cannibalism. We'd heard that fresh graves were found dug up."

The man from the Foreign Ministry asked for a break. When Avery tracked him down later in the men's room, he found him weeping into a tissue.

Chapter 5

Every Monday and Wednesday, Han Chol-Soo was used to coming home to an empty house in Elmhurst, Queens. On those nights, his wife, who had joined him in New York when he was stationed there, took English lessons in Flushing. She rode the bus 40 minutes each way after dropping off their son with a babysitter – a fellow diplomat's wife. Even during her pregnancy, she hadn't missed a single class until the week before she gave birth. During her second trimester, she would often crawl into bed as soon as she returned from class and fall asleep with her clothes on, lying on her side, cradling her stomach. Han hated seeing his wife so tired.

"Why don't you quit the class for now? You can always take classes after the baby's born. You're running yourself ragged," he said to her one night as he peeled off her socks and threw a blanket over her.

Seconds before she conked out, she mumbled back, "It's now or never."

He would sometimes leave whatever cash he could spare under a cup on the kitchen counter so she could take a cab instead. He didn't know whether she ever afforded herself that comfort. He got the sense that she was stashing it away instead. Barely a month after their son was born, she was back to her Monday/Wednesday routine.

On this particular Wednesday, Han got home even later than usual because he had visited Ambassador Kim again in the hospital. By the time he dropped off his colleagues on Roosevelt Island, drove back to Elmhurst and found parking, it was already past 10 o'clock. He expected to see his wife already asleep, her body curled around their son next to her on the bed. But neither was in the bedroom.

He looked at his watch and made a quick check of every room in the house. Empty. His morbid imagination conjured up images of her lying unconscious in the street somewhere, with their son shivering and crying beside her. He looked at his watch again and called the babysitter's house.

"Sorry to call so late, Comrade Rhee. I was wondering whether my wife had already stopped by to pick up Won-Kyu," Han said.

"She didn't stop by at all today. She didn't drop him off. I just figured she was skipping class. You mean she isn't home yet?"

"Oh, wait, I think I hear her at the door now," Han lied. "Sorry to have bothered you so late. Tell your husband I'll see him tomorrow."

Han hung up quickly before she could blurt out another question. He stood with his hand still on the phone as his mind darted through the possibilities. "Where the hell could she be?" he whispered to himself.

As the minutes passed, he became more and more agitated. He began pacing. He looked around the house in search of a note she might have left him. Concern for her safety turned into annoyance as he imagined her losing track of time at a friend's house and blithely chatting away. Mrs. Chung, perhaps; the wife of one of the other young consuls. She was a real talker. Then, when his temper cooled, he knew that kind of happy-go-luckiness was not in her. And she knew that he could not stand it when people got themselves into situations that spawned misunderstandings. Han was meticulous in his personal conduct that way – a trait that gave him a reputation among his coworkers for being a bit unapproachable, brittle even. Deputy Ambassador Kwon, the man that his underlings had gotten to calling "The Pusher" since the incident when Ambassador Kim collapsed, would sometimes say to Han, "You're so thorough." He didn't quite mean it as a compliment. Making sure he wasn't misunderstood was also a survival skill for Han – one that helped him inoculate himself against the deep paranoia in the upper echelons of the Workers' Party.

Han wondered whether his wife had even gone to class today. *Of course not. She couldn't go to class with Won-Kyu in tow. Maybe she found another babysitter that she didn't tell me about? No, it's the fight we had this morning. She's doing this to get back at me.*

He regretted what he had said to her. He had unintentionally re-opened an old wound in the heat of an argument. He had been irritable this morning with lack of sleep. He regretted being dragged out to drink last night. An entourage from his office and the do-gooders who handed over the donations had visited the ill ambassador in the hospital together.

He searched through the house more systematically, checking drawers and closets he rarely opened, taking a mental inventory of his wife's belongings and trying to deduce something of her whereabouts from them. After several minutes, he gave up when he realized he had not even the faintest idea what might be missing, so little had he paid attention to her in the last few years. He could not even remember what she had worn yesterday, let alone keep a tally of her wardrobe.

He then checked the bookcase where she kept her textbooks, stacked side by side with her notebooks. He struck upon the idea to call his wife's English teacher. He recalled that his wife had scribbled the teacher's name in one of those notebooks, a habit left over from her school days. He flipped through them one by one and found it written on the inside flap of the notebook from the first month of class, scrawled in a neat hand.

"I am sorry to call so late. This is Chol-Soo."

"Han Chol-Soo?" It was an older woman's voice.

"Chung Myung-Ae's husband."

"Oh, of course. I'm so sorry, Mr. Han. I didn't recognize the name immediately. It's nice to talk to you finally."

He and the teacher exchanged some pleasantries as he tried to figure out a way to broach the subject of being utterly clueless as to the whereabouts of his wife. The teacher mercifully saved him from the task.

"Is your wife sick again? I didn't see her on Monday either."

Han missed a beat, but the recovery was quick enough that the delay could be mistaken for merely someone who was perhaps distracted, or trying to compose a sentence in a language that wasn't his native tongue. "Yes, she's not feeling well. She has a cold. She asked me to call you."

"Sorry to hear that. I hope she feels better enough to make it next week. You know, she's been making a lot of progress. I think she must have a knack for languages. She's only been in America, what, a year? And she's already quite fluent."

"Yes, she's good with languages," Han said, monitoring his watch as the teacher driveled on about her other students before returning to the topic of his wife.

"Very studious, too, at least more so than Mrs. Koh, though don't tell her I said that. Do you know Mrs. Koh? I mean, she's been in the country more than 15 years, but you'd never know it."

"No, I've never met Mrs. Koh."

"Yes, Mrs. Koh. Oh, those two are like sisters, even though Mrs. Koh is almost old enough to be her mother. Well, not *that* old. Maybe an aunt. But she's got a young spirit. They get along so well."

Han grew impatient that this English teacher was babbling on. He was about to hurry off the phone when a thought struck him.

"Was Mrs. Koh there today?"

"Come to think of it, no. Whatever bug Myung-Ae caught, she must have it, too. Those two, inseparable, I tell you."

The teacher was an interrogator's dream – a leaky faucet that dripped information with minimal prompting.

"Myung-Ae is always coaching her during class, but God knows, it hasn't rubbed off much," the teacher said, then quickly added: "Don't tell her I said that."

"Of course. I keep secrets very well," Han said.

It took him a couple of minutes to extricate himself from the conversation. Han began rummaging through closets, cabinets and drawers, at first in an orderly way, like one would search for a particular shirt or some sugar. Then his search became more frantic. It was not a matter of what he was looking for, but what he was failing to find.

A suitcase was missing, as were a number of the baby's clothes and his bottles and other paraphernalia that accompany newborns. The bulk of his wife's clothes remained in the closet. At least it seemed so. He wasn't quite sure. He clutched a handful of sleeves and yanked them out of the closet in one furious sweep.

"She is out of her mind!" Han screamed. He stood huffing in front of a closet, with a pile of clothes scattered at his feet and dangling from his clenched fists.

It took some time for Han to calm down enough to think straight, and longer still for him to accept the possibility that his wife may have run away with their son. This wasn't just a matter of his family's domestic unrest. This was a matter of life and death. He could actually be put to death for this as soon as he returned to Pyongyang, executed by a firing squad of scraggly young conscripts who barely filled out their uniforms. They would come for him during the nightly curfew. No one would be the wiser. Pyongyang plunges abruptly into darkness at 9 o'clock to save electricity. With no streetlights, no one would even see him being whisked away quietly through the deserted streets. A firing squad would be preferable to ending up in a remote labor camp where he would wither away to nothing, until his emaciated and beaten carcass would be carted out with the daily garbage.

How could she do this? How could she do this to our family? How could she do this to our daughter?

Won-Sook had stayed behind in Pyongyang. Perhaps the Workers' Party would spare her life. But her privileged existence at the Children's Palace would surely come to an end. No more music lessons or dance lessons or choir practice – limited as the repertoire was to pieces honoring the glory of the Dear Leader and the Great

Leader. It would be easy enough for them to concoct a story where both he and his wife die a tragic death. Their absence would also serve as a warning to the comrades closest to them, their sudden disappearance only adding to the clarity of the message.

Han returned to the notebook where he found the teacher's phone number, hoping that Mrs. Koh's number would be there as well. The list of her classmates abruptly stopped – half the page was missing.

Where was this meddlesome woman – this Mrs. Koh? She is at the root of this. He knew her type all too well. There was one of them everywhere. Couldn't keep her nose out of other people's business; self-righteous, yet oblivious to the realities of other people's lives. She was a busybody in search of a cause. It occurred to him that his wife had mentioned her once. She said she met a South Korean woman in her English class, that the old woman had struck up a conversation and had even been so bold as to invite her to her church. *Was that Mrs. Koh?*

"Jesus freak," Han muttered to himself. He forbade his wife to speak to the woman again. She never mentioned her from then on. From what the teacher just told him, it was obvious that his prohibition had gone unheeded.

Han rifled through his wife's other things, hoping for some clue. He came upon one fattened notebook, its worn cardboard covers bulging with clippings wedged and taped inside. It contained pages cut out from glossy magazines showing spreads of manicured homes and luscious gardens – some extravagant, some modest, at least by American standards. They were ghostly spaces, groomed to perfection, sterile in their cleanliness. Most of them lacked any hint of human habitation. Only occasionally did people appear in these pictures, and even then, they were more like mannequins that were carefully posed and placed to give the space a sense of scale. People in these worlds apparently did not suffer the mundane shortcomings of being disheveled or even ordinary, lest they sully the pristine backdrops.

His wife had collected page after page after page of these images, each lovingly pruned. Sometimes she had entire pages. Sometimes she had carefully pruned an element of a page – a shrub here, a lamppost there – pasting it into another page. He noticed in her selections a pattern, a preference for spare design. He felt he was glimpsing into her mind, an album of her desire. It was a mind alien to him.

He continued searching through the house, peeling back the layers of her life to which he had been so oblivious. Each thing that she kept, either by conscious choice or neglect to dispose, illuminated a recess of her mind. There was an ad showing a dishwasher; Han recalled his wife mentioning something about it and how they were a rarity in New York City even though they were commonplace in the suburbs. There were mementos from trips he had long forgotten about. Items of clothing she hadn't worn in years, yet had kept packed neatly away as though they were heirlooms.

Then there were the doodles her notebooks. In their frenetic curves, Han recognized the echoes of the illness that had once led her to recoil from her own daughter when the four-year-old tried to seek some tenderness after falling over and bloodying her knee. Her reaction startled Won-Sook, as though she had been bitten by a dog that had been unwaveringly friendly until then. When his wife realized what she had done, she reached out for Won-Sook, but the girl retreated from her mother, her outstretched arms pulled back awkwardly like a mantis. The memory made him wince.

He had struggled to keep her illness hidden from his colleagues, and even his own extended family, making excuses for her unexplained absences at family and Workers' Party functions. Depression was invented by a self-indulgent West and hence, an affront to the hallowed principles of *juche*, or self-reliance, and by extension, a sign of wavering devotion to the Dear Leader. The stigma on her could have ruined his career.

Seeing her aimless squiggles in the notebooks – sometimes so dense that the underlying page shone through in worn spots – gave him a sickening feeling that he was again about to plunge into those days of living in fear of being found out.

Han kept searching through the house, looking in corners he had never paid attention to before. Then, among all the detritus of her life, he stumbled on a clue that could lead to her whereabouts. Mrs. Koh had sent his wife a card recently, congratulating her on Won-Kyu's birth. His wife had kept the envelope, too. And on it was Mrs. Koh's address. She lived in Flushing. It was easy enough to track down her phone number.

When he called it, there was no answer. Just an answering machine with a message in a man's voice recorded both in English and in Korean. Perhaps it was Mrs. Koh's husband. Han hung up. It was nearly 11 o'clock.

It was time to decide – try to solve this dilemma by himself and keep it under wraps, or confide in someone and improve his odds of finding his wife before the matter spiraled out of control. His immediate urge was toward secrecy. The logical place to start would be to pay a visit to Mrs. Koh in Flushing. But then what? What if his wife wasn't there? Or what if she *was* there yet refused to leave? Han needed a capable backup – capable and, more importantly, discreet. If in fact his wife had run away with Won-Kyu, he was ill equipped to track them down. And if things unraveled badly, he needed an ally to buy some time with Deputy Ambassador Kwon.

Comrade Park. He was the logical choice. But could he trust him? Han hovered over the phone, pondering it as though it were some relic not easily touched. He looked at his watch one more time, then desperation approximated resolve as he picked up the receiver. He called Park's pager. Before dialing the last digit, he paused and took a deep breath.

When Park called him back, he heard a din in the background – music, people laughing, mostly women's voices. It sounded like a bar.

Park finally came on the phone, shouting hello several times before telling whoever was with him to shut up for a moment.

"Comrade Park, it's Chol-Soo."

"Comrade Han? To what do I owe this pleasure at this time of night? Are you alright?"

"Yes, yes. I'm fine."

"What's going on?" Park said, and then, his voice a little muted, said: "Stop that will you. I'm on the phone with my best friend." The women giggling and talking in the background were speaking Korean, decidedly not in a North Korean accent.

There were several things amiss here. The paradox of Park was that he was a hedonist, but born of a time and place that could least afford luxury, and, furthermore, publicly demonized luxury as the ultimate corruption of social harmony. At that moment, Han found Park's transgressions – his penchant for booze and women – rather comforting, even though he could not comprehend how Park could afford it. Park's hypocrisy was especially comforting in light of what he was about to confide in him. Never trust a man without a good vice or two, Park had once said. Han felt as though he had caught Park in a compromising situation, and it immediately put his mind at ease, never mind that Park didn't seem to care and made little effort to conceal it.

"Jun-Young, I've got a bit of a problem and I need your help," Han said.

Chapter 6

Even nearing midnight, Northern Boulevard was a well-traveled road, cutting through enclave after enclave of immigrants in a compressed tour of the world's peoples. There was in fact a mini-rush hour at that time of night created by workers retreating from their night shifts in Manhattan.

On the days that Han took the 7-train late at night from Grand Central, the subway cars were stocked mostly with weary, dark-haired people – Pakistanis and Indians with their matted locks, stout Latinos with aquiline noses and hair gelled back, and the Chinese and his South Korean brethren clutching knock-off designer bags, sleeping with the assurance they would be awoken at the end of the line in Flushing.

One night, not long after Han was first posted to New York, he dozed off and missed his stop in Jackson Heights. When he awoke, he bolted upright in a startled panic, disoriented and unsure of how far down the line he had traveled. When the doors opened at the next station, he dashed onto the platform instinctively without thinking about where he was. His only thought was he had come too far and needed to double back.

It was only after the doors closed and the train rattled away that he realized he was the only person on the platform. The fog in his mind cleared instantly. People had told him that New York was a dangerous place. How much more dangerous then for a citizen of a nation hostile to the United States, he had thought, as though petty criminals were in league with the nation's leaders and chose their targets with deference to international grudges. Even for a Potemkin village as intricate as New York, that level of coordination was a stretch, he later granted. In that moment, as he stood alone on a windy platform, he felt foolish and vulnerable. Everything came into sharp focus. Off in the distance, he saw a stadium.

For a moment he thought of taking a running leap over the tracks to get to the Manhattan-bound platform. Then he saw the stairs leading to an underpass. As he turned a corner to a dimly lit sweep of stairs leading back up, he smelled urine and bleach, a combined odor that he would, from then on, associate with deserted, outlying subway stations, and acute corners of misshapen architecture harboring the city's stains.

Han later learned that the stadium in the distance was called Shea, and that they played baseball there. That game the American G.I.s had implanted in South Korea during their imperialist occupation. On days that they had games at Shea, the 7-train would fill up with an abnormal number of white people. On average, they were louder than the normal crowd that rode the 7. Perhaps they were just more jovial because they were on the train to attend a game, as opposed to the usual straphangers for whom the train was mostly a means of getting to and from work.

After that experience on the empty platform, it took a few weeks for the 7 to shed its menace enough for Han to feel comfortable enough to doze off again.

If the traffic weren't so bad, he would have preferred to drive to and from work most of the time, insulating himself in his car. But Northern Boulevard was a congested mess most of the time. Even now, near midnight, as he and Park drove toward Flushing, the thoroughfare could hardly be called clear.

Park and Han were silent for a good part of the way. When Park spoke, Han smelled alcohol on his breath. And he seemed to be in a good mood. Perhaps that accounted for Park's sympathy for Han's predicament. He didn't chastise Han for letting his life at home get out of control. His sympathy in turn prompted Han to divulge details that, until then, he had kept well hidden.

The problem with keeping secrets is that they isolate you from others. Keeping a secret necessitates evasion. Either that or you have to lie. A lie only works if it is plausible and consistent. The more secrets you keep, the more elaborate the lies must become. Evasion therefore is the surer route to secrecy in the long run. Hence a person with many secrets often finds himself alone and quite often lonely, and yearning for a confidant.

Han was older than Park by several months, but Han often felt unsophisticated and exposed in Park's presence. Even in school, Park was one of those precocious guys who had a worldliness about them, knowing things about girls, politics, and altogether the realm of adults that no nineteen-year-old should rightly know, and hence in their presence one felt immature. It wasn't that Park regaled his classmates with stories of his exploits. Rather, an incidental comment that Park would toss away here and there that spoke of a certain weariness with the world that was the result of it being too familiar. Han, on the other hand, was curious by nature, and curiosity smacked of innocence, if not ignorance. Han couldn't quite comprehend when and where Park was accumulating this grown-up knowledge; they ostensibly spent about the same amount of time in classes and their activities outside of school were fairly limited and structured. But somehow Park was still absorbing dissimilar things. They, on the surface of it, inhabited the same spheres, filtering the world in different ways.

Perhaps it was that Park and Han were not facing one another in the car, or that Han had kept too many secrets for too long, but Han spoke without measuring his words. It was a peculiar sensation.

"When Won-Sook was just a month old – this was when we were in between overseas assignments in Pyongyang – I came back from work one day and found my wife sitting in the bathtub with her," Han said.

Park kept driving and didn't glance over.

"The water was up to their necks. At first I thought my wife was giving her a bath. Won-Sook was crying – I mean wailing inconsolably, like she did when she had a fever – it was like my wife didn't hear her. She was just sitting there, looking off into the distance, holding the baby like a sack of potatoes, like she didn't want her touching her own body.

"Both of them were shivering. I said, 'What's going on? What's the matter?' She wouldn't answer me. So I tried to take Won-Sook away from her and I realized then the water was cold. It wasn't even lukewarm. So I screamed at my wife, 'Have you lost your mind! It's freezing! What the matter with you?'

"She wouldn't let go. I had to pry Won-Sook out of her fingers. I kept yelling at her, 'Let her go! Let her go!' Won-Sook's lips were turning blue. I didn't know if it was from the cold or because she was running out of breath, crying so hard. When I finally pried her loose, my wife made this horrible groan. It still gives me goose bumps when I hear that in my head. She made this horrible sound like some wild animal caught in a trap. Then she started sobbing. It scared me half to death. It was like I'd been living with a total stranger. I didn't want to let Won-Sook out of my sight. And I certainly didn't want my wife to be alone with her when I wasn't there. That's when we moved in with my parents."

"Do you think she would have harmed Won-Sook?" Park asked.

Han didn't answer immediately. Admitting that she might have been in danger was to admit that his wife was capable of infanticide – something so heinous that there wasn't even a word for it in Korean.

Han was silent for so long that Park looked over at him in the passenger seat at a traffic light. Han was staring straight ahead, his face glowing red and then green as the light changed. Up ahead, the signals had all changed in unison, with green lights for at least a mile.

"I don't know," Han finally said. "I don't know what she was thinking."

Someone behind them honked their horn, impatient but not insistent.

Park faced forward and stepped on the gas.

* * *

About half-an-hour later when they pulled up to the curb outside Mrs. Koh's house, Han convinced Park to stay in the car. "We wouldn't want to alarm her by having two strangers show up at her door at this time of night," Han said. Park agreed.

Han smoothed out his clothes before he rang the bell. It was past midnight. The lights were still on inside. Han was expecting to have to explain himself through a closed door, but it opened even without a single question from inside.

The woman answering the door started chatting away even before it had fully swung open. Her husband rarely came home before midnight. "You're early today," she began to say, then stopped herself in mid-sentence when she saw Han. She immediately hid behind the door and pushed it forward as if against a stiff wind.

"Wait!" Han said, stepping forward and putting his weight against the door. "Mrs. Koh? I'm Won-Kyu's father."

She kept pressing forward. He was leaning into it now.

"I'm Chung Myung-Ae's husband. You know Chung Myung-Ae in your English class?" Han said, hoping the different descriptions would help her triangulate him in her startled mind.

"I'm sorry to bother you so late at night. I'm looking for..." he paused in mid-sentence and glanced behind him to check that Park was still in the car, "I'm looking for my wife. She doesn't know a lot of people here, and she talks about you all the time. I was hoping you could tell me where she might be."

"Sorry, I have no idea," she said, still pushing.

Han felt Mrs. Koh's answer was too swift to be truthful. She didn't even ask how long she'd been gone, or any other questions.

"Please, Koh-dongji," Han said, inadvertently calling her "comrade." If his accent didn't give him away, the word pegged him instantly as a North Korean. Mrs. Koh stopped pushing and peeked around the door.

"Do you realize what kind of trouble this could create, I mean not just for my wife and family, but my government as well?"

"I told you, I don't know anything about where she is," Koh said.

"Did my wife ever tell you that she has a daughter, too?"

Koh stood there without responding.

"She does. We do. She's in Pyongyang. And if my superiors find out that my wife has gone missing or even caused some ruckus here in New York, do you know what would happen to our daughter in Pyongyang?"

Koh was still silent.

"Let's just say she'd be in a lot of trouble. Our whole family would be in a lot of trouble. Do you understand? It's a matter of life and death, quite literally."

Something was going on behind those darting eyes of hers, and the effort she was putting in to comprehend the situation seemed to be surpassed only by her effort to silence herself. Han studied her face. She was a woman passing on from middle age. She was old enough to perhaps have a grandchild or two, but they would still be infants. In the background, Han heard the sound of a church choir playing on tinny speakers.

"Koh-dongji. Please help me. You must have children of your own, perhaps even grandchildren?"

"Hold on. I'm not a grandmother yet. Do I look like a grandmother to you?"

"I'm just asking you to imagine if you did, wouldn't you want the best for them?"

"Of course. But as I told you, I don't know anything about where your wife might be. Perhaps you better call the police and report her missing."

"You know I can't do that. You know who I am. Look, you're a Christian, right? You're not supposed to lie. Lying is a sin, no? You're supposed to treat people with compassion. Well have compassion for my family – if not me or my wife, then for my daughter."

Han fished around in his jacket for his wallet. He took out a picture of his daughter – a smaller version of the one sitting on his nightstand – and thrust it toward Mrs. Koh. "This is Won-Sook. If I don't find my wife, her life will be over."

Mrs. Koh took the photo almost as a polite reflex, then handed it back after barely looking at it.

"I'm sorry, I can't help you. I don't know where she is," Mrs. Koh said, and started pushing against the door again.

Han lost his grip on the photo. It fluttered to the floor inside the foyer. Mrs. Koh eased up on the door to pick it up and the door flung wide open. Han almost stumbled in.

Mrs. Koh took the photo and offered it back to Han. When she looked up at him, his gaze was fixed on something inside the house.

Mrs. Koh followed his gaze. On the sofa was a pack of disposable diapers.

"You said you didn't have any grandchildren," Han said.

Mrs. Koh grabbed the door and tried to slam it shut. Han leaned into it with his shoulder and it bounced open and he stepped into the house. Mrs. Koh took a few steps back to regain her balance.

"Stop lying to me and tell me where she is!" Han said, his voice even and steely.

"Get out!" she screamed. "I'll never tell you where she is. I've seen the bruises on her. I know what kind of man you are, you *palgengi*."

"*Palgengi*" was a derogatory version of "red," as in pinko commie.

"Bruises? Did she tell you how she got those bruises? Did she? Did she tell you that she hits herself, sometimes even cuts herself? Have you seen those scars, too? Did she tell you she breaks down crying for no reason at all, and that she'll bang her arms against a corner just so she can explain her crying. Did she tell you that she tried to drown our daughter? Did she tell you that?"

Mrs. Koh stood in the middle of the living room, holding her hands over her mouth.

"Now tell me where she is. Please. I beg you."

"I don't believe you. She's a sweet, gentle woman. She would never do anything like that. Not to her own child."

"Why don't you ask her yourself then? Ask her. She needs help. And running away isn't going to help her."

The church choir playing on the boom box was reaching a crescendo. It was an amateur choir, from the sounds of it, a recording of a church service.

"She wants to live here, in America," Mrs. Koh said. "She doesn't want to go back."

"She can't live here. We have a daughter in Pyongyang. When my assignment is over, we have to go back. We have to."

"She won't go back," Mrs. Koh said. "She's going to seek asylum, and our church is going to help. She's taken Jesus Christ as her personal savior."

Han was about to plead with her one more time and then he heard a man's voice behind him, coming from outside the house.

"Why's the door wide open? I told you not to wait up for me," the man said.

Han swung around and confronted an elderly man in the doorway.

"Who are you? What the hell are you doing in my house?" the man said.

Before Han had a chance to respond, the man walked up to him and grabbed his wrist. Even though he had graying hair, his grip was solid, that of someone who worked with his body for a living.

"Get out! How dare you barge into someone's house at this hour!" the man said.

"Wait!" Han turned around as he was being dragged out by his wrist. "Mrs. Koh. You have to tell me where she is. Mrs. Koh!"

Han then turned back to the man, yanked away his hand and pushed him back. "I'm not leaving until you tell me where my wife is!"

The man swore at Han and grabbed him by his forearm.

Han easily twisted his arm away this time and pushed him back again. This angered the man even more and he tackled Han full on, knocking him back and knocking over a lamp.

Mrs. Koh screamed and ran to help her husband. The two struggling men knocked her backward and they fell to the floor. Mrs. Koh ran toward the phone and began dialing.

Then Han heard a sound like a light bulb breaking, but louder, as though someone had cracked a wooden board at the same time.

Han felt himself being released from the man's grasp. Then the man cried out and grabbed his leg. Han rolled over on his back and saw Park standing in the doorway holding a gun. Mrs. Koh yelped and dropped the phone, rushing to her husband's side.

Park closed the door behind him.

"You're making a lot of noise late at night," Park said to no one in particular.

Han saw that he was wearing gloves. A silvery cylinder lengthened the gun's muzzle. A foreboding came over him. He looked over at the old man. Blood was already pooling on the floor.

"Koh-dongji, please be quiet, or I'll have to shoot him again."

Mrs. Koh closed her mouth, but she was still whimpering, barely containing her hysteria.

Between groans of pain, the man blurted out questions, demanding to know who they were and what they wanted. Spittle ran down his chin.

"Dongji," Park said to Han. "Did you get what you need?"

"No," he said, picking himself up. "She knows where my wife is but she won't tell me. She says my wife's taken Jesus Christ as her personal savior and that she wants to seek asylum here."

Park scoffed. "Listen to me, you Jesus freak. Tell me where his wife is, or your husband might have trouble walking again."

Mrs. Koh whimpered beside her husband, her lips trembling.

Without even so much as a warning, Park shot the husband in the shin. Han recoiled. The man let out another scream, as did the wife.

Park said he would work his way up the leg if he had to.

"No." Han shouted. "Stop it."

"Quiet. We're here to find your wife, remember?" Park said, never taking his eyes off the couple. "Are you in the mood for talking now? Or is your memory still a bit foggy?"

"No. Please don't shoot. I'll tell you. Just please don't hurt him anymore," Mrs. Koh said, throwing her body over her husband.

"She's in Fort Lee, in New Jersey," she said through whimpers. "She's with an elder of a church there."

Han came up to Park's flank, approaching him cautiously. He saw that Park's gun was a well-worn Tokarev, standard issue for North Korean military officers. The silver silencer that jutted out from the muzzle was certainly not standard issue. It had a rough, hand-hewn appearance.

Park asked for a name and address then told Han to write it down as she blurted it out between sobs, like some lost child reciting her name and address to a cop. She had taken Han's wife there herself, just this afternoon, Mrs. Koh said, then, quite incongruously, warned them that they – being Godless Communist *palgengi* – would go straight to hell.

A darkness fell over Park's face. "My family has been building a worker's paradise probably since long before your family has been worshiping foreign gods," he said and stared into her eyes. "You dare lecture me about heaven and hell? Your ancestors are weeping in their graves, Mrs. Koh."

"Why don't you make amends with them right now," Park said, and without warning, fired a shot into Mrs. Koh's forehead.

She crumpled to the floor and her arms twitched a few times. Her husband screamed out and crawled to her side.

Han also yelled out and grabbed Park's arm. He pushed him aside and squeezed off another shot, this time hitting the husband squarely in the back of the head. He collapsed forward, his head resting on his wife's body.

PART II

Chapter 7

In the car as they headed to New Jersey, Han Chol-Soo didn't even venture a sideways glace at Park Jun-Young. For a long while they said nothing. It was the stubborn silence after friends quarrel because they know that he who speaks first concedes defeat. Han felt no satisfaction that it was Park who eventually broke the quiet as they neared the George Washington Bridge.

"You wanted out. This is the only way," Park said. "If Deputy Ambassador Kwon found out, that would be the end of you. The defections in Cairo and Paris have made Kwon even more paranoid and the Party is just looking for an excuse to make an example out of someone. You know very well what would happen to you and your family if the Party found out about this."

He did. Labor camps where men and women faded away, their bodies worn down, their minds withered into pliant vessels for orthodoxy. The prisoners never got enough rations. And never rice. That was too precious to waste on prisoners. They were so malnourished that the young women would stop menstruating, and a harsh blow by a guard or an unlucky fall would fracture their brittle bones. It would not mend properly in the ill-equipped infirmary, which afforded no more lenient accommodations than any of the cells. They were marked with a limp for the remainder of their short lives.

And it wasn't just deserters and captured defectors who earned a trip to one of the labor camps.

One of Han's distant cousins, a mid-level bureaucrat in the agriculture ministry, had almost ruined Han's standing in the Workers' Party by landing himself in a particularly nasty gulag in

North Hamkyung Province, where the brutal and never-ending winter had hardened the guards into vicious taskmasters. Han later learned that his cousin's offense was that he had made what he thought to be an innocuous critique during a ministry meeting of the way barley was being warehoused. By the time the distracted clatter of the room hushed to a murmur, and then to a sobering silence, it was too late. His fate had been sealed by his oversight of the detail that the apparatchik in charge of barley warehousing happened to be a little-mentioned nephew of Kim Jong-Il.

"It was like I cut a fart. People around me were actually shifting in their seats to get away from me," his cousin had told Han when he visited the remote camp after much pleading by his family to pull some strings to get him out, or at least to ensure his welfare.

Han had visited him in early September, before Choosok, the harvest moon holiday. Even then, there was a bite in the wind there. Han hardly recognized his cousin, emaciated and haggard as he was. Even though Han considered himself not the least bit sentimental, he found himself inadvertently weeping as he called out his cousin's name in the meeting room – not as a greeting, more in the form of a question because he could not believe this was the same person who had given him piggybacks and rides on his shoulders to amuse Han when he was a rambunctious boy.

"Is that really you?" Han had said, peering into his cousin's hollow eyes, straining to recognize them.

His cousin told him that he had been chewing grass and tree bark to ease his hunger pangs and that he almost looked forward to being sent out for hard labor. For one, the work kept his mind off his hunger, and it also meant he could forage in the field for frogs in the summer and grasshoppers in the fall. He would have to eat them on the spot because the guards would frequently check for stashed food. He got into the habit of carrying around a small pouch of salt to season the raw meat. His cousin said even frogs and insects were scarcer than the year before.

As Han left the camp, he had furtively handed over a wad of money in an envelope to the warden, not even mentioning his cousin by name, simply stating: "Please use this for the benefit of the camp."

The warden did not even feign modesty. He clawed at the envelope, peeking inside right in front of Han to see how much it contained. Then, with the kind of smile that only a hardened man can make menacing, he said to Han, "A distinguished gentleman such as yourself shouldn't be visiting a place like this," as though Han's mere presence there would somehow sully him. The warden was outwardly deferential to Han's station but simultaneously mocked it, as a laborer might applaud the shoveling of an amateur gardener. There's a particular kind of danger one feels from someone who doesn't give a shit, with nothing much to lose. That's the kind of danger Han felt from the warden.

A similar fate in a labor camp awaited Han, and likely worse, should his bosses find out about his wife's disappearance.

Han glanced sideways at Park.

"What's the matter?" Park asked, returning the glance.

"Nothing."

"Don't be coy. What is it?"

"You look like a different person to me," Han said and looked away.

"How?"

"We've known one another since when? Since university, right? I've never seen this side of you."

Han and Park had fallen into an easy familiarity in New York because they had known one another at school. They had actually lost touch for a decade or so after graduating from Kim Il-Sung University. Han went off to grad school in Moscow. It turned out that Park did a stint in Beijing, though he was never really clear exactly what he did there. Han was okay with not knowing. He appreciated the fact that within the Workers' Party, some knowledge is indispensable for survival; too much makes you a potential threat.

"What is it you think that I do, Dr. Han?" The false formality of calling him "Dr. Han" added a menacing edge to his question.

What is it you think that I do? Han repeated the question to himself. The tone implied something sinister that he had contemplated only in the abstract as being part of Park's job description as security attaché to the ambassador.

"There are people who protect our way of life, buffers against the wind, if you will," Park continued. "They don't always have the luxury of polite methods."

"I'm talking about *you*," Han said. "Look at you. Look at your hands. They're not even shaking." Park had just killed two people – a helpless, elderly couple – and as far as Han could tell, he was as calm as always.

After shooting the couple, Park had methodically picked up the shell casings off the living room floor, as though he were cleaning up lint.

"They would have called the police and then we'd never find your wife, comrade," Park said. "And that would be the end for you. Don't forget I did it for *you*. My conscience is clear. That's why I'm not shaking."

"It's all over for me already," Han said. He wanted to say "over for us" but thought better of it.

"It's not over yet. If you start buckling now, I can guarantee you it will indeed be over – for both of us, and your family."

"It won't be long before someone finds their bodies."

"There's nothing to link it to us. The police will think they were the victims of a robbery. It happens all the time in this garbage pile of a city. Don't you watch television or read the papers?"

This garbage pile of a city – he liked to say that a lot, and with no hint of irony. Considering how Park indulged in every vice and virtue – mostly vice – this city had to offer, he was surprisingly quick to disparage it every chance he got. To be sure, Han also had his misgivings about New York; even held it in contempt at times. But he had to concede the city was audacious if nothing else, even though it always appeared to be on the verge of becoming feral. Wild cabbies menacing faint-hearted drivers; a Brownian motion of pedestrians, some hurried, some impeding others; and cyclists weaving through it all – all of them, the cabs, pedestrians and cyclists, cascading through the streets bathed in chaos. Yet from the vantage point of a jetliner, the very geometry of the city forced some semblance of order onto that chaos, pumping through its grid of streets, like blood through the veins of a writhing colossus.

The bridge he and Park were now crossing embodied that balance of chaos and serenity. Han recalled seeing the George Washington Bridge from afar when he first arrived in New York and thinking how the lights that dotted the suspension cables and towers evoked beads of dew. The bridge spanned the darkness over the Hudson like a cobweb, shimmering and alive with headlights crawling over the expanse of crisscrossed cables and girders.

As a scientist who studied the physical world, it was hard not to be impressed by it, even though Han was no stranger to massive public works projects. The late Great Leader, Kim Il-Sung, had been a visionary of such displays of engineering prowess. Yet the works he was familiar with in Pyongyang were more akin to solitary jewels, ostentatiously mounted and on display. The George Washington Bridge seemed to him more like a cutting diamond, its edges alive with labor, even if its presentation was compromised by its practicality.

During Han's first month in the United States, he and his wife took the A train to the Rockaways, the thin peninsula in Queens that juts into the Atlantic. It had been foggy and drizzly that day. From the station they walked by the ruined houses and the stray seagulls pecking through the litter gathered in the leeward gutters. It reinforced his prejudices about New York – how a supposedly rich country like America could turn beachfront property into something bleak, so unlike anything he had seen in his travels around the world.

The beach itself was relatively clean, possibly because there were hardly any people there that day. A man with a greying beard so thick that it threatened to conceal his face entirely was walking along the waterline. He was topless, even though the wind had a bite to it. The waves broke on jetties stabbing out into the grey-green winter sea. It was grave, solemn. His wife took his hand in hers. It surprised him. That was one of the few times Han had taken his wife on anything resembling a trip simply for the pleasure of it. Perhaps if had indulged her just a little bit more, she wouldn't have felt the need to run away. But they could never be tourists, especially not in this land.

The U.S. State Department allowed North Korean diplomats to travel up to 25 miles from New York. However, the natural border formed by the Hudson River and the cliffs of the Palisades felt to him a more obvious marker of his circumscribed life – much more so than the invisible perimeter drawn arbitrarily by his host nation.

He had once heard a fellow U.N. diplomat – a sullen Russian fellow prone to bouts of dramatic pessimism over soggy cafeteria food – refer to the GWB as the K-19, a sly reference to a steel construction of another kind; his country's notorious submarine that killed and poisoned so many of its crew in a hushed-up reactor accident, hence dubbed the *Widowmaker*. In the case of the bridge, the Russian had said, it enabled the daily evacuation of those satellite bedroom towns in northern New Jersey, their able-bodied workforce pouring into Manhattan, leaving diurnal widows to roam the leafy suburban roads.

Han had laughed at that. "You Russians are melancholy," he had said. He was garrulous, with a quick wit, and hopelessly flawed – in other words, Han liked him instantly.

The Russian sang the praises of the Short Hills Mall in New Jersey. "Have you been there? Very nice. Expensive, yes, but very nice."

Han told him he had yet to venture so far from the city.

That Russian – who hailed from Vladivostok and seemed to feel entitled to familiarity with Han because of the port's proximity to Korea – would accost him in the hallways of the Secretariat Building and demand to debate him in Russian after he learned that Han had studied at Moscow University.

"Doctor Koreitsi," he would call Han, using the Russian word for 'Korean'.

"Your Dear Leader has the right idea. Hang onto Communism for as long as you can. Everything went to shit in Russia after Gorbachev," he once said in what seemed to be a moment of frustration and nostalgia. "Bloody gangsters all over the place now. It's all bloody gangsters."

The more Han thought about the Widowmaker comment, the more that story seemed an oblique warning directed at him about the dangers of toying with the atom. The GWB had just been a convenient excuse to bring up the topic. The man claimed he was the cultural attaché with his Mission, but over the course of several meals, studying the folds of his face in the U.N.'s brightly lit cafeteria, Han suspected his real post was a great deal more serious, and hence, infinitely more dull – which is why he craved conversation with strangers.

The man was much too eccentric to be a cultural attaché. People who truly held that position were unfailingly the most tedious Han knew; their dullness surpassed only by their caution--caution of words, caution of gestures, and most of all, caution of their politics. This Russian's verbose eccentricity was that of a man who had been encumbered with a secret for too long.

Han entertained the thought that this man was his Russian counterpart. Han wouldn't have been surprised if the Russians had a running dossier on him going back as far as his student days when he studied physics in Moscow. That's how the weasel knew to bring up the Widowmaker reference, he suspected. It would make sense. If he was in fact Han's counterpart, they were both men who knew the state's dirty little nuclear secrets and spun those secrets into elaborate veils for the state's advantage. And these meandering debates over curried chicken on rice pilaf, preferably at a table overlooking the roiling East River and the industrial shores beyond, were just the Russian's way of lifting the veil ever so slightly.

The difference between them was quantitative. Han's country had a lot less fissile material to work with, whether it was uranium or plutonium. Naturally, the veil Han spun was appallingly thin in places – a flaw that could only be remedied by the masterfully timed bluff every once in a while. Brinksmanship – that's what the West called it.

Fortunately, the canny rocket scientists back home in North Korea had multiplied the effectiveness of such bluffs. They had made remarkable progress in developing a reliable way to launch what little fissile material they had further and further into enemy territory. South Korea was not an issue. The People's Army didn't need a missile to obliterate Seoul. It was in easy reach of their artillery. The missiles were needed to keep off balance the imperial powers that surrounded the peninsula.

A communiqué Han had received from the home office had mentioned that their long-range missile project, code-named *Taepodong*, was nearing completion and could be ready for a test firing as early as next year. It would be a worthy addition to the shorter-range *Nodong* missile, which had proved profitable on the international arms market as a successor to the Soviet-era Scuds. There was a nice little niche for the surface-to-surface *Nodongs*, which flew considerably further than Scuds. Iran and Yemen were satisfied customers, as was Pakistan. It had excited Han to think of the diplomatic leverage the *Taepodong* would create. Lobbing one over Japan into the Pacific would do the trick.

* * *

As their car reached mid-span of the George Washington Bridge, Han asked Park whether he remembered the time Park drove to Washington with the ambassador during a specially authorized trip.

"Sure," Park said.

"What were your impressions?"

Park glanced over at Han as if to say, *why are you asking me this now?* He pondered the question, then said: "It's a big country. That was my impression. The distance between here and there is about the same as the distance from Pyongyang to Shinuiju. When you look at a map of the U.S., however, New York to Washington, that's just a short hop, isn't it?"

Shinuiju was a city on the Yalu River, bordering China. In ancient times, Korea had built its own northern barrier, one-tenth the scale of the Great Wall of China, to keep out marauding barbarians. It stretched a thousand "ri," roughly 500 kilometers, about the distance that a Scud could fly.

"What do you suppose is in all that space?" Han said, his voice distant as though his mind was wandering over the American landscape.

"Lots of deserts and farms. Lots of empty space, dotted by garbage-pile cities," Park said.

The over-arching feeling Han had when traveling across a desert – be it the American West or the Gobi – was one of being small. The Americans had given him a brief tour of the Very Large Array in New Mexico as a side trip during a visit to Los Alamos. The vastness of the high desert was the terrestrial echo of the infinite heavens being probed by the radio telescopes lined up in three spokes, the dishes facing skyward in unison like rows of colossal white sunflowers. When Han was younger, he felt enlivened by this sense of being small in the universe, buoyed by the sense that the world was boundless and open for exploration. Only later did he understand that not everyone felt as he did; some just feel lonely and diminished by the solitude.

"It's a big country," Han said.

"Shouldn't you be thinking more about the predicament you're in now?"

"I am. I was just wondering, if she's violated the 25-mile perimeter, she'll have a lot of places to hide, won't she? Like you said – there's lots of empty space here."

"People don't just disappear like ghosts. We've already found out where she's going. Let's see what this Jesus freak minister has to say first."

"And what if he plays dumb? Then what, Jun-Young?"

As soon as he uttered the question, Han wished he hadn't asked it. He didn't want to know the answer. He asked another question instead to change the topic. "Is it true that Deputy Ambassador Kwon got a consul recalled to Pyongyang when he was in Berlin?"

"Where did you hear that?" Park said.

"Small office, isn't it?" Han said and smiled. "Rumors. Just because I don't gossip, doesn't mean I'm deaf." Han wasn't the only one who had detected a hawkish alertness that had been awakened in Kwon lately in the ambassador's absence. Perhaps what had until then seemed only a theoretical possibility – taking over the top spot at the North Korean Mission to the U.N. – seemed within reach.

"And what else do these rumors say about Kwon?"

"That the consul eventually got sent to Camp 14," Han said.

A trip to that notorious labor camp in Kaechon was usually a one-way trip.

Park said nothing.

"Well?"

"Well, what?"

"Is it true?"

"I knew that consul. He wasn't the smartest guy in the world," Park said.

He didn't have to elaborate further. Han knew from that answer that the rumors were true in essence if not in every detail.

Chapter 8

Every man can be broken, given enough time. But how do you break someone *quickly*, especially a person of faith. The difficulty in eliciting information – or rather, *accurate* information – from a man of faith is that the source of his resistance lies beyond the reach of reason, even bodily pain. Everyone has a limit on how much pain he can endure. However, a man can bear almost any amount if he knows it is temporary. When he believes there is no relief in his future, even minor discomfort can defeat defiance.

The problem with using pain to extract information is that the person may at first rebel fiercely. They may also feed you disinformation just to stop the torture. Disinformation is more harmful than no information at all because it leads you down the wrong path. When pressed for time, this is a problem.

It didn't take long for Park to figure out that the Reverend Baek Sang-Min was a zealot of the most incorrigible kind – one who came to his faith in spite of the most horrific of personal circumstances, rather than by way of some vague sense of altruism fostered by privilege.

"What makes you think I'm afraid of you? I have the Lord on my side, gentlemen," Baek said, peering over his gold-rimmed glasses. They were perched on the tip of his nose, which was slick with perspiration. He was bound to a wooden chair in the kitchen, his hair a mess. Wisps of gray that barely concealed his scalp were congealed into sweaty clumps. The top three buttons on his pajama shirt had come undone as the result of a scuffle.

"I was orphaned in the war. I almost starved to death. I scrounged through trash piles for food. By rights I should have died twice already. I live only as long as the Lord finds it useful to keep me in this world," the minister said, gently blinking as a bead of sweat trickled along his brow and joined a rivulet of blood running down from a gash on his forehead into the corner of his eye.

Park looked over at Han and shook his head, as would a parent stumped by a misbehaving child.

"I know you don't care about your *own* life," Park said, "but surely you care about your wife's."

Park had found a bag of M&M's in the kitchen and had dumped them on the dining table, sorting them into lines by colors, as if to check the randomness of the mix. He began popping the M&M's into his mouth, starting with the most numerous color, until all colors reached parity. He paused to admire the symmetry of the lines of candy, like soldiers in formation. He would devour them one color at a time until they were gone.

Park and the minister both glanced over to the quivering woman bound to another chair. Her bare ankles were taped to the chair's legs, and she had somehow managed to keep on her slippers. There was a pillowcase over her head. The striped fabric billowed and receded with each distraught breath.

It had been easy enough to get into the minister's home. They didn't even have to force their way in. Park told the minister that he was on an urgent errand from Mrs. Koh.

"How incautious you have become in your plenty," Park had said before pistol-whipping him. The handle caught the old man on the forehead and it instantly started bleeding. By the time the minister regained his wits his hands were already bound.

It would be easier still to torture him, with his neighbors none the wiser. The very things that made the suburbs so private would conceal all but the loudest of disturbances. The detached homes were discreetly shaded from each other with greenery or fences, and sealed tight even in summer with the chill of air conditioning. Neighbors could live years next door and never glimpse the insides of one another's homes. They minded their own business, taking care to honor the boundaries of the groomed lawns.

The more affluent the suburb, the farther apart the homes, and the further removed from the soil were their owners, tending the land by proxy with the unwashed labor of illegal immigrants. They could know little of nature's brutish whims – the kind that had ravaged North Korea lately, the kind that unfurled slowly, laying waste to entire crops upon which farmers relied for their livelihood and a people for their sustenance.

Like most boys in his homeland, Han had often been recruited as a child to help farmers plant their crops. He marched along shaded country roads flanked by towering trees, shouldering a shovel like a rifle.

The wind stirs the leaves into a sound of waves coming ashore. The air is dense with the hum of cicadas and the scent of acacia blooms. At dusk, after a hard day's labor, the chorus is taken over by frogs and crickets. The boy is enveloped in a cacophony of life lurking in the darkness. He and his fellow young patriots sing a rousing ode to the Great Leader as they return home, tired yet proud, their path lit by starlight, fireflies and the steely determination of innocence.

The lush vegetation in Han's homeland was a pale memory. Mountains and hills within a day's walk of the smallest of villages had become brown and bare, and obscured by a dusty haze kicked up by the slightest breeze. The denuding of the land was due only in part to repeated droughts. Most of the damage was caused by famished villagers scavenging every piece of vegetation for food, however unpalatable. They even stripped the bark off trees, to a height of about seven feet – as high as most could reach without exerting themselves – leaving trunks that resembled a pale leg exposed by rolling up one's trousers. The trees soon died off, leaving the land barer still. The haze was worse in the late spring, when the easterly winds scoured China's vast deserts and dumped layers of fine yellow grit on the Korean peninsula. Laundry hung outside on lines took on a jaundiced hue.

"It appears that your wife's faith may not be strong as yours, Baek-*dongji*," Park said and took a place behind her chair. Her breathing became even more frantic when she felt Park's presence behind her.

"Don't call me comrade, you insolent fool. I'm not your friend," Baek shot back. "Don't Communists have parents? Did they teach you nothing about respecting your elders?"

Anger flashed on Park's face. As quickly as it emerged he calmed himself with a sigh. "You are a human trafficker, reverend," he said, pointing to a messy pile of documents on the kitchen table. Han and Park had rifled through the minister's house looking for clues to the whereabouts of Han's wife and son. Phone lists, itineraries, pamphlets, spreadsheets – all pointed to one thing: Baek was part of a network of Christians who had taken it upon themselves to help North Korean refugees and defectors, mostly through an underground network in China.

Han went upstairs. He hesitated at the door of the bedroom when he realized he still had his shoes on. It was a reflex to remove his shoes at the threshold, as was the custom in traditional homes. He had to consciously override it to step into the carpeted room with his shoes still on, treading as though he were on virgin snow. The scent of cold cream lingered in the air. The woman had just removed her makeup. He surveyed the room, then approached a desk in the corner and checked the messages on the minister's answering machine. There were several calls coordinating visits to sick parishioners.

He hit the redial button. An answering machine picked up.

"Welcome to the First Baptist Church of Fairfax, located in beautiful Springfield, Virginia," the recorded message said in Korean, also giving the hours of its services and directions. He also dialed *69 for the last incoming call. The same answering machine picked up.

"Virginia," Han whispered to himself.

When Han returned downstairs, he found Park and the minister trading verbal barbs.

"Even if they make it to China, or even Thailand, then what?" Park asked rhetorically. "Languish in jail? Meet their miserable end? Have you been to that Suan Phlu prison in Bangkok? Quite the place, isn't it? Thirty people to a cell. Lucky if you can find a place to lie down. Oh, and let's not forget the wonderful smells. Charming."

"No worse than any of your labor camps, I imagine."

"Even if they do manage to make it to South Joseon, then what?" Park continued, using the 19th-century dynastic name for Korea still used in the North. "They're treated like spies and second-class citizens. The only jobs they can get are cleaning toilets or hauling off trash."

"Mr. Park. You don't have to regurgitate Party propaganda here," Baek said. "It's just us. There's no one else here. You don't really believe that stuff, do you?"

"You're a learned man in your own way, Reverend. You, of all people, should know what a cesspool South Joseon has become. If it's so great there, then why did you leave?"

"I left *South Korea*," Baek said with special emphasis on *Namhan* to correct Park's usage, "because I'm on a mission for the glory of God. I'm spreading his word."

"Jesus freak," Park muttered under his breath.

"Comrade," Han said, motioning to Park for a word in private. "I checked the reverend's phone messages. Looks like the last incoming and outgoing calls were to this place." Han handed him a slip of paper.

Han and Park together rifled through the documents strewn across the dining table, looking for any names linked to the First Baptist Church; something more than the address – a church member's name, a phone number, anything. There were too many pages. It would take all night to properly scrutinize each one.

"Even if we go to the church, there's no guarantee your wife and son are going to be there," Park whispered to Han outside of the earshot of the elderly couple. "We need to know who's harboring them. Some church elder, maybe."

Park and Han looked over at Baek.

"First Baptist Church of Fairfax," Park blurted out.

The minister's face betrayed him. The slightest of twitches in his eyebrow.

"Who is she staying with there?"

Baek's face hardened, as though he had made a silent vow to himself.

Park said nothing further. He walked over to the kitchen cabinets and searched the drawers. He pulled out a knife and scraped its blade with his fingertips to check its sharpness. He discarded it and eventually settled on a blade about six inches long then walked over to the minister's wife.

"Wait!" Han called out to get Park's attention. When Park turned to him, Han was at a loss for words.

"Watch out for our good reverend here," Park said, handing his pistol to Han.

Han felt simultaneously reassured and unnerved by Park's composure. Park placed the blade against the woman's neck. She recoiled from the coldness, and when she realized what the object was, she began to sob.

"Park-dongji!" Han said, somehow hoping that the formality would deter his partner.

"You're the little boy's father, aren't you?" the minister said to Han. "Your wife and son are long gone. Nothing you or your friend does here will bring them back to you."

"Reverend Baek. I beg you, please tell me where my wife and son are. I give you my word they won't be harmed. We have to act quickly, before my superiors find out. As long as they don't know, we can make this problem disappear."

"Your wife was baptized two months ago. Your son, too," Baek said. "They're God's children now. We had a baptism just for the two of them. It was a beautiful ceremony."

Baptized? Han couldn't believe what he was hearing. Baek might as well have said she had turned into a fairy of some sort, so outlandish was the concept and so remote the possibility. Han tried to remember whether there had been any telltale signs of her conversion two months ago. There were none that he could recall. It was chilling to him that his wife could have kept such a radical change in her life to herself without even a hint. Or had his neglect of her been so wanton?

"Han-dongji, what are you doing?" Park said, gesturing with the knife for Han to raise the muzzle of the gun toward the minister.

How do you break a man, quickly, and a defiant man of faith at that? Without the benefit of time and fatigue, exploiting empathy is often the quickest path. Even the obstinate and those that find solace in self sacrifice find it hard to endure pain inflicted on others on their account.

Park lifted the pillowcase off the minister's wife's head. Her mouth was covered with duct tape. Her tangled hair was matted in clumps against her sweaty forehead and her overfed, plump jowls.

Then, without hesitation, Park sliced off her left ear cleanly with the deftness of an assembly line worker, the stroke merely a matter of routine. Her scream barely registered as a groan. The wound bled profusely, the burgundy flow fanning out over her neck and following the contours of her collarbone. It wasn't until she saw Park holding out her ear in front of her that she became hysterical.

The minister writhed in his chair.

"You crazy son of a bitch!" he growled as he fought against his restraints.

Han knew there was no turning back now.

Even after Park had shot Mr. and Mrs. Koh, Han maintained the illusion that he could somehow tiptoe through this whole ordeal, come out clean through the other side, as long as he found his wife and son. That illusion had made him behave effetely, a dandy caught in a rainstorm who scurries for cover. Now he knew he was sullied beyond salvation – drenched. There was no longer any need for caution.

It was an artificial line he had drawn; he knew that. Seeing Mrs. Baek's ear lopped off – a raw violation of her body – created a gut reaction he couldn't ignore or explain away. He felt resigned and at the same time liberated – the comfort afforded a man left with but one choice. For the Reverend and Mrs. Baek, it was the beginning of the end.

Han raised the muzzle of the gun to Baek's forehead and told him to shut up. He glanced at his watch. It was nearly 3 a.m. The time for compromise had passed.

Chapter 9

As Park Jun-Young and Han Chol-Soo drove away from the minister's house, Han felt his chest grow cold and he wondered whether that was how a heart attack begins. His mind raced back to the night before, when he had returned home late in the rainstorm after stumbling out of the room salon with the people who had visited Ambassador Kim's hospital room.

Han recalled the chilly downpour driven by winds that gusted unpredictably from all directions and how he felt suddenly awake as he inhaled the moist air. He thought he could smell the ocean. On the drive back to his apartment in Queens, he had to rub the windshield with his hands to clear the fog that had steamed off his body. By the time he reached his front door, he was shivering so hard that he had trouble threading his keys into the lock. He stabbed at the keyhole a few times. Then blowing into his palms, he warmed himself enough to insert the key using one hand to steady the other.

He tiptoed by the room where his wife lay curled around their infant son. He did not enter. He instead went to the living room, where he peeled off his drenched clothes into a puddle beside the sofa, and collapsed half naked into the cushions, exhausted by the cold. How he wished he could turn back the clock just one day.

He recalled falling into the sofa, after peeling off his drenched clothes, being unable to stay asleep, despite his fatigue. The storm assaulted his senses all night. Thunder echoed through the apartment periodically and rattled the windows. He tossed and shimmied on the sofa, still clammy from the moisture he had worn in from the night. He found himself counting the seconds between the lightning and thunderclaps, calculating the storm's distance, until he was wide awake.

The lightning was so sharp between the darkness that Han could read the eyes in the photograph propped up on a side table. The image appeared in flashes, surfacing from a deep shroud and flickering on with a ghostly persistence of vision. It was a studio portrait of himself with his wife and their daughter, Won-Sook, five years old at the time, perched on his lap. It was a stiff, formal sitting, taken before Won-Kyu was born, chronicling the measure and appearance of his family. Neither he nor his wife was smiling, not because they were unhappy, but because the formality of the occasion demanded they be properly somber. It was not every day that one sat for a family portrait.

Han's posture was upright and so was his wife's, as though they had been lashed to wooden boards running the length of their spines, like in those daguerreotypes. He wore a grey pinstripe suit, slightly oversized, as if he expected to grow into it. On his lapel was a coin-sized pin showing a miniature portrait of the "Great Leader," Kim Il-Sung, set against a scarlet background, advertising his allegiance to the Workers' Party. His wife wore a *hanbok*, the traditional two-piece Korean dress. When standing, the flowing burgundy skirt pitched all the way up from her ankles to her armpits. The white V-neck top had sleeves that billowed out and then tapered back in to the wrist, forming a half-moon shape on the bottom. His daughter wore the state-sanctioned preschool uniform – a blue skirt and a white shirt, accented with a scarlet scarf around her neck, worn girl-scout style.

Han studied that picture all through the night, lying on his side, anticipating the next brief illumination from the lightning. The thunderclaps grew less frequent as the night wore on, and he fell into a fitful sleep. The distant rumbling wove its way into his dream and continued to plague him.

Han woke up to the sound of a baby's crying. He wasn't sure at first whether he had dreamed the sound or it was the sound that awakened him. It was still dark outside, but the storm had passed and the darkness was uninterrupted by lightning. He had slept only enough to feel groggy, not rested. He tossed around for several more minutes, his mind wandering that foggy realm between sleep and awakening until he heard the sound of footsteps on a creaky wooden floor. He opened his eyes and saw a ghostly figure walk by. It was his wife, in a white nightgown, walking down the hall with the baby in her arms, trying to console his crying.

Opening his eyes was an exertion for Han, made more difficult by the headache that seemed to surface along with his consciousness. He swung his legs off the sofa with a groan and was shocked by a cold sensation on the soles of his feet. He was stepping on the pile of clothes he had discarded on the floor.

"It was almost 3 o'clock when you got in," his wife said from the hallway over the baby's crying.

"You were awake?" Han said, kneading his temples.

"The baby was crying all evening. I finally got him to sleep just before you came home. I didn't want to wake him, so I didn't get up." She paced up and down the hallway, patting the baby's back. "I don't know what's wrong with him. Maybe I should take him to a doctor."

"It's probably nothing. Remember the trouble we had with Won-Sook?"

"He's even worse than her. He won't sleep. I can't sleep either," she said. "I'm worried about him."

Han picked up his soggy clothes and turned them inside out – or rather, right side in.

"Did you clean my grey suit?" he asked, glancing over at his wife standing in the doorway. Her hair was disheveled, her complexion uneven. A cruel thing happens to some women as they age – they lose the vitality that made them charming even if they had not been natural beauties in their youth. Han feared that cruelty was visiting upon his wife prematurely. "Maybe you could take him to that clinic in Flushing."

She stood in the doorway in silence for a moment as the baby seemed to calm down. "I hate that place. You wait two hours to see the doctor for three minutes. And all those miserable, sick people coughing in the waiting room."

"I know," he said.

"You work so hard," she said. "Shouldn't there be some reward for that? All you say is that it'll get better, but when?"

The baby started crying again when she raised her voice. "If we can't even pay the ambassador's hospital bills, what chance does our son have?" she said, talking louder to be heard over the baby.

"Perhaps it's not Won-Kyu who needs to see a doctor. I think you should keep things in perspective. We're all under a lot of pressure," he said.

When Han was a teenager, his father had chided him about his short fuse. "You get it from me, I'm afraid," his father had said. "You're going to have to work hard all your life to keep it in check, I hope better than I have." Han had mellowed a bit with age, thanks mostly to the constant husbandry of his own prickly nature, as his late father had admonished him to. He had also noticed that a part of that edge had returned of late.

"Don't try to brush this off by suggesting it's just in my head. That's not fair."

"Fair? What was the reason that we waited six years to have Won-Kyu, anyway? It wasn't the flu. You tried to kill yourself, remember?"

As soon as he blurted that out, he wished he could have taken it back. The image of that day when he found his wife on the floor was seared into his mind. She had vomited up scores of pills, half-digested and foaming like soap.

His wife's presence in the room felt suddenly still. Han glanced over at the family portrait on the side table, more so to avoid eye contact with his wife, who now stood in the doorway mumbling to find the right words.

"Look, if you think he's really sick, take him to that doctor in Flushing. I'll think of some way to pay for it," Han said.

His wife turned her back and walked away. He felt a knot in his stomach when he recalled those confused days leading up to her suicide attempt. He struggled to comprehend why she refused to even see her newborn daughter, let alone suckle her. He'd never heard of post-partum depression before then. It caught him completely off guard. When he looked at his wife these days, there was a twinge of guilt at having been ignorant of her ailment. There was also dread, seeing the same early symptoms emerge again after Won-Kyu was born. Even when Han and his wife slept in the same bed, they neatly lay side by side, like stone effigies atop medieval tombs. Sometimes in the middle of the night he would touch her hand. She was a light sleeper; more often than not, she quietly pulled away as if bashful for the contact.

When he caught glimpses of her looking at herself in the mirror lately, she would carefully examine the wrinkles fanning out from the corners of her eyes and test the elasticity of the skin around her neck. He could not gauge now whether it was resentment or depression that was eating up the forbearance that had made her so charming at one time.

If only he could take back what he had said.

Chapter 10

In all the years the clerk at the deli had known Mr. Koh, the owner, he had called in sick only twice that she could remember. There was something inspiring about his unrelenting presence in the store. Early mornings, in the deep of night, weekends and holidays, the stout man always seemed to be there, haunting the narrow aisles, sweeping the sidewalk, moving supplies in the dank basement, or gazing out from the elevated platform behind the counter. He was not invulnerable to illness, just determined not to yield to it. On one occasion, when a cracked-out robber had stabbed him in the belly with a screwdriver, he was back at the deli later that very day – after a stop at the ER and then a sporting goods store, where he bought himself an aluminum bat. Even when the clerk was mad at him for some reason, it was impossible not to respect his determination. He would never ask one of his workers to do something he had not already done any number of times.

Mr. Koh was a civil engineer by training and, as a younger man, had landed a job at one of the larger Korean construction firms; one of those *jaebol* companies – conglomerates that undertook everything from shipbuilding to semiconductors. When Mr. Koh immigrated to the United States, he took on the more humble identity of a deli owner. Perhaps it was this sudden diminution in his social status that made him so reluctant to take time off. It was as though by dint of will he could overcome illness or injury. That triumph over his bodily weakness was crucial in his drive to elevate himself once again, if not through the perplexing social strata of his adopted home country, then for reasons of redemption through labor. And during those rare times that he was not at the store, his wife was there in his stead.

That's why it was so strange that neither Mr. nor Mrs. Koh had called in to the deli to say they would be late. In fact, it had never happened before, so it was cause enough for alarm. The clerk called their house several times, but no one answered. When another clerk came in for work, she quickly handed off the reins to him and went to their house in Flushing. The door was ajar when she arrived. She did not stay long to inspect the mayhem inside. The moment she saw two motionless bodies lying sprawled on the living room floor, she immediately ran to a neighbor's house, where she collapsed into the neighbor's arms and whimpered: "911. Call 911."

* * *

It was dawn, yet Jenny looked as though she had just walked out of a cocktail party. She was wearing a short, black dress and heels so delicate that the straps appeared to be painted onto her pale ankles. She wore her hair up in a French twist. Her bangs had come loose, covering one eye when she caught a breeze the wrong way. She fussily combed them back behind her ear each time with the same hand in which she held a lit cigarette. Even with a shawl covering her shoulders and arms, she was shivering. She paced back and forth on the sidewalk in front of a parking garage for Avis Rent-A-Car, pausing when she felt a warm draft from somewhere inside. She couldn't stand in one spot for too long because the drivers kept moving cars in and out, screeching the tires.

It was much too early – or rather, much too late – for such chic glamor. For a passer-by who didn't know what Jenny did for a living, it would have been natural to assume she had stumbled out of an all-night party. Jenny worked at a room salon. She was the hostess that Park called his "girlfriend." Her real name was Jin-Hee. But it sounded close enough to "Jenny" that she adopted the Anglicized version as her *nom de guerre*.

When she spotted Park and Han walking toward her down the street, she chucked her cigarette on the ground and stomped on it as though it were an offending bug.

"I've been waiting here for 30 minutes! I'm freezing!" she yelled as soon as they came within shouting distance. She crossed her thin arms and shot him a disapproving look. She was a slip of a girl.

Park apologized several times and dashed the final few yards to her in simulated slow motion with open arms.

"Enough with the show," she said, slapping away his hands when he tried to embrace her.

"Come on. Who gets cold in the middle of September anyway?" Park said. Teasing was as good a method as humoring when it came to coaxing Jenny out of a bad mood.

"It's six o'clock in the morning! Look at what I'm wearing!" she said.

It was only after Park had sufficiently lightened Jenny's mood that he introduced her to Han. She nodded to Han in a truncated, wary bow. Han nodded back.

Han recalled meeting her briefly once before. She was a girl from Seoul who had come to the States under the guise of attending a language school. Perhaps that was her sincere motive in the beginning; perhaps it was just an excuse to escape whatever was ailing her back home. Whatever the reason, she had strayed into the world of the not-quite-legitimate. She couldn't have been more than 25, but she exuded a kind of world-weariness that belonged to someone dulled by alternating indulgence and disappointment.

"How is it that you can even afford her?" Han had asked Park once.

"Oh, no. I *can't* afford it. I'm not a client. She *likes* me," Park had said.

Han knew that wasn't quite true. Every time Park returned from Macao, he would become a big spender for weeks and made it a point to visit his girlfriend. Han also noticed that much-needed supplies in the office tended to get purchased during those profligate binges.

"I admire your energy," Han had said when he learned of Park's mistress. He had felt a twinge of envy. He tried to recall the last time he had felt desire for his wife. It had taken years after their daughter was born for her depression to subside. Han remembered those few precious years of warm affection after she emerged beyond her despair and her newfound clarity beckoned him to her. She crawled under the blanket with him one night after years of keeping separate beds. He dared not let his desire take over lest he break the spell of her intimacy. He was content at that moment to warm himself against her affection. At dawn he was awakened by her kisses on his neck. He grappled with her underwear, ripping it a little when he couldn't take it off fast enough. Later that morning he wondered whether he had dreamt the whole thing until he saw her lying next to him. The next few months were the happiest of his marriage. It was as though a fever had broken.

It didn't last, however. Even before she discovered she was pregnant again she had begun to slip away. There were parts of her mind that receded back beyond the reach of reason or affection.

Han wondered what it must be like to have a mistress, but he knew he was ill equipped to handle such an arrangement. Han was inclined toward self-reproach. And besides, a mistress like Park's required means. Han had long suspected that Park had resources at his disposal beyond what was available to everyone else at the Mission. But showing curiosity about topics beyond one's own purview could be hazardous to one's career. Still, Han didn't need someone to spell it out for him. Park was the one person at the Mission that was afforded a long leash by both the ambassador and the deputy ambassador. When Park returned from his business trips, he was flush with cash and often sported a rugged tan. He would regale Han with stories of his exploits. There were also inexplicable gaps in his itinerary. Han knew enough not to pry.

Han had traveled widely himself, both during his studies as a physicist and later for his work. However, his destinations never measured up to the glamour of Park's trips. And more often than not, they involved trips to northern locales in cold seasons, with the exception of the time he was in Islamabad. Even then, he had managed to time his trip with the monsoon.

The Urdu he had picked up then he was unexpectedly putting to use now in New York, surprising shopkeepers and restaurant owners who often heaped extra helpings on him just for the novelty of his talent. Han had a facility for language. It gave him an urbane sophistication that belied his dire financial need, much like that of a well bred, highly educated young man who takes a not-so-lucrative job.

It didn't take long for Jenny's mood to sour again, however, when Park explained that he needed her to chaperone Han on a road trip to Virginia, and that she would have to rent a car on her credit card.

"Why do I have to put it on *my* card?" she protested, almost storming off.

"Listen to me, Jenny. This is probably the most important thing you'll do for me," Park said. "I promise it will be worth your time."

When Jenny started to object, Park reached for her hand and held it tightly. He took out an envelope from his jacket pocket and placed it in her palm, clasping her fingers around it.

When Park let go of her, she could feel there was a heft to the envelope.

"What's this?"

"Just something for your troubles."

She was about to open the envelope. Park stopped her. "Not here. Look at it later. Just accept it and do this favor for Dr. Han and me."

"How long is this going to take? What about school and work?"

"Just call in sick. Shouldn't take more than a day or two. You'll be back before the weekend," Park said, glancing at Han as if to impress the deadline upon him.

It was killing Jenny not to be able to look inside the envelope. She didn't have to, really. Even by the weight, she could tell it was a considerable sum, assuming they were $100 bills, which, knowing Park, they likely were. The bulge of the crisp envelope, the unyielding solidness of what was inside was thrilling. It also frightened her a little – the burden of it. Park was generous with her, but he wasn't in the habit of dropping large wads of cash for no good reason. Being in the business she was, she had long been disabused of the notion of generosity for the sake of altruism. In her world, gifts came with strings attached. That was okay with her; she much preferred a frank quid pro quo to kindness cloaking ulterior motives. In her calculation, the magnitude of the gift implied a larger favor in return.

"Your colleague must be in a lot of trouble," Jenny said.

"He will be if you don't help him," said Park.

The weight of it. She gave some thought to handing the envelope back. It was just an envelope, after all. But it was not so easy. In the short instant that she had held on to it, she found she had grown attached to the idea of all the things she could do with such a sum. Cash was freedom; freedom from the relentless hours she kept, from the late-night subway rides, and especially from the sweaty-palmed old men clumsily groping at her.

"I have one condition," she said.

"Alright. Name it," Park said.

"I want *that* car," she said, pointing to a lipstick red Mustang convertible that had just been washed. Water trickled off the paint in fat rivulets.

Park glanced at Han with a look of resignation and smiled at Jenny. He reached out his hand to Han and asked him for his IDs and his Kim Il-Sung lapel pin. "Just in case," Park said.

Jenny tossed the envelope in her bag and asked, "Where are we going again?"

* * *

At the Kohs' house in Flushing, a crime scene investigator rolled out a shell casing from under the sofa. Using the bare end of a wooden cotton swab, he speared the hollow end and got up from his knees with a groan.

"Looks like they missed one," he said and handed the swab and the shell over to a detective named Jack Finister.

"Not your garden-variety Saturday night special, is it?" Finister said as he used his bifocals like a magnifying glass with one hand. He walked over to the window for more light. "Let's get a better look at you."

He had grown accustomed to speaking to objects and corpses.

"What you got there?" his partner asked, closing in for a peek.

"What we have here, my friend, is a 7.62 Tokarev round – a Russkie favorite," Finister said and then took another glance at the victims. "Full metal jacket, not hollow point."

"Military surplus? Maybe we got some Brighton Beach boys branching out to Flushing," Finister's partner said.

"Brighton Beach, maybe. Boys, unlikely," Finister said. "Dunno about your boys, but mine certainly don't pick up after themselves like this."

Finister didn't like neat crime scenes. Messy crimes spoke of haste; haste caused mistakes; and mistakes left clues. Neat crime scenes spoke of calculation; hence they were a pain in the ass.

"Better put in a call to the FBI field office to see if they have anything on the Russian mob butting heads with the Asians," Finister said.

The house had been ransacked. It would be hard to tell what was missing until a relative came. However, the chaos seemed too – *manufactured*. Finister knew from experience that even a half-witted crackhead doesn't go to the trouble of exhaustively rifling though every nook and cranny of a house. Burglars are selective, picking the low-hanging fruit, unless they're hunting down a particular item. Anything that will score a few bucks with a fence will do.

There was too much disorder at the Koh's house. It looked more like a domestic violence scene – fury unleashed on inanimate objects when brutality on the living exhausted itself. Something didn't sit right.

On the porch, the clerk had reached one of the couple's children on the phone. It was their son, who was away at college in Princeton – the embodiment of their sacrifice. The clerk sobbed on the phone. Finister could hear an escalating hysteria on the other end. For a moment, Finister couldn't tell whether the clerk was speaking English or Korean because she was so distraught. Finister took the phone from her and spoke to the son. He said his name was Steven. He said he would be home in a couple of hours.

After he hung up, Finister took the clerk by the elbow and sat her on the steps outside the front door. She was trembling.

"Were they in any kind of financial trouble that you know of?" Finister asked.

"No, I don't think so. They never spent any money. They saved a lot," she said.

"Anyone come around the store asking for money? I mean people asking for money in exchange for protection, that kind of thing?"

"No. Everyone liked them. I mean, they had a few robberies over the years, that's about it. Mrs. Koh didn't speak English very well, but everyone still liked her, especially the Mexicans. She was like a mother to them, the employees. She spoke better Spanish and she did English. She'd finally found enough time to take some English classes, and now *this*."

The clerk broke down again. She folded into Finister and unburdened herself into his coat. Finister clutched her with his beefy hands and stood her up. She was so light, like a bird. He nudged her toward one of the cops wearing a blue jacket emblazoned with "Community Affairs" across the back. As the officer led her away, Finister felt a twinge of guilt. Every time one of these Asian shopkeepers got punched, stabbed or shot in their stores, he had come away with some stubborn part of himself – the part that had lived in Bay Ridge all his life and felt territorial about it – thinking that in some way, the victims had it coming. He knew it was irrational. No doubt the perps were scumbags. And as a cop, he knew better than to blame the victim. He also knew that a truly random crime was exceedingly rare. With shopkeepers, there's usually a history of bad blood with the customers-turned-perps. Some follow the black customers around to make sure they don't shoplift. Rudeness begets rudeness. No point trying to figure out who started it. The irreverent punk in Finister felt the shopkeeper had it coming. The cop felt guilt at thinking that way. A crime at your shop is one thing; when it follows you home – well, that was something entirely different as far as he was concerned.

Finister walked back into the Koh house to examine the crime scene again. He scanned the piles of books pulled from the shelves. Once again, the thing that struck him was how it looked as though they had been scattered out of spite, rather than as the aftermath of a hasty search. The books were mostly in Korean. One of the exceptions was an English-as-a-second-language study book. As the clerk said, it seemed that Mrs. Koh had finally found enough leisure in her life to expand her English beyond the necessities of commerce. Inside the front cover of the book, Mrs. Koh had neatly printed her own name and the name and phone number of her teacher, a Mrs. Janet Klondyke – like the ice cream, except with a "Y."

Chapter 11

When Han first arrived in New York, he had bought a map that showed the city and its surrounding counties. With a pencil and length of string, he measured out 25 miles on the legend and drew a circle centered at the United Nations. *This is the boundary of my life for the next few years.* He studied the circumference.

To the north, he could legally venture into the southern part of Connecticut – that rectangular outcrop of the state that jutted toward the city; to the east, he could go just shy of the border between Nassau and Suffolk counties; to the west, a place called Morristown in New Jersey; and to the south, approximately the banks of a river called the Raritan.

When he and Jenny passed a sign on the highway stating they had now entered the Township of Edison, just north of the Raritan, Han felt his pulse quicken.

"Crossing the Rubicon," he muttered to himself.

"What?" Jenny asked.

"The Rubicon. You know, Julius Caesar?"

"Yeah, I know him. I took world history in high school. Roman emperor, right?"

"That's right."

"What's the Rubi – whatever?"

"The Rubicon. It's a river in northern Italy. When Caesar crossed it with his army heading toward Rome, it meant he couldn't turn back. Everyone knew at that point that he was mounting a coup d'état."

"So? What's that got to do with you?"

Han could feel himself breaking out into a sweat. He wiped his brows with his sleeve.

"What's the matter with you? Are you ill?" Jenny asked.

"Nothing. I'm just a little nervous," Han said.

"About what? Why do you keep looking at the dash board?"

"I'm looking at the odometer. I've never been this far from New York City – at least not without permission. That's what I mean by Rubicon. I can't turn back now."

In spite of himself, Han found himself smiling. Perhaps what he was feeling wasn't fear after all, but exhilaration. This was the first time he had crossed the 25-mile boundary without being accompanied by an entourage of diplomats and security personnel.

"You have to get permission from your boss to travel?" Jenny asked.

"No. Not from my boss – from the American government. The State Department."

"You're joking, right?" Jenny blinked at the road as though the blinking somehow aided comprehension. "What happens if you get caught?"

"I'd be in a lot of trouble."

"How much trouble?"

"Getting kicked out of the country, for starters."

"That's it?"

"That's just the beginning."

"Yeah, but it's not like the Americans would put you in jail, right?"

Han gave Jenny a look as though she were a misbehaving child. "No. The Americans wouldn't." He said it with a gravity that he hoped would pierce her blitheness.

She was a puzzle to him. At times she spoke like a petulant teenager, clueless to anything except her own desires. At other times she spoke with the weariness of a spurned adulteress.

"You mean they'd put you in jail in North Korea?"

"Something like that."

Jenny blinked at the road again, then, unsolicited, launched into a story that Han could only guess was her attempt to relate to him.

"When I was in middle school, the teachers used to tell us stories about how bad things were in North Korea – stuff about neighbors informing on each other; on their own family, even. I figured it was just bullshit stuff, you know, government propaganda, to keep us from complaining too much.

"I hated school. I mean, I got decent grades, but I couldn't stand all the crap from teachers. Bunch of hypocrites, if you ask me. There was this one teacher – this woman music teacher – who used to smack the girls around all the time. See, the guy teachers, they'd go easy on you because they didn't really want to smack girls around. They'd just make you stand with your arms in the air until they felt like they were gonna fall off, or something like that. This music teacher – she was a real bitch. She figured that because she was a woman, she could slap you around and nobody could say anything."

"So, did you believe them?" Han asked.

"Believe who?"

"Your teachers – about the propaganda?"

"Oh, that," Jenny said. "Yeah, I suppose I did. Honestly, I didn't think much about it. So what if the North Koreans were ratting each other out? I had my own more immediate problems."

"I'm sure you did," Han said benignly.

"So, is it true? I've asked Jun-Young *oppa* about it, but he never talks about political stuff," Jenny said.

The fact that she called him *oppa* – a word reserved for older brothers or boyfriends – immediately confirmed them as intimates.

"I suppose it depends on what you've heard," Han said.

"Okay, for example, do you get sent to jail for criticizing Kim Jong-Il?" she asked.

Han's cheeks reddened.

This was the interrogation of a guileless child. The only defense against such unwittingly profound inquiry is frankness. But even when he resolved to tell the truth, he found his own body unyielding with the years of conditioning toward obliqueness. He stammered and stuttered for the right words. He was so out of practice at frankness.

* * *

One of Han's favorite things to do when he first arrived in New York was to drive across the upper deck of the Queensboro Bridge just as dawn's first light ignited the peaks of Manhattan's tallest skyscrapers. Beneath the glowing crowns of the buildings, the island was in shadow, veiled in purple as sunlight inched its way down the forward edge of a world stretching itself into morning. Moments later, sunlight would sparkle off the uppermost windows in shards of gold, as though the glass were sheets of ice capping the precipitous summits of snowy peaks, hardened and polished by the repeated cycle of thaw and freeze.

From this vantage point on the upper deck of the bridge, Han could take in a panoramic length of Manhattan, from the Upper East Side to the Con Edison smokestacks on that hip of the island jutting out into the East River. The skyline was never more dramatic than after foul weather had blown through as it had last night. In the streets, mangled umbrellas lay strewn across the sidewalks and gutters, their broken limbs flapping in the breeze, like the carcasses of birds.

Even after a sleepless night, Han had a feeling he was starting over, that the whole city was starting over. Dawn gave you that sense.

When Han first came to New York City, he regarded it with abundant suspicion, as a kind of Potemkin village—impossibly prosperous and busy, its denizens possibly shipped in by government edict, like the tens of thousands of men, women and children in North Korea conscripted into rehearsing mass games in stadiums and performing them with terrifying precision. Whether they were stacking themselves into outlandish formations on the field or composing heroic murals in the stands with a flawless mosaic of placards, their minds and motion were as one. To behold one of those mass games was to be awed by the unity that could be achieved by will and labor properly pressed into service.

As a fake city, New York lacked that kind of flawless coordination. Then again, precision would not be the desired effect when trying to simulate something breathing and alive. Even so, Han was struck by how persistently messy the city was. Plastic wrappers and other kinds of detritus of conspicuous daily consumption always churned about in vortexes. The contrast with Pyongyang was stark. There, the streets were remarkably free of trash, not necessarily because of some preternatural leaning toward cleanliness but because plastic wrappers, and the things they encased, were themselves rare.

What New York lacked in pristine precision, however, it made up for with audacity of scale. There were enough absurd extremes here that Han found it convenient to convince himself that it had been erected for the purpose of fooling the rest of the world. He imagined that America's prosperity hardly extended beyond the 25-mile radius of daily life to which he and his fellow North Korean diplomats had been confined by agreement with the State Department. The alternative to believing that New York was an elaborate lie was to ask too much of the imagination.

On one occasion last year, Han was invited to the baronial Upper East Side townhouse of a corporate titan who, like many men of newfound wealth, took up philanthropy to ingratiate himself into the upper strata of society. He had accumulated his considerable fortune with a chain of supermarkets, so Han was told. And the man had offered to donate foodstuffs to relieve the hardships in North Korea in the wake of devastating floods.

That wealth can drive social mobility wasn't a unique feature of class in America, but America stood apart from the Old World in that the depth of one's pocketbook had such an inordinate bearing on one's status. Many people elsewhere comprehended the possibility of an aristocracy of meager means. Communism had tried for five decades to purge North Korean society of the concept of class, but traditional mores proved inconveniently enduring, even for a Party loyalist like Han. Jane Austen's stories of struggling gentry, seeking to fortify their standing through wily marriage, was entirely believable and familiar to him. Scholars whose tattered robes scarcely diminished their nobility populated his own folklore.

Han had always wondered what those Upper East Side mansions looked like on the inside. The fundraiser for his countrymen afforded him the chance to peel back the curtains of privacy that the rich protected so dearly. Who could blame them? From Han's point of view, what man with a conscience would not be embarrassed by the absurdly unequal distribution of wealth?

The fundraiser was staged in the vaulted "Great Room" of the townhouse. Dark wood wainscoting curved in unison with a grand staircase to the second floor, which overlooked a rear courtyard hemmed in by cloisters. In that room, nestled among the oil paintings, was a tapestry depicting a unicorn, its hues made subtle by time measured on the scale of lifetimes of dynasties rather than mere mortals. All the trappings of the estate spoke of refinement. Yet it appeared that too was purchased, for the tycoon he himself turned out to be a bit of a boor. Well-meaning as he was, he missed few opportunities to put his foot in his mouth, stumbling over history and culture alike. He was apparently of the belief that opinion, if held strongly enough, was a proper substitute for fact. In the end, Han decided the thing that bothered him most about the tycoon was a kind of fakeness – not of pretense to refinement, but a bending-over-backwards coarseness. It was as though he were *playing* the role of a garish American mogul rather than being one. Perhaps he had figured out that he would never be completely accepted by the old money crowd, so he might as well strive for the polar opposite of pedigree and go for the crude, self-made man persona.

This nagging feeling that things weren't quite what they seemed in America – that a veneer had been applied to hide their true nature – extended to inanimate objects as well. For instance, Han found it curious that many buildings in the city had a name – even newly constructed apartments that were rather dull, architecturally. At first he conjectured it was an American custom to name the structure after the architect who designed it. He soon learned that had nothing to do with it. As far as Han could discern, whether a building had a name did not depend on the age of the edifice or its architectural significance – at least by the admittedly haphazard knowledge he had accumulated on his visits to mostly Eastern European cities in the former Soviet bloc. In spite of New York's much ballyhooed ethnic diversity, the names of the buildings were almost without exception Anglo-Saxon, leading Han to his next conjecture that those of British ancestry had a stranglehold on the city's real estate market. Many of the names were also agricultural in origin – Millhouse, Hayfield, and such – or evoked the names of noble houses – Braithwaite, Spencer – spawning another hypothesis that there were competing clans of expat Brits vying for land-holding supremacy on this crowded island, one group descended from aristocracy and another from peasant stock that had made good through shrewd investments.

The supermarket tycoon did live up to Han's expectations in two respects: He was outsized and loud. In America, that was true even of the youngsters. Boys were already strapping hulks by the time they were 16, garrulous and irrepressible, like horses gone wild for want of saddle and harness. Same for the girls– the sheen in their hair yet to be dulled by the trials of life, somehow supremely confident in their own opinions and unafraid to share it, noisily. Where did they find the sense of entitlement?

Then there were indulgences of a more absurd kind. Han would sometimes walk by a shop called the Doggy Gym on East 45th Street, just a few of blocks from the North Korean Mission on Second Avenue. On one occasion, he saw a cab pull up in front of the store and a gangly woman draped in a long coat got out with two excited dogs tugging and biting on their leashes. Han didn't know dog breeds well, but they resembled greyhounds, except with long fur that fell neatly parted from the centerline of their lanky bodies, fluttering in unison with their owner's coat. She chattered away at them, bending down to let the dogs lick her face. On closer inspection, the cab turned out to be a car service called Pet Chauffeur, which purported to specialize in transporting dogs, cats and other domesticated animals that Americans seemed so fond of inviting into their homes, treating them with a kindness that they did not afford even fellow humans.

Another woman walked toward the store with a tiny dog barely larger than a rat. It was wearing a high-collar leopard-print coat and its eyes were bulging. Its twig-like front legs marched as though it were doing a military goose-step. Han watched incredulously. It was too absurd to be true. *They're just trying too hard,* he thought of the charade. Just another example that New York is a fiction, concocted by some cloistered committee with precious little knowledge of what the rest of the world would accept as plausible.

But what if it were true, this absurd New York?

What if there actually were people so wealthy and bereft of perspective that they would pamper animals with luxuries beyond the reach of most people in the world. This thought angered Han more than the idea that what he was watching was a display staged for his benefit. How could a nation that nurtures such absurdity have survived the Cold War and remain the world's last superpower? How could a nation of such indulgence demand austerity from its foes? Han felt his pulse quicken.

This is why he chose to reject the possibility that the Doggy Gym and the Pet Chauffeur – and New York City, for that matter – were real. It offended him; and he knew he wasn't alone. If it came to a choice of living in a city of false facades or a city of absurd excess, he chose the former. The motive to fool others—*that* he could at least fathom.

Living in New York was a daily exercise is temperance, since much appeared to be formulated to antagonize nations such as his. Han would feel a twinge of envy as he walked by the South Korean consulate, which was housed in a stand-alone building with its U.N. Mission on a prime slab of real estate between First and Second Avenues. The South Korean colors flew on a flagpole next to its street-level entrance. The North Korean Mission, in contrast, occupied a drab box of a building overlooking Second Avenue, also occupied by the U.N. missions of countries such as Nepal, Micronesia and Syria. The twenty or so employees at the North Korean Mission were crammed into an office that was not even permitted to announce its presence with a flag because the nation lacked normalized relations with the United States.

On more than one occasion when Han was riding the elevator up to his office, a random stranger had felt compelled to point out that he was heading for the thirteenth floor. The first time it happened he just nodded, not understanding why the person had made the comment. The streets of New York were full of people who were either talking to themselves or talking out of turn. It wasn't until it happened again that Han became perturbed.

"Thirteen floor, eh?"

The person who had pointed it out the second time used a decidedly disapproving tone that made Han wonder whether the thirteenth floor suffered from a dangerous structural flaw that he was unaware of. The man got out of the elevator before Han could ask him a question.

When it happened a third time, not three months after Han's move to New York, he made a point of asking him.

The man replied: "You know, thirteen? Unlucky number?"

The funny thing was Han already knew that some Westerners considered thirteen to be inauspicious. Its real-life application just hadn't occurred to him until then. The irony was that the man who finally explained it to him got off on the fourth floor – a number so ill-omened that the fourth floor didn't even exist in many buildings in China, Korea and Japan, where the words for "four" and "death" were homophones in all three languages.

The North Korean Mission's suite might easily have been mistaken for the back office of an insurance company or a real estate firm if not for the ubiquitous portraits of Kim Jong-Il and his late father, Kim Il-Sung, adorning the walls. Those beatific images of the Dear Leader and the Great Leader were less portraits and more iconography, set upon scarlet backgrounds, their chins jutting out and gazes fixed upon some distant goal, high above the horizon, as though the elevation of the eyes signified the loftiness of purpose. If they had started as photographs, any trace of reality had been airbrushed to extinction. What remained were flawless illustrations in hyper-real hues, with rosy cheeks and bleached smiles, reminiscent of American print ads in the fifties, peddling domestic bliss through the latest detergent or home appliance.

* * *

Detective Finister knew his limitations as an investigator. He wasn't brilliant, but knowing that about himself, he wasn't lazy either. What he lacked in natural ability he made up for with thoroughness. Call every number, knock on every door, exhaust every lead – that was a way of working that made sense to him. It did not depend on sparks of inspiration, hence it allowed him tranquility in what was usually a chaotic mess of inane motives and ill-conceived plots to carry them out.

At his desk at the 109th Precinct, Finister opened up the English-as-a-second-language study book he had collected from the Koh residence and called the teacher whose name Mrs. Koh had written inside.

"Mrs. Klondyke?" Finister asked when a woman picked up the phone.

"Yes."

"Mrs. *Janet* Klondyke?"

"That's me. Who's this?"

Finister explained who he was and why he was calling. Klondyke went silent on the other end of the phone for a while after he told her that Mrs. Koh had been killed.

"Who would want to kill someone like Mrs. Koh? I mean, she was an absolute *angel*," said Klondyke. She sounded like an older woman, in her sixties, perhaps.

"I don't know, ma'am. That's what I'm trying to find out," Finister said. "Did she mention anything to you? Anything out of the ordinary? Anybody she was having trouble with?"

It seemed that Mrs. Klondyke didn't hear his question. She just kept saying, "Oh, dear. Oh, my God."

"Mrs. Klondyke, I know you're upset, but I need you to gather yourself and think for me."

It's hard to tell how people will react to such news. The death of someone close can be upsetting under any circumstances. A brush with *wrongful* death disturbs the core of a person. Some get angry, some become mute, some weep quietly, others wail. A good deal depended on how close the victim was to them, or whether the person had anything to do with the victim's demise.

"Can you think of anything out of the ordinary?" Finister pressed after she composed herself.

"Well, she wasn't in class yesterday," Klondyke said. "*That* was out of the ordinary. Mrs. Koh never missed a class."

"Did she say why?"

"No. I'm afraid not. I was going to ask her the next time I saw her."

The teacher gave a good account of Mrs. Koh's personality – such as her study habits during the year she had known her, and her propensity toward being early. However, she offered nothing much in the way of leads. Certainly nothing that would account for why anyone who knew her would want to kill her, not to mention her husband.

"Oh, goodness," Klondyke said. "This is horrible. They're such a devout couple, too. Devout Christians."

As the teacher rambled on about the couple, Finister leafed through the pages of a Bible he had also brought back from the Koh residence. It was a bilingual Bible – one side of each page was in Korean, the other side in English, with blank spaces interspersed to keep chapter and verse aligned between the two disparate languages. Many of the passages on the Korean side were underlined. The English side was mostly bare. The Bible was well used but clean, with the kind of honest wear that spoke of the user's benign habits, like the rounded edges of a desk. The wear on the gold-edged pages showed that she favored the New Testament, in particular, Matthew and First Corinthians.

"Thank you very much for your help, Mrs. Klondyke. Like I said, if you remember anything else, please call me," Finister said.

As he hung up, his eyes landed on an underlined verse in Matthew, Chapter 7.

Wherefore by their fruits ye shall know them.

Chapter 12

After slogging through morning rush-hour traffic on the outskirts of Philadelphia, Han and Jenny reached the Maryland border by late morning.

Being brought to a standstill on a city street by bumper-to-bumper traffic was annoying at best. For Han, it was both daunting and impressive at the same time to behold miles of a highway before him clogged with cars, undulating over the landscape and shimmering with tailpipe exhaust like the scales on a squirming snake.

The highways that lead out of Pyongyang into the countryside were normally so deserted that the concept of rush hour did not exist there. Drivers could even stop in the middle of the highway, rather than having to pull over to the shoulder, and walk about on the road itself with no concern of being run over. It was as though the infrastructure had been built for an industrious civilization that vanished abruptly and completely, leaving a ghostly network of pristine roads.

"This is the Mason-Dixon line," Han said when he saw a billboard on the side of the highway welcoming motorists to Maryland.

"What?"

"The Mason-Dixon line – the northern border of Maryland. This is where the South starts," Han said.

"The South? Like in the Civil War?" Jenny asked. The Korean term for the American Civil War was the South-North War.

"Yes, that South."

A civil war – brother killing brother; a people devouring itself. In this, Korea shared a painful chapter in common with the history of the United States. It is a thing that changes a people; casts a long shadow across its heart and from then on, the heart is slower to take joy in things.

The difference between the U.S. and Korea was that in the latter, the civil war was still a living memory, not a trauma lingering as the tales of forebears. A generation still lived in Korea that had endured the cataclysm and its effects had not healed with the passage of some fifty years. Rather, it had been amplified through and by the Cold War.

This journey Han was taking – his posting to New York, this unauthorized crossing of the Mason-Dixon – was the result of that cataclysm. He couldn't shake the feeling that the ghosts of one civil war were communing with those of another that happened half a world away and almost a century apart.

"I thought the South was like Georgia, like in *Gone with the Wind*?" Jenny said.

"Yes, but this is the dividing line between that North and South."

"You sure know a lot about history. You are a doctor, after all. At least, Jun-Young *oppa* keeps calling you Dr. Han. What kind of doctor are you, anyway?"

"Physics."

Jenny frowned as though she had bitten into something sour. "Ugh, I hated physics in school. The teacher was an asshole."

"Was there *any* teacher you liked?"

"Sure, I adored my Korean language teacher. He was this wiry old guy. He loved what he did. That kind of passion, it's infectious you know."

Passion – it was a curious choice of words. It wasn't that Han couldn't fathom the importance of enthusiasm in doing one's job well, but passion? Perhaps it was just a sloppy inflation of words. He had to remind himself he was speaking to a South Joseon woman. More and more, South Joseon was becoming a cultural outpost of the United States, susceptible to the same appeals to emotion and desire, even though its people were hardly a generation removed from a time when ascetic ideals ruled supreme, particularly in the education of children.

"Passion is nice. What about hard work and focus?" Han asked.

"I didn't mind working hard, but I need a reason to. I just had a hard time figuring out how all of that stuff in school would help me later in life," Jenny said. Then her voice grew wistful. "I see it now, though. It's not that it's any use to us, other than for winning money on a quiz show, maybe. I can see now it was just about getting good grades to get into a good school. A crappy school got me a bad job and that led to another bad job, and one thing led to another and now I'm here, working in a room salon."

Han looked out his side window, unsure of where else to put his gaze in the face of such honesty.

"Hey look!" Jenny said, pointing to something ahead, her voice instantly exuberant.

There was a group of children gathered at the back window of a yellow school bus in front of them. One kid with a mop of sandy blond hair had a pink Post-it note pressed up against the window with something scribbled on it. Jenny accelerated to get closer. The Mustang growled as Han felt himself squeezed back into the seat.

When they got close enough, they could see the note read: "Nice Car!" with a smiley face in the dot of the exclamation point.

"Oh my god, how cute is that!" Jenny said, the mood in her voice suddenly upbeat as though the bleakness of her confession just seconds ago was a distant memory. She started to wave at the children. They enthusiastically waved back.

"I still remember those poems I memorized in high school," Jenny said cheerfully. "Wanna hear one?"

"Sure, why not."

"Oh, wait, I wanna listen to this song first," Jenny said as she cranked up the radio. She shouted over the din, "You know the Spice Girls?"

Han shook his head.

"You don't know this song? Where have you been?"

Jenny sang along with parts of the song she seemed to know. *If you wanna be my lover/ you gotta get with my friends. Make it last forever/ friendship never ends.*

"This is one of my best karaoke numbers at the room salon. My clients love it. I've got this whole dance number I do with it," Jenny said. She took both hands off the wheel and mimicked holding a microphone in one hand and gestured with the other.

An alarmed Han lunged for the wheel and held onto it has Jenny continued her dance number. "What the hell are you doing?"

"Oh, calm down," Jenny said and took the wheel back.

"Don't do that again please."

"Okay, okay," she said and turned off the radio. "Where was I?"

Han took a deep breath. "You were about to recite a poem."

"Oh yeah. That's right. You know '*Azaleas*' by Kim So-Wol?"

"Of course."

It was a poem from the 1920s that every Korean man, woman and child would have to recite at least once during their school years. Few would go to the trouble of memorizing it but it was so ubiquitous that most people could still mumble a line or two.

Jenny cleared her throat and sat up in her seat before launching into it.

When you grow weary of me
And walk away
I shall send you off without a word.

The azaleas
From Yongbyon's Medicine Mountain
I will pick by the armful
To scatter in your path.

On those petals placed
Step by step in your retreat
Tread lightly as you leave.

When you grow weary of me
And walk away
I shall die before I shed a single tear.

Jenny's delivery was straight, and matter of fact, without the dramatic affectations that normally plagued the reading of this poem. She spoke the words as one would carry on a conversation and they felt entirely contemporary, even though the expressions were dated – much like the speech of 1920's English would seem to a modern speaker.

Han found himself suddenly perturbed, or moved – he wasn't quite sure which. He dismissed it to being tired. He hadn't slept more than brief catnaps since he had gotten up at dawn the previous day.

Yongbyon – what was the setting for one of Korea's most beloved poems, was now the home of North Korea's nuclear program, including a reactor capable of producing enough plutonium to make at least one nuclear weapon a year.

Was Jenny's choice of this particular piece just uncanny coincidence or was she wilier than she was letting on? Han stole a glance at her. His eyes drifted down and lingered on the hemline that was riding up her thighs as she worked the gas pedal and brakes. He remembered then what desire felt like and imagined what her skin tasted like. Was Park babbling state secrets to her in those quiet lulls after lovemaking? Even the most taciturn of men feel compelled to share his heart, or at least some intimate detail, in those tender moments after sex.

"Did you know that Kim So-Wol was born in the North? In North Pyong-ahn Province, actually," Han said. "That's where Yongbyon is."

"Really? You know, I must have recited that poem a thousand times. I never really thought about Yongbyon being a real place before," Jenny said. "Have you been there?"

"Yes, quite a few times."

"What's it like? Are there really a lot of azaleas there?"

"Yes. It's very pretty."

Once, on a rare day off between projects while visiting Yongbyon, Han had ventured out of the dimly lit warren of reinforced concrete labs and corridors and scaled Medicine Mountain – Yaksan, as it was called in Korean. It was one of those April afternoons when the sun first hinted at the relentless heat it would deliver later that summer. The azaleas were in full bloom, along with unruly waves of forsythias, begetting a riot of pink and yellow across the hills.

In the middle of that, in a denuded valley, was the dull, concrete bunker that housed the storage pond for the thousands of nuclear fuel rods. Every time a truck pulled up along the unpaved road, the facility was shrouded in dust for a while.

On his hike back to the facility, Han saw a white SUV pull up to the storage pond building, also kicking up a trail of dust. It was the daily visit from the monitors from the International Atomic Energy Agency. Even from that distance, Han could spot the Swedish man. His hair was so blond that it glowed white in the sun.

He was one of the Westerners who had been keeping an eye on them for some three years now, making sure they didn't tamper with the seals around the pool and smuggle the spent fuel rods to a reprocessing plant off-site to convert them into bomb-grade plutonium.

How far Han had strayed from his training. His work now had little to do with furthering science. Instead, his job was to further his country's posture against its neighbors. Where the nuclear program excelled, they could use it to bolster the impression that they were further along than they really were. Where the program was wanting, Han would advise his superiors to avoid discussion with the outer world to obfuscate its shortcomings. It was a delicate balance. Disinformation works only if you mix enough truths with half-truths and lies.

"Jun-Young *oppa* likes that poem," Jenny said. "He laughed the first time I recited it for him. I was *so* mad. I punched him – really hard, too. I guess he figured I was talking about him, and that I wouldn't hang onto him if he left."

Kim So-Wol was a man, but schoolteachers usually characterized this work as written in the voice of a woman, though it was ambiguous enough to allow for both interpretations.

Perhaps the poem was so beloved because it tapped into a peculiarly Korean sensibility called *hahn*. There was no corresponding English word for it. It described a sense of stubborn sadness rooted in unresolved wanting or deep emotional wounds. It was fatalistic, but at the same time, resilient because of its stubbornness. *I shall die before I shed a single tear.* The one who is abandoned is defiant, and at the same time, he or she accepts the lover's departure. The sendoff is a mixture of fare-thee-well, have-a-nice-life and bitter loss.

"Do you feel passionate about what *you're* doing?" Jenny asked, doubling back to a previous topic.

Before Han had a chance to answer, Jenny suddenly jerked the Mustang to the right lane, toward an exit ramp.

"What are you doing? Where are you going?" Han demanded.

"Look, I've been in these ridiculous clothes all night. I have to change out of them. I can't breathe any more," Jenny said.

She was already on the ramp. Han didn't bother objecting.

* * *

Han was startled to full attention by a scream. He bolted up in his seat and saw Jenny pointing to something outside the car.

"Look! There's a BJ's Wholesale Club!" she squealed, steering the car toward a warehouse-like structure.

"What club?"

"BJ's – it's this store where you can get makeup and electronics and food and all these other things for really cheap. We *have* to stop by. I can change in their bathroom," Jenny said. "I don't usually have a car in the city, so I never get to go to these stores. It's kinda like a Costco, but different. Have you been to Costco?"

Han shook his head.

"Ooh, look, everything looks so new. It must have opened recently," Jenny said, pulling into the parking lot. They were in a town called Abingdon.

Han couldn't quite understand her excitement. She greeted it as though she had chanced upon an old friend she hadn't seen in a while.

Jenny entered the store first, her stilettos clacking on the floor with every enthusiastic stride. Han hesitated at the entrance as though briefly snagged by a cobweb. He was a non-believer about to intrude into the sacred sanctuary of a rival religion, this cathedral of consumerism.

When Jenny noticed Han wasn't by her side, she spun around and waved to him to hurry up.

There is a scent peculiar to new things, modern things. This store was redolent of newness. Music echoed through the cavernous space, over the persistent hum of the air conditioning. That hum was the ubiquitous undertone of office buildings nowadays, unnoticed until it is switched off and absent, a kind of cosmic background radiation of noise. Han got goose bumps as the frigid air engulfed his damp clothes. Some employees wore sweaters or fleece jackets.

"Meet me here in about 10 minutes," Jenny said and dashed off to the bathroom, her heels tip-tapping all the way.

Han stood awkwardly next to the cash registers for a while, thinking he would stay there until Jenny returned. But after an employee asked whether he needed help, and moments later he declined a second offer, he decided to wander through the aisles rather than make himself an easy target for their helpfulness.

Shelf upon shelf upon shelf of products were laid out before him. This was more of a warehouse than a store. He picked up one gadget in the home and garden department and puzzled over what it was for. He couldn't even venture a guess. He passed an obese woman whose shopping cart was piled with toilet paper pressing up against a toddler seated in the cart, his legs dangling through the wire frame like dough spilling over the edge of a table. The boy was stoic, even though the pile behind him forced him to hunch over. It was as though he was carrying the weight of it on his back. It reminded Han of the rotund statue of Atlas shouldering the globe at Rockefeller Center.

Han roamed further into the store. So many different varieties of the same thing – that was the thing that struck him. Electrical power strips with six sockets in single file, another with the sockets in two rows of three, another in gun-metal grey, yet another with a plug that would fit at a right angle to the wall, and so on. The choices were bewildering.

He turned another corner and was confronted with a fleet of baby strollers. Most had four small wheels, one had three big ones, formed like a wheelbarrow, with seat harnesses as one would find in the cockpit of a jet. He briefly wondered whether Americans were indeed so militaristic, as the Party had so frequently told him, that they were giving their infants a head start with some rudimentary form of flight training. Another stroller carried a price tag so absurdly high that Han dismissed it as a typo. Han gave each one a little push to gauge their mobility and heft.

His daughter, Won-Sook, had been raised on the backs of her mother and indulgent relatives. No one in North Korea pushed their children around in prams or strollers. He remembered the time when his wife threw out her back lifting Won-Sook when she was about four years old. She was bed-ridden for two days. He couldn't help but wonder whether his wife might have felt less worn down had she had the benefit of one of these contraptions. He entertained the thought of buying one of them so he could give it to her when he eventually found her.

Han was no stranger to opulence. Even the most impoverished of nations has the pride and means to gather its wealth into a showcase for visitors. Pakistan, Libya, Nigeria – each had their favorite tourist spots where it showed off its treasure and tradition. His country did the same itself in Pyongyang and at the International Friendship Exhibition, where all the gifts from around the world to the Great Leader and the Dear Leader were collected in granite-floored chambers, deep underground.

What was on display here wasn't so much opulence as abundance, verging on wastefulness. Why would anyone need the choice of fifteen different kinds of power strips? As absurd as it was, it was in keeping with the country's nature – profligate and easily bored. Even at the Friendship Exhibition, the chambers were kept in darkness until a tour guide manually switched on the lights as she led visitors through the halls. And even though the rooms were kept immaculate, there was a mustiness that hung in the air, unlike the astringent odor that permeated this store. He wondered whether the Americans noticed it as well, or whether they were inured to it.

"I told you to meet me up front. I've been looking all over for you," Jenny said. She took Han by the elbow.

Han looked Jenny up and down with an expression that suggested he didn't recognize her. She had changed into a pair of jeans and a tight-fitting, pastel-blue T-shirt with a pink heart bordered by silver sequins over her chest. She had also let her hair down, though the remnants of her French twist remained as wavy curls, the sheen catching the light in dense rows.

"You look …" Han caught himself before he said "prettier" and said instead, "different."

In the parking lot, Han saw a woman emptying her shopping cart into her car. She couldn't close the trunk because it was too full. She had to unpack and repack some of the bags to make them fit. A few cars away, a man who was wearing suspenders with sweatpants climbed into the driver's seat and molded the folds of flesh on his belly to one side to make himself fit behind the wheel.

Han hung his head and looked down at the asphalt and shook his head.

"Let's get back on the road, shall we?" Han said to Jenny.

Chapter 13

Janet Klondyke, the English teacher, called Detective Finister about an hour after their first conversation. Her voice was placid and composed.

"I'm sorry I didn't recall this detail before," she said. "You know how I mentioned that Mrs. Koh wasn't in class last night?"

"Yup."

"Well, it just occurred to me that another Korean woman that she's good friends with also wasn't in class – for the second time in a row, as a matter of fact, and she's *always* there. Her husband called saying she was sick. She took a semester off when she had a baby. Before that, even when she was out-to-here pregnant, she never missed a class."

"Who's this other Korean woman?"

"Ms. Chung. Her name is Myung-Ae Chung. She and Mrs. Koh were pretty close. I don't think they knew one another before they started taking my class last year, but they became good friends. They always sat next to one another – at least recently. And they'd giggle like little schoolgirls. It was pretty cute, actually, considering Ms. Chung was so much younger than Mrs. Koh; almost young enough to be her daughter."

"Do you have Ms. Chung's phone number and address?" Finister asked.

"Sure, I have it here somewhere," Klondyke said.

Finister could hear her footsteps over the phone, growing distant, and then getting closer again. She picked up the phone and gave him the information.

"God, she's going to be so upset when she hears about this. You will try to break the news gently to her, won't you, detective?" Klondyke said.

Finister said he'd do his best, but he knew there was no way to soft-pedal that kind of news.

* * *

Finister called Chung's apartment a few times. There was no answer, so he and his partner took a ride out to her place in Elmhurst. They rang the bell and knocked and rang the bell again. No one came to the door. A curious neighbor peered out of his chained door.

"Why you making all this noise?" the old man said.

"Police," Finister's partner said flatly, flashing his shield.

"Do you know where your neighbors are?" Finister asked.

"If they're not answering, figure they're not home. They in some kinda trouble?"

Finister's partner, Rick Martinez, flashed Finister a look that suggested they had a live one here. Finister talked the man into undoing the chain. The man stood in the doorway in his sweats. Over the man's shoulder, Finister saw a television flickering in the darkness.

"You know Ms. Chang, the Korean lady who lives here?" Finister asked.

"Chang? Nah, the couple that lives there aren't the Changs. They're Korean, but the last name is Han."

"You sure?"

"Yeah. They keep to themselves, but I know their last name. It's Han. Trust me, I've seen it on their mail in the lobby. He works for the U.N. is what I heard."

"This is the lady who had a baby not long ago, right?"

"Yeah, that's the one. Cries all the time, as a matter of fact. Walls are pretty thin here."

Outside of the building, Finister spotted a Ford Escort with diplomatic plates; well-worn, yet clean. He tapped his partner on the arm and pointed to it.

"I guess the world-peace business ain't none too prosperous," Martinez said as he scribbled down the plate number. "You sure know how to pick 'em. All we need is some snooty prick with diplomatic immunity to gum up the works."

"I don't pick 'em. They pick *me*," Finister said.

"Why do you figure this lady's using a fake name just to take classes?"

"Probably her maiden name," Finister said. "Chinese do the same thing – keep their names after they get married. That's just the way they do things."

* * *

"Say again?" Finister said into the phone back at his desk. He scribbled something down and then waved to Martinez across the room.

"Yeah, got it. Thanks," Finister said and hung up. He looked at Martinez without saying anything for a while.

"What?"

"Our Ford Escort is registered to a Mr. Chul-Soo Han, a consul at the Democratic People's Republic of Korea's Mission to the United Nations."

"*North* Korean?"

"Uh-huh."

"Jack, you outdid yourself," Martinez said.

* * *

Having grown up in a large family as one of six boisterous siblings competing for attention, James Avery wasn't easily distracted, even in noisy settings. The offices where he was temporarily assigned were normally so quiet that anything above the clicking of keyboards or hushed cubicle conversations instantly registered as noise. But with the General Assembly to start in less than two weeks, there was a palpable buzz around him. Perhaps it was this skill that Avery had developed – the ability to filter out ambient noise, like the brawling of two brothers, yet pick up on vital sounds, like his mother calling him to dinner – that made his ears perk up at the mention of a particular name.

A colleague of his was talking with a section chief over some last-minute assignment – a "babysitting job," as his colleague called it. The volume was escalating, rising above the background.

"I've got nearly ten thousand pages to go through before the G.A. This is gonna eat up my whole day," Avery's colleague said, his voice getting tight with frustration.

"It's a murder investigation, for Chrissake. Just go over there with these detectives and stick around as they interview the guy. Look, it'll just take a couple of hours," the section chief said and handed over a folder.

"Who is this Han Chol-Soo, anyway? Why do they wanna talk to him?"

"He's some consul. It's not actually him they need to talk to, it's his wife. She apparently knew one of the victims."

The man tossed the folder on his desk. "You've *got* to be kidding me," he said.

"The sooner you head out, the sooner you can get back to what you were doing."

Avery almost tripped on a stack of binders as he rushed out of his cubicle toward the arguing pair. "Hold up. Hold up. Did you say Han Chol-Soo?"

"Yeah. Why?"

"Han Chol-Soo – late thirties, attended Moscow University?"

Avery's colleague flipped through the folder. "Yup. That's the one. Know him?"

"His name's come up on something I worked on before," Avery said, then pointing to the folder, added: "You want me to take that off your hands? I've been dying to check this guy out first hand for some time now."

His colleague's face brightened. "You magnificent son of a bitch, Avery," he said, then promptly held out the folder to the section chief. "He wants it. Let him have it."

"By all means. It's yours," the section chief said. As he walked briskly away, he called out to Avery over his shoulder, amiably pledging to buy him a drink after they come up for air.

Avery waved a distracted acknowledgement. He was already flipping through Han's file and was immediately disappointed at how incomplete it was.

* * *

When Finister and Avery arrived at the North Korean Mission, they were ushered into a windowless conference room. All activity in the office seemed to come to a standstill as the two were escorted past the rows of desks, uniformly positioned to face the wall that was bare except for the portraits of the Great Leader and the Dear Leader. They felt the eyes of the workers following them. Avery ignored it; Finister stared back.

"Jesus Feckin' Christ," Finister said to Avery when they were left alone in the conference room. "I've seen more joy in a freakin' morgue."

Avery looked at Finister, motioned up to the ceiling with his eyes and then shook his head. Finister instantly caught on that the walls might have ears.

When a man walked into the room, Finister immediately stood up and reached out his hand. "Mr. Han?" he asked.

"No, I'm sorry. Dr. Han is not here today. I am Consul Park Jun-Young."

When they shook hands, Finister quietly took note of Park's firm and calloused grip.

"I was told on the phone that we could meet Mr. Han – Dr. Han – here. I'm Detective Jack Finister with the New York City Police Department."

"Hello, I'm James Avery with the State Department. It's a pleasure to meet you."

"Nice to meet you," Park said. "I'm sorry, Dr. Han is not here today."

"Yes, you said that. Well then, how about Dr. Han's wife? Can you put us in touch with her? It's actually her that we need to speak to," Finister said.

"I'm afraid that is not possible," Park said. His accent was relatively thick but easily understandable thanks to his propensity for pronouncing every syllable evenly.

"Perhaps I'm not making myself clear. I'm investigating a homicide in which Mrs. Han may have vital information."

Park opened the door behind him and called out to someone.

"Park *youngsa-nim*," Avery said, using the Korean word for consul, tacking on the honorific "*nim*," then continued in Korean that his cooperation would be much appreciated.

Park's face stiffened. "You speak Korean," he said.

"*Neh. Hankook-mal hamnida*," Avery replied. Yes, I speak Korean. He then bantered about, explaining how he came to learn the language.

Park's demeanor changed. It's easier to play dumb when you can pretend that you don't understand the language. It's a ruse that Park used to great advantage a number of times. Now he was naked and without a fig leaf.

Park thought of an adage in Sun Tzu's *The Art of War* that is used so widely in the Far East that it has taken on the authority of gospel. *If you know the enemy and know yourself, you will be victorious in each of a hundred battles.* Like sayings in the Bible often quoted in the West, people used this saying without even knowing its origin because it was so ingrained in the culture. It was more commonly used nowadays as a dictum for triumph in things as mundane as school exams or soccer matches. Avery's mastery of the language struck Park as an example of the phrase closer to its original military usage. Speaking an enemy's language was tantamount to deciphering a code.

"Mrs. Han is not well, I'm afraid," Park said.

Avery translated for Finister.

"We went to Dr. Han's home. She wasn't there," Finister said.

"Yes, she's not there," Park said, then told someone outside the room not to bother getting the translator. "She is in a hospital."

"I'm sorry to hear that. Do you think we might be able to speak to her for just a few minutes," Finister asked, glancing over at Avery as though he was making sure he was translating properly.

"No, I'm sorry. She's very ill. She can't have any visitors," Park said.

Finister pressed him, asking for just a couple of minutes, explaining how the success of an investigation depended on speed, that if a crime isn't solved in the first 48 hours after it is committed, its chances of ever being solved dropped dramatically.

Park was stubborn. Talking to him was an exercise in circular logic. Finister sighed and looked over at Avery, who was sitting upright in his chair with his forearms on the table, studying Park, even as he translated his words. "I'm afraid it's impossible. All we can do is hope her condition improves quickly. Perhaps tomorrow," Avery translated, trying to capture the inflections of his artful dodging.

With that, Avery looked over at Finister and both men knew the interview was over. Avery took out his business card and offered it to Park with both hands. Finister put his card on the table and pushed it toward Park.

"As soon as Mrs. Han is well enough, we'd like to speak to her," Finister said.

As soon as Finister and Avery left the Mission, the deputy ambassador intercepted Park in the hallway and motioned for him to follow him into the Faraday Cage.

Deputy Ambassador Kwon insisted on carrying out any conversation with even a hint of sensitivity in the cage, a small chamber tucked away behind the conference room. The cage was completely encased in wire mesh that blocked electromagnetic signals coming in or out. It was a 19th-century invention yet few countermeasures worked as well in neutralizing late-20th century eavesdropping. Its effect was dramatic as the principle was simple. A radio or a cell phone that worked perfectly well would fall mute when you closed the door. The room had an eerie quiet about it that Park found disconcerting. Even though it was not insulated acoustically, the texture of the wire mesh – which resembled shiny layers of window screens – muted the echoes that would have bounced off normal walls. The simplicity of the cage appealed to Kwon. He understood it; therefore he trusted it.

For some minutes after he sealed the door, the deputy ambassador had Park stand in the corner as he sat there, bristling with anger, saying nothing for some time.

"Consul Park, you were a member of Room 35 before, were you not?" Deputy Ambassador Kwon finally asked.

"Yes, sir."

Room 35 was a unit within the Workers' Party that specialized in abducting Japanese nationals with an eye to assuming their identities. A fisherman from a remote village in Shimane Prefecture, a college co-ed visiting a coastal town on summer break – the kidnappings had a peculiar calculus; their identities on paper were more valuable than the sum of their lives. The agents of Room 35 trained for years, mastering the language and customs, then posing as Japanese nationals with forged passports, traveled freely to South Korea or other countries.

"Then you must understand the paramount importance of not letting one's personal emotions or affiliations put a mission in jeopardy," Kwon said. "Just because you think you saw a moment of frailty at the hospital the other night, it doesn't mean I've gone soft."

Kwon had wept during the visit with Ambassador Kim. Park still couldn't quite believe it. That was what Kwon meant by the "moment of frailty."

When a wolf's paw is caught in a snare, some have been said to gnaw it off to save its own life. Park wondered, if a beast is capable of such terrible resolve, why not a man? This was the choice Park faced – cut Han loose and live with the damage, or be slaughtered for fear of losing an ally. For a moment, Park entertained a third option – lie in wait for the trapper and mete out one last satisfying revenge. He quickly dismissed it as quixotic.

"Of course I understand, deputy minister. It was foolish of me to try to deal with this on my own," Park said. "I underestimated the trouble that Dr. Han would cause."

"I know Dr. Han and Ambassador Kim saw eye to eye on many things," Kwon said. "They would both have us open the country's doors a little wider to international inspectors in exchange for some measly food aid. I think both are beyond help now. With all the unwelcome attention the ambassador has stirred up here, I wouldn't be surprised if he gets called back to Pyongyang the moment he gets out of the hospital."

"As for Dr. Han, it is quite unfortunate. You will tell me everything now," Kwon said and casually turned his back toward Park, supremely secure in his advantage now.

* * *

Finister kept his silence until they walked out of the lobby onto Second Avenue, not because he feared any real threat of eavesdropping, instead to digest what had just happened.

"You buy that crap?" Finister asked Avery.

"Not for a moment," Avery said. "Pity, really. I was really hoping to meet this Dr. Han."

"What for?"

Avery explained how he had been searching for years for a man who might be the nexus of connections in North Korea's nuclear program and how he believed that this was one of those behind-the-scenes guys who knew where all the bodies were buried, or in this case, where all the plutonium is buried.

"This guy Han. *He* could be that guy," Avery said.

"So, he's one of those schlubs who does all the work but gets none of the glory," Finister said with a hint of recognition.

"That's what I'm thinking."

Finister took out a notepad from his inside jacket pocket and leafed though it. "North Korea's an old Soviet-bloc country, right?"

"About the last of its kind standing. Why?"

"Ever hear of a pistol called a Tokarev?"

Avery shook his head. "My dad was a missionary. Not exactly a gun person."

"It's originally a Russian model. There were a ton of 'em made in Eastern Europe, as well as China. Standard issue in Communist-bloc countries. Kinda like the Beretta is for the U.S. military now."

"So? What about it?"

"We found a Tokarev shell casing in the Koh residence. Don't see a lot of those. Mainly .32s, .38s or 9 mils. We figured it may have been a Russian mob thing – maybe the Kohs pissed off the wrong supplier, something like that. But something wasn't quite right about the crime scene. It looked like they'd cleaned up after themselves. And both Mr. and Mrs. Koh got one to the head and one to the heart. Thorough."

Avery looked at Finister and then looked up at the exterior of the building where they had come from, gauging where the thirteenth floor may be.

"I think I need to look into Mrs. Koh's extracurricular activities a little closer," Finister said.

Chapter 14

On the outskirts of Baltimore, I-95 runs through a landscape of smokestacks belching plumes of white steam, metal towers crowned with open flames, and hulking cranes off in the distance leaning over the waterfront like a row of boney white praying mantises in single file.

The setting was hardly picturesque, however, for Han, keenly more interesting than the glitzy locales he would normally be escorted to as part of his itinerary as a diplomat visiting foreign countries.

From an early age, he was intrigued by how things worked beneath the surface, and that curiosity often got him into trouble. He picked up the habit of taking things apart, and putting them back together in sometimes unconventional, yet still functional, ways. His mother once whipped him mercilessly with a forsythia branch after she discovered that he had taken apart the only radio in the house and tinkered with it to pick up more than the single authorized government channel. It was an offense that could have sent the whole family to a labor camp. She ordered him to fix the tuner back to the original channel, which he did, with a handful of leftover parts for which he could find no practical use in the re-assembly.

This industrial enclave that he and Jenny were driving through was to America what the circuit boards were to that radio – the unglamorous yet functional inner workings that made the larger machine tick. There was an understated grandeur about this landscape. Han imagined it dutifully grinding away, day and night, unnoticed by the masses, supplying this hungry nation with its wares.

Han knew this was no Potemkin village. Neither was that wholesale store in Abingdon. They existed, in darkness and in light, on rainy days as on clear, whether Han or his colleagues saw them or not, or whether they believed, in jest or sincerity, that the wealth of the United States had been assembled around New York City as a showcase for the benefit of their eyes. What we tell ourselves to avoid the reality – we don't believe it, not really. But we repeat it anyway, because to accept the reality in earnest is to accept humiliation.

In his mind's eye, Han pictured a map of America and imagined the 25-mile circle around New York City – tiny in the context of the country as a whole – and he picture a hundred, a thousand such industrial enclaves across the map that he would never see, churning away in obscurity, producing immeasurable bounty, mobilized to feed the bottomless appetite of its decadent populace and to subjugate other nations such as his own.

His own personal efforts to combat that juggernaut seemed suddenly insignificant, as though he were trying to scoop out an ocean with a pail.

"Is the famine in North Korea as bad as they say in the news?" Jenny asked, proving yet again that she had an uncanny sense of timing.

"Do you believe everything you see on the news?" Han countered sharply.

"No, of course not," Jenny said. "I did watch this documentary once on cable about these boys who would cross the border into China looking for work. It was really sad. The boys would beg on the streets and stuff, or get whatever jobs they could, and the Chinese police would chase them around, so they would sleep huddled together in some basement somewhere.

"And when they got enough money, they would go back to the border, along the Tumen River, where it was pretty shallow, and they'd cross back into North Korea. If they got caught, they'd get all their money confiscated by the border guards. So just before they would cross the river, they'd roll up the money into these little tight wads. They packed them really small using pliers and they would wrap it in some scavenged plastic and then seal it with a lighter. Then they'd swallow it. The younger kids – I guess they were about 10 or 12 – they'd gulp it down with lots of water. You could see their necks straining. Some of them would massage their necks, like they were milking a cow, to make the wads go down. The older ones, they'd gotten so used to the whole thing that they'd just swallow it without anything, just their spit, I guess.

"The narrator said when they get to the other side, they'd just crap it out and then they could use that money. It was so sad, these little boys, huddled in the bushes, swallowing plastic-wrapped pills of money. Some of them were so young, they were at that age when they didn't even know to be shy in front of girls. You know what I mean?"

"That's a bunch of nonsense – useless South Joseon propaganda," Han said.

"I dunno. It looked pretty real to me. I'd never seen North Korea on TV before. They had these long telephoto-lens shots of watch towers."

"That's enough. I don't want to hear any more," Han said.

Jenny persisted as though she hadn't heard him. "And the boys would scope out the river from the bushes to look for a good time to cross. They said in winter they could just walk across the ice."

"Enough, I said."

Han's objection wasn't particularly loud, but it was resolute. Jenny recoiled.

"I was just telling you what I saw on TV," she mumbled, hurt.

They did not speak again until they crossed into Virginia.

Han hadn't seen the program Jenny spoke of, but he recalled the documentary he had seen in that hotel room in Zurich. Most of these so-called news programs were in a hurry to forecast the imminent collapse of North Korea. From the fleeting glimpses captured in video, they divined the future of a nation that had withstood the encroachment of superpowers for five decades, even though the provenance of the footage was always a bit murky, be it of barefooted children begging for food in the streets or of graffiti scribbled under a bridge criticizing the Dear Leader.

They were lies, Han told himself.

* * *

Had Han gotten to know Mr. and Mrs. Koh, before his fellow consul had killed them, he would have discovered they shared his asceticism. They had done well for themselves in the New World, but you'd hardly know it from the frayed hems of their clothes or their tired shoes, which had been re-soled so many times that layers of the cobbler's handiwork appeared on close inspection like geological strata. The fruits of their labor had been poured mostly into the education of their children. Now that the kids were grown and out of the house, their industry needed a new outlet. As Detective Jack Finister delved into what he called their "extracurricular activities," details about their lives aligned and misaligned with Finister's own expectations in peculiar ways.

That Mr. and Mrs. Koh were devout Christians was not a surprise. Their well-used Bible said as much. The darkened edges of the pages revealed an affinity for the early sections of the New Testament, in particular the gospels of Matthew, Mark, Luke, and John.

Koreans, far more so than their neighbors in China or Japan, had embraced Christianity with gusto. That was especially true of those who emigrated abroad. Perhaps it was that they felt besieged in a new land and needed familiar companions, or that they needed some reassurance that their hardships would be rewarded, if not in this world, then in the next.

There are devout Christians and then there are Evangelicals, and Finister was beginning to learn that the Kohs were more of the latter. They were members of the Bethel Baptist Congregation, a church in Flushing that the couple's son, James, spoke of rather disapprovingly. When pressed, James pointed to what he called the pastor's "militant streak." Like any good evangelical, the pastor did not believe in the principle of live and let live when it came to faith. That kind of compromise was not a part of his theology. A failure to convert someone reflected poorly on one's own faith, and like other charismatic evangelical leaders, he rallied his congregation around his own passions, one of them being the salvation of his godless North Korean brethren.

"When I was in high school I hated going to church," James Koh told Finister, occasionally wiping away tears with his shirtsleeve. "I didn't have the heart to stop going because it would have crushed my parents. When I left home for college, they got even more involved in their church."

After decades of quietly building up an admirably profitable business, and, along the way, affording their son and daughter the best schools, the Kohs belatedly found a penchant for proselytizing if not altruism.

"I never could tell if they really believed in whatever the cause of the month was," James said. He himself rarely attended church any more, unless he was home for the holidays.

His parents threw themselves into each cause with as much zeal as they did when building their business, or when drilling into their children the paramount importance of Ivy League credentials – "not just any old college degree," as they called it. The couple made it clear that their children's future success depended on it, and furthermore, that it was also as an affirmation of the fruits of their sacrifice.

"You don't seem too happy about being at Princeton, son. Some people would kill for that opportunity," Finister said to James.

"Of course I'm grateful. It's just that my parents wanted it so bad – more than I did, in fact. Now they won't even see me graduate."

Kids, Finister thought, they never want what the parents want.

The church's latest pet project was collecting donations to send relief shipments to famine-stricken North Korea, James said, though he couldn't recall much detail beyond that.

The words "North Korea" jumped out at Finister. He called Avery and told him to meet him at the Koh residence. They needed to go through the paperwork in the house again.

Chapter 15

The First Baptist Church of Fairfax was located in a neat white clapboard building on a well-traveled suburban road in Virginia just outside the Beltway. Its grey slate steeple towered above most other structures around it. The notice board outside the church indicated that there were services in both English and Korean, on Sunday and Wednesday, with Bible-study groups on Saturday. The English-language services catered almost exclusively to the second-generation children who had lost their facility with Korean. Occasionally a non-Korean would wander into the English-language service. The congregants were invariably nice to them, knowing the visitor must feel out of place. Very rarely did any of them return for a second time.

Unlike upstart congregations that normally gathered in improvised spaces, such as former restaurants in strip malls, this ministry had done well for itself. It had bought the property from an atrophying local congregation of elderly European stock and made it theirs, most certainly to the chagrin of the last remaining stalwarts who remembered when Asians were rare in town. Nearby homeowners had mixed feelings about it – secretly cheering that their sagging property values had been buttressed by a rejuvenated church, yet outwardly complaining at every town meeting about the horrendous Sunday traffic.

It was just past lunchtime when Han Chol-Soo and Jenny Rhee arrived, and there were a few cars in the parking lot. The front door of the church was locked, so Han and Jenny went around the back. They heard the chatter of children as they approached a rear entrance. When they opened the door, the chatter turned into a cacophony of a dozen willful toddlers. Jenny and Han peered into a room just down the hall. It was full of kids, maybe four years old, unsupervised. Han was disappointed. He half expected to see his wife sitting there, holding Won-Kyu in her lap.

"Can I help you?" a voice from behind them asked in Korean.

Jenny and Han turned around. It was a young woman, in her twenties, holding the hand of a boy who was diligently picking his nose with his free hand. Tears glistened on his cheek, evidence of a very recent bout of crying.

"I'm here to see Pastor Kim Yoon-Kyu," Han said.

"He's on his way back from visiting a parishioner who's in the hospital," the young woman said. "You're welcome to wait here if you like. Is he expecting you?"

"Yes. Yes, he is," Han said. He looked at Jenny to make sure she would not contradict his lie.

Han had rehearsed this encounter in his mind on the drive down from New York, trying to cover every permutation of questions he could imagine. He understood himself well enough to know that he was not a very good liar. His limitation for moving up through the ranks in the Workers' Party was partly due to this unintentional candor of his face; how his emotions seemed to have unfiltered access to it. He dealt with uncertainty in the best way he knew how – preparation. He would pose as a messenger from the Rev. Baek Sang-Min, the man whose corpse now sat side by side with his wife's in their tidy Fort Lee tomb.

Han had a general idea of how these underground networks of Christians were helping North Korean refugees in China. Most of the time, the fugitives would make their way to South Korea via a third country, such as Thailand, Vietnam or Mongolia. In rare cases, they would go to South Korea directly from China, though that was a dicey option that would keep diplomats up at night.

One of the folders that Han had taken from Rev. Baek's house contained enough of a paper trail that Han managed to piece together how these churches based in America were helping out those underground networks. Often the support was monetary. In some cases, parishioners who were U.S. citizens would conduct missionary work in China, using their citizenship as a shield against the hazards that such work entailed – unpopular as it was with the Chinese authorities.

Han even found a few snippets of correspondence pertaining to his wife: A letter from one of the church elders suggesting he was anxious about the novelty and risk of her case – the defection of a North Korean diplomat's wife here in the U.S. – and the controversy it could ignite. An enterprise that relies on clandestine maneuvers does not succeed by calling attention to itself, the church elder wrote. The correspondence showed it was Rev. Baek who seemed to be cheerleading his parishioners and other members of the network, to take this case on. Han recalled the disheveled old man starting back at him, defiant to the end.

* * *

"These folks have been waiting for you for about half an hour, Pastor Kim," the young woman said by way of introduction, with a hint of disappointment in her voice, ostensibly at Kim's tardiness. "They said you were expecting them."

The Rev. Kim Yoon-Kyu was a much younger man than Han had expected. For some reason, he had envisioned him as a contemporary of the Rev. Baek, but he looked to be about the same age as Han. If Han had met Kim randomly on the street, he would never have pegged him as a man of the cloth. He was dressed in a crisp, navy blue suit and looked more like a well-heeled professional.

Kim looked dazed and he seemed to be searching his memory for an appointment he had possibly neglected.

"I'm so sorry. I must have completely overlooked this. Please sit down. I'm afraid you'll have to indulge me," Kim said. "Can you tell me what we were supposed to meet about?"

"We're here on an errand from Pastor Baek Sang-Min," Han said. "Did you get his call?"

"I spoke to him late yesterday. He didn't mention that he'd be sending anyone."

"Really? He said he was going to call you first thing in the morning. I'm Deacon Lee Tae-Yon and this is my wife," Han said, gesturing to Jenny. He had picked the names off one of the spreadsheets he had found in Pastor Baek's house. "We've been members of Pastor Baek's church for several years now."

Rev. Kim must have seen something register on Jenny's face – perhaps a note of surprise – because he looked at her for a good long while. Then, as if to correct his faux pas of staring, he offered a compliment that ended up coming out as rather wicked. "My goodness, Deacon Lee, your wife is so young."

"He always was a bit of a charmer with the ladies," Jenny said, and surreptitiously pinched Han's arm.

Perhaps Han had stretched the truth a little too much, or at least too much for Jenny to let it pass without at least some form of objection. Han was genuinely grateful to her at that moment for playing along. Han continued with the ruse. "Pastor Baek asked us deliver a package to Ms. Chung Myung-Ae."

Kim stiffened at the mention of Han's wife's name. "I see," he said, and then began shuffling through some folders in a drawer. "Well, if you give the package to me, I'll make sure she gets it."

"Pastor Baek asked us to deliver this in person to Ms. Chung," Han said. "I don't even know what's it is. He was quite adamant that we hand it to no one but Ms. Chung herself. You should check with Pastor Baek yourself, of course. Why don't you try him now."

Kim begged Han's pardon and picked up the phone. He passed his finger down a list of phone numbers that had been taped to a pull-out shelf on his desk and dialed one number. Han could hear it ringing, and then a voice.

"It's the answering machine," Kim said to Han, and when the recording ended, he left a brief message telling Baek that his messengers were sitting in his office and asked him to call him back as soon as possible, even bowing into empty space, a sign of polite deference, as though the old man were standing there.

"Let me try the church as well," Kim said, and dialed another number from the list. This time, he got someone live on the phone.

Han's heart began to race. What if someone had gone to Baek's house already? Han sized up Kim, taking measure of him, wondering if he could overpower him if he had to, if the voice on the other end of the phone suddenly grew frantic. But nothing in Kim's eyes betrayed a sense of urgency.

"Alright. Please tell Pastor Baek that Deacon Lee Tae-Yon is here on that errand of his," Kim said.

The woman's voice on the other end of the phone got a little animated.

"Yes, he's here, with his wife. They're sitting right next to me now," Kim said.

Han heard faint laughter on the phone.

"So, you know them," Kim said, momentarily looking up at Jenny and Han. Kim's face softened. Han looked over at Jenny and managed a smile.

"Very good. Thank you very much," Kim said, and just before he hung up, added: "No. That won't be necessary."

"I'm sorry about all that. It's just that we're all a bit jittery about Ms. Chung's defection. It's something entirely new for us," Kim said. He scribbled something down on a piece of paper and handed it to Han.

"She's staying here. It's the home of a friend of one of our parishioners in Albemarle County, near a town called Charlottesville. It's about two hours south of here," Kim said. "Have you heard of it?"

Han felt as though a heavy weight had been lifted from his chest. For the first time since the ordeal had begun, he knew where his wife and son were.

"Yes, I've heard of it, but I haven't had a chance to visit. It's where Monticello is, right? Jefferson's estate?" Han said.

"That's it," Kim said. "The parishioners from our church live not too far from there, actually."

"Jefferson?" Jenny chimed in. "As in President Jefferson?"

"Yes, honey. That Jefferson," Han said.

"The one who's on the twenty-dollar bill?" she said brightly, excited to finally join the conversation.

"I think that's another president," Han said, chuckling amiably.

Jenny tilted her head in puzzlement. She reached for her purse.

"I'll call them and let them know you're coming," Kim said, giving them directions.

"Oh, it's Jackson," Jenny said. "Jackson, Jefferson – they both start with 'J' and end with 'son.'"

In the church parking lot, Jenny tossed her bag into the back seat of the Mustang. She was annoyed. "This is my wife?" she said, mocking Han's performance. "Hey, I'm no Christian, but even I know that you're going straight to hell if you lie to a minister."

"Careful. He's still watching," Han said as he exchanged long-distance bows with Kim, who was standing at the doorway to send them off. Han motioned one more time for Kim to go back inside, waving his hand in a kind of underhand throw. Five decades of Communism hadn't attenuated the elaborate dance of two Koreans trying to out-polite one another – one man insisting on not going back inside until the guest was comfortably out of sight, the other urging the host to return to the comfort of their abode.

When Han visited a cousin in a rural village once, the cousin had insisted on standing outside the house for their long goodbye until Han disappeared over the crest of a nearby hill.

It is a warm evening some ten years ago. Every time Han looks back, the cousin is standing there, even though Han keeps waving for him to go back inside. When he looks back one more time before he descends the other side of the dusty road, his cousin is still there, waving at him with his arm reaching skyward like a reed in the wind. He sees the cousin's smiling face even now. In his mind, he is still standing there, forever a genial totem pole.

When Han climbed back into the Mustang with Jenny, his forced grin melted away with a sigh as though to hold it longer would have caused him discomfort.

"Going to hell?" Han said glumly. "The afterlife is the last thing I'm worried about right now."

* * *

Avery stood in the middle of the Kohs' living room, looking down at the dinner plate-sized stains on the carpet. Earlier in the day, the pools of blood had been dark and deep. Now, they had turned a shallow brown, the hue of fallen oak leaves.

That a struggle between two rivals half a world away could have followed this couple home and intruded into this inconsequential outpost of the Cold War, seemed surreal and unfair to Avery. The evidence suggested that was a distinct possibility. The Tokarev shell casing; the correspondence between the Kohs and other members of the church on their charitable work to help refugees; the fact that Mrs. Koh and Mrs. Han were classmates; and now the "unavailability" of Dr. Han and his wife.

Avery tried to make sense of it. His neck began to ache.

"So what's the deal?" Finister asked Avery. "Is this Han character trying to defect with his family?"

"A guy with this kind of pedigree – unlikely," Avery said, still looking at the blood stains. "This guy's the cream of the crop. There's no reason for him to risk everything by defecting. And he's been stationed all over the world. He's had plenty of opportunities to defect before if he wanted to. Why now? It doesn't add up."

"Hear me out. Just thinking out loud here," Finister said. "Let's just say Han *does* want to defect, for whatever reason. What does he do? First, he makes sure his wife and son are some place safe, then he reaches out to you guys, right?"

"In theory," Avery said.

"What if that some place safe was supposed to be Mr. and Mrs. Koh's house?"

Avery nodded, tacitly encouraging Finister to continue.

"Mrs. Han, a.k.a. Myung-Ae Chung, starts taking English lessons and gets friendly with Mrs. Koh. Now, it doesn't take long for Mrs. Koh, who's found Jesus and has recently taken to helping North Korean refugees, to find out that our Mrs. Han is in fact the wife of a North Korean diplomat. She starts evangelizing to Mrs. Han and soon she's drinking the Kool-Aid."

"Wait. Kool-Aid? Aren't you Catholic?"

"Yup. I was born into it. We don't drink Kool-Aid, just the blood of Christ. Catholics don't do evangelism. What are *you*?"

"Lapsed Presbyterian," Avery said. "Former Kool-Aid drinker."

"Anyways, so now Mrs. Han is born again. She goes home and preaches to her husband, and gets *him* to drink the Kool-Aid, too," Finister said.

Avery had to stop him there. "No, no, no. Now *that's* a leap," Avery said. "I don't think you understand the kind of vetting and selection these guys go through to get where they are. These guys are ideologically pure as the driven snow. If there's even a hint that they're wavering, they get sent back for re-indoctrination."

"Didn't you say that the Number Two guy in the Workers' Party defected this year? What's his name?"

"Hwang Jang-Yop," Avery said.

Hwang had made headlines in February, when he showed up in Seoul as the highest-ranking defector from North Korea. He was a very big fish indeed. In the late 1950s, as deputy chairman of the Workers' Party propaganda section, he conceived the Pyongyang regime's official ideology of *juche*, or self-reliance.

Through the '70s, he was a three-term chairman of the Supreme People's Assembly. In 1980, he rose to chief secretary of the Central Committee.

"Plus another two ambassadors or something? I'm thinking they were also ideologically pure as the driven snow," Finister said, mimicking Avery's accent to throw the phrase back at him.

Avery nodded. He had to concede that in the universe of insiders, those men were more on the inside than even someone like Han. An American newspaper likened the impact of Hwang's defection to what might have happened to the American Revolution if Thomas Jefferson or James Madison had defected to the England of King George.

"Go on," Avery said.

Finister cracked a grin, knowing he had won the point.

"So now Mr. and Mrs. Han have both found religion and they decide it's time to walk into the arms of Christ in their new, free country. Mrs. Han takes the baby and stays with the Kohs so that Mr. Han can bail out at a moment's notice when he gets the green light from you guys." Finister pointed to Avery.

"Except *someone* at the North Korean Mission finds out about this defection plan before Han pulls it off. They detain Mr. Han, find out where his wife is, and send someone to get her back. They off the old couple – I dunno, maybe they put up a fight or maybe a cleaner goes in from the get-go, intending to kill them to hush things up. Mr. Cleaner gets Mrs. Han back, and Mr. and Mrs. Han are sitting in a room somewhere under lock and key, waiting for a long trip back to North Korea.

"And maybe *that's* why Mrs. Han can't have any visitors; not because she's ill, like our Consul Park says," Finister said. He turned his palms up as a signal that his story was done.

Avery walked over to the window and looked out into the small and tidy garden where the Kohs had planted rows of chrysanthemums, mostly white and yellow varieties that were just beginning to bloom.

The mums would be flowering in his parents' garden in Seoul as well. The seasons there and in New York mirrored one another uncannily. It was one reason Avery felt at home in New York. The weather also provided a perennial topic for polite conversation when he spoke to his parents.

"Even if Dr. Han has become 'born again' – which, I have to say, I find hard to believe – there's another thing that makes it unlikely for him to defect," Avery said.

"What's that?"

"Han has a daughter in Pyongyang. Would *you* defect if you knew you'd never see your child again? And not only that, if you knew she'd be screwed for life because her parents were traitors."

"Shite," Finister said. He walked over to where Avery had been on the rug and stood over the bloodstains, staring into them as though they would surrender some insight. "Kinda blows that whole defection theory out of the water, doesn't it?"

"Well, not necessarily. I just had a horrible thought," Avery said, looking over at Finister. "You ever see that movie *Sophie's Choice?*"

Finister's eyes met Avery's for a moment. Avery looked back out the window and Finister back down at the bloodstains.

Even though Avery had turned away from religion, it seemed he could not quiet escape it. It kept on intruding into his life, like a jilted lover stalking him, keen to remind him of what he had left behind. That his work would force his life to intersect with the lives of Christian missionaries from Korea in New York, of all places, seemed bizarre. It was as though God were playing a prank on him.

"There's two people who can make all of this add up – Mr. and Mrs. Han," Finister said. "I'm putting a tail on Park. If he won't tell us where they are, maybe he'll lead us to them."

Chapter 16

The road to Charlottesville from northern Virginia was dotted with reminders of the Civil War. Every few miles Han spotted a signpost with the name of a town; person or landmark that he recognized from history books he had read when he found out he would be stationed in the United States. Manassas, Lee Highway, and Fredericksburg – each time he saw a familiar name on the side of the road, he followed the signpost until it passed from his sight.

"What do you keep looking at?" asked Jenny from behind the wheel.

"Oh, it's all these signs. The names – it's like pieces of history sprinkled along the highway."

Han explained to Jenny that it was like the jolt of recognition he felt as a schoolboy when he visited the USS Pueblo for the first time after years of seeing it only from afar and in textbooks. Every North Korean child knew the story of how the U.S. Navy vessel was captured in 1968 while spying in North Korean waters. Han recalled the pride and satisfaction he felt as he watched a video presentation on board, showing how American negotiators groveled for the return of the 83-member crew. *The enemy knelt down, as the myth and might of the United States crumbled before the will of the Korean people,* the narrator said in a voice on the verge of breaking with emotion.

America often seemed a land without memory, especially when one lived in a city like New York, constantly remaking itself, forgetting itself in its haste. There was something about Virginia, however, that spoke of age, now that Jenny and Han had ventured off the main highways and onto the roads that passed by solitary barns on meadows lush with centuries of toil. These trees were nourished on fallen soldiers. *Lacrimae rerum* – the tears for things. The landscape seemed familiar to Han, green and fertile as it was, the way he remembered his country being in his childhood. He felt melancholy and simultaneously at home.

Jenny turned up the radio again as she complained of being tired. It was understandable. She had been up almost as long as he had, going on 30 hours now, with a restless night that preceded it. That life, a day ago, seemed like someone else's. She asked Han if he knew the song now blaring from the speakers. This time he did. He recognized it even through the wind and road noise from having the Mustang's top down.

"It must be *really* old if even *you* know it," she said.

"It's on TV all the time these days," he said. "Whenever they show Princess Diana's funeral."

"Ooh, you *do* know it," she said, genuinely impressed. "Yeah, Elton John changed the lyrics for Princess Diana."

When Han and his fellow members of the Mission went to the room salon with the local businessman after visiting the ambassador at the hospital, an inebriated Deputy Ambassador Kwon had spoken mercilessly about Diana; how unbecoming it was that the princess had been "gallivanting around with that Arab," as he put it.

"Is that really how the mother of the future king of the British Empire should behave? Hitching rides on his yacht, half naked?" Kwon said as he waved his shot glass around, spilling half of it.

Images of Diana had been hard to escape since her death a few weeks ago – whether in the form of photos splashed across the front pages of newspapers or video clips on TV, spanning the time from when she was an ingénue bashfully showing off her engagement ring to when she was a sullen divorcee staring out with those hurt eyes sunken further by mascara.

"She had bad karma," Kwon said, slurring his speech. "Sure, she may have been miserable. She made everyone around her miserable as well, and brought them nothing but bad fortune. She dragged the royal family through the mud. And think of it from the Al Fayed family's point of view. They had more money than they knew what do with. What the hell did *they* get out of it? A dead son, that's what."

The room salon hostesses, with their moth-like tropism toward banter, nodded and giggled in agreement. One of them refilled the spilled portion of Kwon's shot glass.

The other ubiquitous image in the media these days was that of the mangled sedan in that Paris tunnel. How frantic those last moments must have been before the crash, with paparazzi racing the car on motorcycles, firing their flashes into the back seat, engines revving, tires screeching, before everything came to an abrupt and smoky standstill.

Han bumped his head against the passenger-side window. He had dozed off and was awakened by the sound of screeching tires. He bolted to attention and saw Jenny fighting the wheel, steering the Mustang off the dusty shoulder and back onto the asphalt. He felt his heart thumping.

In the left lane, a black pickup truck swerved back onto the road from the opposite shoulder. A flap of the rear fender was jammed up against the wheel, spewing a cloud of grey smoke. The acrid taste of burning rubber quickened Han's senses.

"I must have nodded off!" Jenny screamed. "We could have died!"

The pickup truck slowed down and pulled up alongside the Mustang. The man in the passenger seat waved his cap out the window, motioning Jenny to the side of the road.

"What should I do?" she asked frantically.

"You'd better pull over," Han said. "Let's settle this quietly. We don't want to get the police involved."

The truck pulled in front of the Mustang and they both rolled onto the shoulder. The pickup stopped a little further into the road with its left tires on the asphalt, as though the driver were preemptively blocking the way should Jenny change her mind and make a break for it.

A tall man leisurely got out of the driver's side of the pickup and walked around to inspect the damage. His passenger, a man with skinny limbs and a disproportionately big gut, joined him, pushing the cap he had waved moments before back onto his balding head. He took a lugubrious drag on his cigarette before flicking it to the ground. The driver tapped the back tire with the toe of his scuffed boots several times, took off his cap, and fanned it to get a better look at the smoldering tire. Unlike his passenger, he had a head of thick, sandy brown hair. It stood up as though it was charged with static.

Han told Jenny to stay in the car as he got out. He walked a few steps toward the two men, patted his pockets, then doubled back.

"How much money do you have?" he asked Jenny.

Jenny looked through her purse. "About two hundred dollars – my tips from last night."

"What about the envelope that Jun-Young gave you?"

Jenny was deflated. She sighed and fished out the envelope from her bag. She gauged the weight of it once again in her hand. She hadn't had a chance to see how much was inside. She opened it and flicked through the bills. They were all C-notes.

"There's enough in here to buy that damn junker," she said confidently. "But this is *mine*."

"Don't worry. I'm sure there's more where that came from," Han said. "Give me five hundred. Consider it a loan."

Jenny hesitated, like a child reluctant to open a bag of candy, only because to disturb the completeness of it would diminish its value. She licked the tip of her index finger and peeled off five bills, counting it twice. Han had to give them a little tug out of her grip. Before turning around, he divided the bills into a batch of two and three and stuck them in opposite pockets.

"What the hell is your problem, mister?" the balding passenger said as Han approached the pickup. Han couldn't help thinking that the man looked like a tadpole because his limbs were so slender and his girth so ample.

"Sorry. I'm sorry," Han said.

"Sorry ain't gonna begin to cut it, my friend," the man said, his face reddening.

"We will pay for damage," Han said.

"Damn right, you're gonna pay for it."

"How much?"

Tadpole man chuckled and looked at the tall man. "How much? He wants to know how much, Dex. Mister, you just ruined my friend's truck and messed up our day. You wanna try a little foreplay before you try to fuck us over?"

Han didn't quite understand what he was saying, partly because of the drawl and partly due to his unfamiliar figures of speech. Han stuttered, not quite sure how to respond. He must have looked sufficiently puzzled because tadpole man took a step toward Han, stuck out his face, pushed the rim of his cap back, and offered another explanation.

"I'm saying I don't think I like your attitude, sir. You can't just throw money at a problem."

"I don't mean to offend. We are just in a hurry."

"Sure looks that way," the tall man named Dex finally chimed in. "For starters, how 'bout an explanation from your driver friend there?"

"She made mistake," Han said.

"No shit, Sherlock," Dex said. "But I'd like to hear it straight from the horse's mouth."

Han was completely lost now. Who was Sherlock and what did horses have to do with this? Han wondered whether he was referring to the Mustang. A Mustang was a horse, wasn't it?

Dex muttered something to tadpole man and then added, "Let's see what the little lady has to say." He grabbed the waistband of his jeans and hitched them up as though preparing for heavy lifting, and walked over to the car.

"What do you have to say for yourself, miss?" he demanded.

Even though the soft top was down, she had gone to the trouble of rolling up her windows as some measure of protection.

She kept on apologizing, and that only seemed to make Dex angrier.

"Why don't you step out here for a moment and talk to me face to face. I ain't gonna hurt you," he said as he opened the door. She smelled booze on his breath.

"Hey, you are drunk!" Jenny said, her demeanor changing swiftly from meek to pugnacious. She repeated that in Korean for Han, standing up on her seat and yelling over the windshield.

"I ain't drunk, bitch! You're the one who slammed into *me*, remember?" Dex said. His hair seemed to stand up even more as he got agitated.

Jenny's eyes grew wide and her lips taut with indignation. She was about to climb out of the car when Han came up beside Dex and pushed the door closed. Jenny fell back into her seat.

"We said sorry. We give you three-hundred dollars," Han said, quickly pulling out the bills from his pocket.

"That's not gonna cover it, mister," Dex said, reaching again for the door handle. Jenny was right; Han could also smell the alcohol on his breath.

Jenny was having none of this now. "Fuck you! You are drunk. You should not drive!" she screamed, standing up in her seat again, pointing an accusatory finger at Dex.

"You got a mouth on you, lady," Dex said and lurched forward.

Han grasped Dex's forearm, not firmly enough to hold him back, just enough to get his attention.

"Get your damn hand off me!" Dex said, shoving Han's chest.

Han stumbled back. He heard footsteps behind him on the gravel. He turned and retreated a few steps to make sure he had both men in view. He wanted to be out of reach of a wild hook. The last thing he wanted was a brawl on the side of the road, but he wasn't about to let himself get blindsided.

Han had put in 10 years in the People's Army for his mandatory military service – five on active duty and, in recognition of his academic talent, five in the reserves while he pursued his Ph.D. Any group of men in their prime – let alone a military outfit – will harden each other, test one another's mettle, even though individually they may be temperate and even tender. During those early years in the army, Han earned a reputation for being tough, though it was based on a rather unrepresentative cross section of his deeds, public and dramatic as they may have been. In addition to his aptitude for pushups and chin-ups, Han's notoriety was solidified when he knocked a guy out cold with a back kick during a Taekwondo sparring session. His foot caught his opponent squarely on the chin, dropping him to the mat like a rigid stump. Han recalled feeling exhilarated and simultaneously shocked at the way his opponent fell without trying to protect himself. He noticed from then on he was treated with a certain deference in the mess hall and the barracks. If one is to earn such a reputation, he learned that it was useful to do it earlier rather than later.

Han took the remaining two hundred dollars out of his pocket and held it out in his hand.

"This is all I have," Han said. "Five hundred dollars. Enough to fix the truck."

"What're you doin' with all that cash anyway? You a drug dealer or somethin'?" tadpole man said. "You got your fancy car and New York plates. And you're in an awful hurry. Dex, you smell something fishy here?"

"Damn right I smell somethin' fishy, Tommy," Dex said.

So, tadpole man's name was Tommy. "Here, take five hundred. It's fair, yes?" Han said.

Jenny yelled in Korean not to give him the money; that the tall man was drunk, so they should call the police. Han shouted back in Korean that the last thing they needed was for cops to get involved.

"Where y'all from, anyway?" Tommy said.

Han belatedly realized that in his haste to settle the matter he had seemed desperate. It was clear now that Tommy and Dex smelled an opportunity.

Greed – Han was sick of it. Even here, in a land of plenty, it was alive and well, always hungry for more. At every turn in his home country, it was impossible to get anything done without greasing the wheels with some kind of bribe. At least there he understood the need for it. There is so little available above board that daily life would grind to a halt if you refused to deal under the table. The black market and the grey area between gift and bribe – those were the safety valves. But why here? Did they not have more than they needed? Were Dex and Tommy not comfortably swaddled in the largesse of the state? Why would they not want to settle this quietly and expeditiously?

"We don't want trouble. You don't want trouble. Please take it. It is enough," Han said.

"You just don't get it, do ya? This is *America*," Tommy said emphatically, pointing at the dusty ground.

Han couldn't understand why he felt the need to state the obvious fact of which country they were in. Was that supposed to explain something?

"Is this their way of asking for more money?" Han asked Jenny in Korean.

She implored him not to give them any more and then added: "If you give them one more cent, you can walk back to New York because I refuse to drive any more."

Perhaps Tommy and Dex were being coy, like those North Korean bureaucrats sometimes are when they deem a bribe insufficient. Some insist on privacy when being handed an envelope; others feign modesty, politely declining the gift, forcing you to be more insistent than they are pretending to be modest; some refuse to take the envelope directly from your hand, asking instead that you lay it down on a table. An overt hand-off was perhaps too uncouth for them, though they obviously did not think it uncouth to take the money for doing something that was ostensibly part of their job.

Han often found Americans too direct – at least the northerners he was used to dealing with. Perhaps these southern men were more circumspect. They also seemed to have an exaggerated sense of honor, much like Koreans.

It's customary in Korea to quarrel for the privilege of picking up the tab at the end of a meal. This stems in part from the tradition that those who are higher on the social ladder are expected to pay for their subordinates. So, to pay for someone's meal denotes a superior position in the hierarchy. Once, this quarrel of generosity between Han and his cousin actually turned into a shoving match, with Han trying to stuff money into his cousin's pocket after the cousin clandestinely settled the tab while faking a trip to the bathroom. The reason it had degenerated to that extent was that Han and his cousin were the same age and of similar social stations, so there was no convenient measure to decipher who was higher on the social ladder. Even a year of seniority would have been a clear enough differentiator. The quarrel was settled only by subterfuge, when Han pretended to acquiesce but secretly slipped the money into his cousin's briefcase. Han later got an angry call from his cousin when he found it. The cousin vowed that he would now have to treat him twice.

If the land shapes its people and this was a terrain that Han felt a kinship to, perhaps it made sense to deal with Dex and Tommy as kin, prickly as they were.

Since Dex had pushed him away once already, Han approached Tommy instead and offered a handshake. The man seemed puzzled at first and then torn, as though he could not quite summon the heart to reject the peace gesture. He looked at Han and at Dex alternately a couple of times, perhaps seeking a sign from Dex that it was okay to make nice. An exaggerated sense of honor also meant a man does not refuse to shake another man's hand.

"I am sorry," Han said.

As Tommy extended his hand, his fingers trembled ever so slightly with the exertion of swallowing his belligerence. When the two finally clasped hands, Han felt the calluses of someone who worked with his hands for a living.

Han then tightened his grip so Tommy couldn't retreat, and he moved in close to stuff the money into Tommy's jacket pocket.

In retrospect, it was a stupid, impertinent move, based on a gross misunderstanding of those men, and triggering a further misunderstanding, this one catastrophic.

In the holding cell, Han had ample time to ponder how he had so badly miscalculated the situation; how he could have allowed himself to be lulled to a feeling of kinship with these strangers based on some fuzzy romantic notion of the land and the body being one; how desperation had so clouded his judgment. His country's penury, and his own meager means, had obscured his mind to the simple solution of dipping deeper into that envelope of cash, notwithstanding Tommy's protestations that you can't just throw money at a problem. In the real world, you can. It was just that Han and his countrymen usually didn't have enough of it to throw around, so they were forced to resort to cheaper alternatives. Sometimes those alternatives were ingenious. Sometimes they were just plain kooky.

The scuffle between Han and Tommy prompted Dex to join the fray. Jenny kicked open the car door and rushed toward the brawl, then bounced on her toes looking for an opening into the confusing mess of grunts and flying limbs. Had the sheriff not pulled up to break up the melee when he did, the list of injuries would most certainly have been worse. Han came out of it relatively unscathed – partly a testament to his early, harsh training in the military, but more so to the natural knack he seemed to have for fighting, infrequently tested as it was. The tally included a couple of bruised lips, scratches and a black eye. Tommy got it the worst, with two broken fingers.

Chapter 17

The odor in the jail cell reminded Han of the disagreeable mix of urine and bleach he smelled in the stairwells of less-frequented subway stations around New York City. There was a stainless steel toilet in the corner. It didn't have a seat, let alone a cover. He was sharing the cell with a man who smelled like he had taken a bath in stale beer, sleeping it off on the bench bolted to the cement floor. He had yet to stir from under the plaid shirt he used to cover his face.

Han couldn't see Dex in the adjoining cell but he could hear his voice, loudly protesting that he wasn't drunk.

"What the hell are you talking about? He was speaking English fine before y'all showed up," Dex said.

They'd taken Tommy away in an ambulance, cradling the hand with the broken fingers close to his chest, and Han hadn't seen Jenny since they parted ways at the front desk of the police station, when he had called out to her not to reveal who he was.

During questioning, Han was put into a stark, windowless room. Han obstinately pretended not to speak the language. When Han responded with only puzzled looks, the young deputy spoke slower and louder. He seemed to believe that that could magically overcome the language barrier. He had a kind face, so open and devoid of menace that Han wondered how he might possibly excel in this line of work. When Han still gave him a confused look, the deputy sighed in frustration and stomped out of the room, leaving Han handcuffed to the chair. Perhaps the ruse worked, perhaps it didn't. He was curious what Jenny had told them.

The deputy returned shortly, mumbling to himself. He escorted Han to a phone in the hallway and handcuffed him to a metal bar next to it.

Han called Park Jun-Young for his one phone call. He expected Park to be furious, but he sounded disappointed more than anything else, deflated, perhaps. Park spoke with the weariness of a parent let down by a troublesome child. He told Han about the detective and the man named Avery from the State Department who had come to see him.

"Couldn't you have been more careful?" Park said. "This was your chance to make things right."

"I know. I have no excuse," Han said. The Korean phrase he used literally meant *I have no words to say* – the ultimate disclosure of contrition. He reached for his head, trying to scratch it as a reflexive gesture of embarrassment. The cuffs jerked his hand back with a clank.

"I *did* find out where she is," Han said in his own defense. "I was so close."

"I know. Jenny just called me," Park said.

"She did? Where was she calling from? I haven't seen her since I came to the police station."

"She said they released her because she wasn't involved in the fight."

"What did she tell the police about me?"

"Don't worry. She's a shrewd girl – a lot more so than she lets on. Told them you were an acquaintance visiting from Seoul. They told her to come back with your passport if she wants to bail you out."

Han explained how he was playing dumb with the cops.

"That's good," Park said. "Don't tell them anything. If we do this right, there's still a chance we can take care of this. They don't know who you are, so let's keep it that way."

"So what do I do now?" Han said.

"Just sit tight. I'll get your passport to Jenny. Your name is Kim Kwang-Il. You own a printing shop in Seoul and you're here on a B-1 visa."

"I understand," Han said, nodding to himself, now feeling reassured rather than troubled by Park's fluency with things illicit. "How soon, do you think?"

"Look, I'm not a miracle worker. Good quality takes time."

"What about the deputy ambassador. Has he caught on yet?"

There was a pause on the phone, as though Park had become momentarily distracted.

"Don't worry about the old man. I've got you covered," Park said.

Han felt a pang of gratitude. Tears welled up in his eyes. "Jun-Young. I don't know how I'm going to repay this debt to you," Han said, his voice quivering.

"Don't be stupid," Park said and rushed him off the phone.

Han felt embarrassed by the abrupt end to the conversation, and he was left to wonder through the restless night in the jail cell whether he had been too sentimental.

He found himself contemplating the day before his life had turned upside down; swept away, as his umbrella had been on that fickle gust of wind that smelled like the ocean on that night he and the other visitors had shuffled out of Ambassador Kim's hospital room.

They told the old man that the drink of choice for their impromptu gathering would be beer. The ambassador seemed crushed that he couldn't join them. If he hadn't been tethered to an IV, he would have hobbled out of there with them. He craned his neck to get a parting glimpse of them going out the door and called out to Kwon. "Drink some for me," he said forlornly.

Beer was just the beginning, though. In the course of toasting one another's health, they soon switched to soju, its harder edge better suited to the barbequed ribs and *bulgogi*. The smoke and sizzle of marinated beef on the tabletop grill demanded soju, its punch being a perfect palate cleanser between morsels.

Choi, the local businessman, had enthusiastically offered to pick up the tab. It was a rare treat for Han, Park and Deputy Ambassador Kwon. The people at the Mission so rarely dined out. Most of them packed their lunches from home to avoid having to pay the scandalous Manhattan prices. The three diplomats enthusiastically partook of the feast, even though Kwon was in practice a joyless eater. He shoveled food into his mouth as though famished and gave no hint that he tasted any of it. Kwon's face glowed red with alcohol and his complexion was better for it. Han's face, on the other hand, never got red when he drank. That had been a mixed blessing for him over the years. It earned him a reputation that he could hold his liquor, even though the effect was largely cosmetic. The downside was that his drinking partners sometimes branded him reluctant or incapable of letting himself get drunk. *You're too cautious, Dr. Han. You should let yourself go every now and then,* they would say as they badgered him to have another drink, radiating affability with flushed faces. As a younger man, Han had tried to shed this impression of himself as overly concerned with self-control. He at times drank more fiercely than others to prove his point. Over the years he grew weary of trying to prove them wrong.

Han looked younger than his years, due in part to his thick head of hair, unruly as it was. When he was a child, his nickname was *Bamsongee*, or "chestnut" – a reference to the way his hair would stand up like spiky bristles. The effect was amplified by the way his mother insisted on keeping his hair at a length too short to tame with gravity.

In addition to his aptitude for back kicks, he discovered a knack for push-ups and chin-ups when he was in the army. That prompted him to practice even more on his own time. He did it for the same reason that any young man concentrates on things at which they excel – it earns them recognition among their peers. An unintentional yet natural consequence was that it made him rather muscular, in a wiry way unlike the bulky physiques of western bodybuilders. His slender build reflected his self-denial.

Choi kept refilling Han's glass with soju. And, as was the custom, Choi insisted that Han empty his glass completely before each refill.

The custom mostly allowed the senior members of the drinking party to hasten their juniors' pace. Not entirely emptying one's glass was a signal that you were not ready for another refill. But it could be ignored by seniors if they wished. And no one refilled their own glasses. Only alcoholics and dead-end loners poured their own drinks.

By the time they stumbled out onto 32nd St. they were bracing themselves against one another to steady themselves. As they composed themselves to say goodnight, they milled about on the sidewalk among the detritus of a day's worth of commerce – piles of garbage bags and bundled cords of collapsed boxes.

"I'd feel a bit sad to end the night like this," Choi said. "When are we ever going to have an opportunity to meet like this again?"

He checked his watch. "The night's still young. How about a second round, eh?" Choi said, his lips a little numb with the soju. Now that he was good and soused, his childhood Hamkyong accent started to leak out.

The clergyman politely excused himself at this point and after he was out of earshot, Choi said: "I know this fun little place only a few blocks from here. Liquor tastes a little better when a pretty girl is pouring it for you, no?"

The three diplomats paused momentarily and looked at one another. An evening at a room salon could easily run up a bill of $1,000 a head. As if sensing their reluctance, Choi reassured them. "Don't worry about that. I'll take care of everything tonight."

"We couldn't impose on you any more than we already have," Kwon said. "You've already done so much for us."

"Nonsense. It's no imposition at all. As I said, when are we going to have an opportunity like this again?"

Kwon declined ceremoniously one more time before relenting. And being the most senior of the three diplomats, that meant Park and Han had relented by default.

"It's decided then. I'll tell them to get ready for us," Choi said and excused himself to make a phone call.

Kwon patted his pockets looking for cigarettes. He reached into one of his outside jacket pockets and instead of cigarettes, he pulled out the envelope he had received from Choi in the hospital room, now crinkled and a bit damp. Park had told him earlier that the local Korean-Americans had raised enough money for the ambassador not to worry about his medical bills, but he didn't know the exact amount. The envelope wasn't sealed, so he lifted the flap and peeked at the check after discreetly checking that Choi wasn't around. It was in the amount of $50,000. He nodded and put the envelope back into his pocket.

He patted down some other pockets for cigarettes and turned up empty. "Give me a cigarette, will you, Consul Park," Kwon said.

Park tapped one out of the pack and also lit it for him. Kwon took a deep, long drag and exhaled high into the air.

"This man used to live in a village just a few hours on foot from mine. Now we meet here, of all places," Kwon said. "As a merchant, he's done well for himself selling groceries."

The centuries-old prejudice against merchants was reinforced in the communist North by its hostility to the bourgeoisie.

"Are you still upset about getting a hand-out?" Han said.

Kwon squinted at Han through his cigarette smoke. "That smart mouth of yours is going to get you into trouble one of these days," he said.

Park cut off the conversation when he saw Choi returning. The man's tie was crooked and he couldn't walk a straight line. He had a mischievous grin on his face.

"Let's go have some tasty liquor, shall we?" Choi said, pushing the others forward.

As Han sat in jail, it seemed unbelievable to him that it had been barely two days ago. The dark came slowly in the cell, the way dew falls, and Han found no refuge from his thoughts.

Chapter 18

The ache in James Avery's neck woke him up at four in the morning. It had turned into a throbbing knot that wouldn't let him turn his head to the left. He had been dreaming that he was swimming in molasses. As soon as he crawled his way out of one pool, he fell into another. And a giant version of himself was watching from overhead. Each time he turned his head to take a breath, pain shot through his spine. That's when he woke up.

Avery tried to go back to sleep but it was useless. He lifted himself off the bed at an awkward angle using his arms and then stood in front of a mirror, grimacing each time his chin approached his left shoulder. This knot wouldn't go away without some deep heat. He was up anyway, so Avery went to a sauna in Manhattan's Koreatown that he knew was open around the clock. He was the only white guy soaking in the hot pool at that hour, and seemingly the only one who had gotten any sleep, however unsatisfying. For everyone else, this was probably the last stop in a night of pub-crawling. Thirty-second Street catered to those one-stop shoppers who didn't want to venture far: Start with dinner, second round at one of the bars, third round at one of the karaoke joints, late-night chow at one of the 24-hour restaurants, and then soak out some of the alcohol at the sauna.

By the time Avery walked onto the street, his cheeks were an alarming pink, but he could turn his head with only mild discomfort. The sun was just beginning to rise through some clouds. Avery could tell it would be a warm day for September. He had changed into his suit, and was beginning to regret it because he was still sweating from the residual heat from the sauna. The collar of his shirt was already damp. He undid the top button and was moving his head from side to side to loosen his collar when one of the Korean-language newspapers caught his eye.

The headline read: "Four local Korean churchgoers slain." And the sub-head was: "Fort Lee minister and wife slashed; Flushing couple shot."

Avery grabbed that paper and started reading it in front of the newsstand. The vendor shouted out, "Quarter! Quarter!" until Avery fished a ten-dollar bill out of his pocket. The annoyed vendor asked him if he had anything smaller. Avery snatched up copies of all the daily newspapers and walked off without waiting for change. The vendor shouted after him to take his change.

The article's tone was spare and to the point.

The Rev. Baek Sang-Min, 67, pastor of the Hanwoori Church in Fort Lee, N.J., and his wife, Kim Ok-Soon, 62, were found slashed to death in their home yesterday, just hours after two members of a Flushing church were found slain in their home, police said.

Koh Pil-Yoon, 54, and his wife, Lee Jung-Sook, 50 — both members of the Bethel Baptist Congregation in Flushing — were shot to death at their Flushing home, police said.

The Rev. Baek, a member of the Fort Lee Board of Education, was also known for his efforts through his church for famine relief in North Korea.

The grisly scene was discovered by a church staff member who went to Baek's home at about 5 p.m. after trying to reach the pastor all day, police said. The victims were tied to chairs and their throats had been slashed, a law enforcement source said.

Avery hadn't realized until then that Mrs. Koh's maiden name was Lee. She had apparently embraced the Western custom of adopting her husband's last name. He skimmed over the parts about Baek's biography and the anguished quotes of parishioners mourning the loss of their pastor and his wife.

An eerily similar case played out in Flushing earlier yesterday when an employee at Koh's bodega in Manhattan discovered Koh and his wife at their home after being concerned about their whereabouts, police said.

Koh and his wife were shot multiple times, including execution-style shots to the head, a source familiar with the case said. The house was ransacked, but it was unclear what had been taken, a family member said.

The Daily News, *The Times* and *The Post* all had articles of varying length about the Kohs. None of them spilled any ink about the Fort Lee minister and his wife. In the calculus of local media, that was a non-story. If it happened across the Hudson, it might as well have happened in Kansas. Two different cases in two different jurisdictions with two different methods. The only thing linking the two cases was the fact that the victims were Korean Christians. Even the article in the Korean-language paper did not suggest a link beyond that.

Avery went to the nearest pay phone and called Finister to tell him about the Fort Lee case.

"You thinking what I'm thinking?" Avery asked. "Can you pull the recent phone records from the Kohs' house when you get to the precinct?"

"Got 'em right here."

"Talk about taking your work home with you."

"Nah, my wife would kill me. I'm at the office."

Avery looked at his watch. It was just past 6 a.m. "And I thought *I* was obsessive,"

"I know. Tell me about it. It's a curse," Finister said. "Let's take a look here."

Avery heard paper rustling over the phone. He imagined Finister sitting at a desk piled high with files, save for a spot for the typewriter.

"Yup. Bunch of calls to and from 201 area code numbers, plus all the calls to South Korea, a few to China even. They racked up quite a bill this month. Lemme find out who these 201 numbers belong to."

"Page me if I'm not at the office," Avery said.

Avery's mind was racing, playing out the permutations of possibilities if the two cases were indeed linked. If the Kohs' residence and the Rev. Baek's home were two stops on an underground railroad that Han was using to defect, then it appeared that someone was on his tracks.

"We need to take a closer look at this Consul Park Jun-Young character. I'll ask our guys at INR to see what they can dig up on him," Avery said.

"INR?"

"Sorry. Intelligence and Research."

"You guys have your own spooks?"

"Everybody has their own spooks. We like to think of ours as gentlemen spooks. You know, tweed jackets and sweaters."

"Sounds like a bunch of Ivy League old boys," Finister said.

"You're smarter than you look, Jack," Avery said and heard a bemused grunt over the phone. "It's the old pipelines. They keep making 'em and we keep taking 'em. Discretion is bred into them. And if there's something I've learned about the privileged in any country: Crooked business dealings? No problem. Gambling habit? Look the other way. Mistress? That's almost a pre-requisite.

"That's the one thing, Jack. If your suspect is someone at the DPRK Mission, I'm afraid you might be digging a dry well. You can forget a collar. The most that'll happen is they get kicked out of the country."

"I just wanna see the creep responsible for this taken out of circulation," Finister said. "If he gets sent to the big house or his home country, still gets him off *my* streets. That's all I care about. I'll call Federal Plaza."

After Avery hung up, he stood by the phone, holding onto the receiver for some time, immobilized by thought. If Han *was* defecting and he had made overtures to State, chances were that Avery would have heard about it. But Han's contact didn't necessarily have to be someone at State. It could have been any number of people at half a dozen agencies. With so many moving parts that spoke to one another only on the most cosmetic of levels, it was impossible to tell who knew exactly what, even if you were ostensibly batting for the same team. Most calamities in an organization of any appreciable size are not the result of any one person dropping the ball. Small mistakes and banal neglect have a way of accumulating.

Avery's neck began to ache again. He had worked up a sweat for nothing.

* * *

Back at his office, Avery managed to get his hands on Park Jun-Young's dossier. The only item in his thin file that Avery found even remotely interesting was a notation that Park had traveled several times to Macao. A State Department analyst based in Rosslyn, Virginia, had remarked, matter-of-factly and without any sense of urgency, that Park's travels to Macao could bear looking into in the future, if the opportunity arose, because it was a known hub of money laundering and "because DPRK's foreign personnel are operating in an increasingly unfavorable financial environment." Translation: North Korea was strapped for cash, and Park could be laundering money in Macao to fund its struggling foreign diplomats. Park could easily blend in with the day-trippers from the Pearl River delta or Hong Kong. If in fact the DPRK was laundering money there, they could find themselves in even more dire financial straits after Portugal returned Macao to Chinese rule in a couple of years.

If the U.S. government could prove that Park was funneling ill-gotten gains into the U.S., the State Department could expel him for what they would euphemistically call "violating his privilege of residency."

That would take time; too much time to be of any use to Han if he was indeed on the run from Park. Avery concluded the key was to tail Park. This was beyond Finister now. It was time to call in some favors.

Chapter 19

Park Jun-Young had known Jenny for more than a year, but he never had the occasion to visit her apartment before. Even after they became lovers, Jenny's place remained off limits, like the backstage of a theater was to outsiders. Jenny never invited Park home and Park never asked to be. There was the practical reason that she had a roommate. There was also her line of work. When one entertains the opposite sex for a living, feigning intimacy, one needs a sanctuary to unravel that persona. Entering that private space isn't like entering any other person's home. It's an intrusion into their inner sanctum.

Now that Park was in her apartment, he felt a voyeuristic thrill in seeing the articles of her unvarnished life – the dishes in the sink, her pajamas, and her bed, adorned with a menagerie of stuffed animals. But the more he took in the banality of it, the more the thrill turned into something sad. The space was discordant with what he knew of her, at the room salon or even on their trysts on neutral territory. He started feeling a twinge of guilt.

Jenny came out of the bathroom with wet bangs of hair framing her reddened face. She was sniffling as she toweled off. Park couldn't tell whether she had been crying. She hung the towel to dry on the bed frame and turned to him. They looked at one another for some time without saying a word. She walked over to him, put her arms around his neck and buried her face in his chest. Park put his hands on her midriff. He liked the feel of her hips flaring out from her slender waist. He moved his hands up her torso, riding the peaks and valleys of flesh over her ribs, lifting up her t-shirt with them. She raised her arms straight up and let him undress her, resigned to his desire though she had none herself, except a need for comfort.

His thrusts were urgent and hungry, as they used to be when they first became lovers. Instead of the anonymous scent of hotel sheets, the bedding was suffused with her essence. The stuffed toys fell to the floor in ones and twos like despondent jumpers. Park was never really a tender lover. Today he was particularly ferocious. She cried out, then gasped for air as she felt his weight bear down on her just before he climaxed. Everywhere he buried his face – the pillows, the comforter, the sheets – he could smell traces of that Chanel perfume she favored, the one he bought for her.

When Park returned from the bathroom, Jenny was prostrate on the bed, her face buried in a pillow. He rolled her over to kiss her. She was weeping.

Park was taken aback. "What's the matter?" he asked.

"I'm sorry," she said, rolling away from him.

"For what?"

"I know how important this was. I've messed up the whole thing. What's going to happen to Dr. Han now?"

"Nothing, I hope. You're going to bail him out of jail."

She turned back to face him, tears still welling from the corners of her eyes. "What do you mean? Isn't he going to get sent back home now? Back to Pyongyang?"

"Not if you bail him out. You want to make this right, don't you?" Park said, wiping her tears away with his fingers. "You're the only one who can get him out of there. You know I can't go there myself."

Jenny sat up in bed and curled up under the comforter as though she were watching a scary movie. "So you made him a fake passport?"

"A very good one."

"What if I get into trouble for it?"

"You won't. They won't know the difference."

Jenny suddenly regretted having had sex with Park in her own bed. It felt like he had spoiled a moment that no one could ever make right. It was the feeling of telling someone you loved them, but the confession was unreciprocated.

"I really can't afford to get into trouble with the law, *oppa*. You know that, don't you? I've already overstayed my visa. I can't go back to Korea. I'd rather die than have to go back."

"Don't talk nonsense," Park said. "I told you, you won't get into trouble. Look, I need you if I'm going to clear this up. I can't do it without you."

Jenny hated it when people tried to talk her into doing things she didn't want to. In high school, her best friend talked her into playing hooky to go on a double date. When Jenny refused, her friend wore her down for three days until she said yes. Jenny's date turned out to be a gangly, awkward boy, smothered in oversized clothes that his mother had obviously bought for him with the expectation that he would grow into them, and with a face erupting with acne. That wasn't the worst of it. Someone from their school apparently saw them roaming the streets of Seoul on the day they were supposed to be sick. Jenny's parents were notified. Any punishment the teachers could have meted out paled in comparison with the withering rebuke her parents delivered. Jenny was no longer close friends with her after that. In fact, they hardly exchanged two words for the rest of high school.

Park tossed the passport onto the bed. Jenny picked it up and opened it to the photo page. There he was, Han Chol-Soo, peering out, unsmiling, in a tie and jacket, masquerading as one Kim Kwang-Il, a citizen of the Republic of Korea. Jenny wondered, why did these guys all turn into mirthless automatons whenever they got their pictures taken?

Park tossed something else onto the same spot on the bed--another envelope. Jenny knew instantly what it was. She didn't reach for it. It sat in the bottom of a crater in the down comforter, like a fat stone tossed onto loose sand.

"If it's a matter of money, I can get you a little more than what's there," Park said as he started dressing.

An old Chinese adage came to Jenny's mind: *To see something is to covet it.* Jenny closed her eyes. So loathsome, this temptation; even more loathsome, this want. She wished to be clear of it, this whole mess *and* the money.

"You really don't think much of me, do you?" Jenny said forlornly, tossing the passport on top of the envelope and gently kicking them from under the covers.

"Jin-Hee, why would you say that?" Park said, deliberately using her non-Anglicized name to ply his intimacy on her. "I know you need the money and I need you. We can help each other out."

"Would you go to these lengths if *I* was in trouble," Jenny asked, then quickly added, "No. Don't answer that."

She threw the covers off and grabbed the passport and envelope with gusto in one hand and a gown in the other. The final verse of the poem "Azaleas" popped into her head – the poem she had so earnestly recited to Han before their road trip had taken a turn for the worse.

"I shall die before I shed a single tear," she breathed into her gown as she walked naked to the bathroom.

* * *

The sunlight was broad and warm when Park stepped out of Jenny's house onto the quiet street in Flushing. A sheen of sweat instantly formed on his forehead, fueled by the carnal heat that had yet to dissipate.

At the end of the block, he passed a drab, two-story commercial building topped with an unlit neon crucifix jutting into the sky. Each of the window panels on the upper floor was pasted over with a silvery material with cutaway Korean characters forming the name of the church.

Park wiped the sweat from his face with the palm of his hand and was suddenly overcome with a sense of loneliness, and then paranoia. It was as though a close friend had left him, and then remained at a distance to watch him. The sensation was peculiar enough to make him stop in his tracks and take stock of his surroundings, as someone lost in the woods might do to reorient oneself.

It dawned on him that he recognized one of the men he had just passed on the street. He never forgot a face. A white man, with curly brown hair, in a dark suit, on a quiet residential street in Flushing in the middle of the day. He was out of place. When Park looked for him again, the man was all the way at the other end of the block, turning a corner. Park chased after him. By the time he reached the corner, he had lost sight of him. He felt himself become impatient with the rising irritation of a clumsy hunter who has startled an easy target. An old Asian lady with a wire shopping-cart approached him.

"Did you see a white man in a suit coming down that way?" Park asked her in Korean.

The old lady looked at him askew and veered away from him.

It took Park Jun-Young a couple of hours to return to his office in Manhattan. He took wild detours in hopes of catching someone on his tail. He saw no one. That only made him more paranoid, because it's what you *can't* see that can hurt you. He called Jenny from a pay phone a few blocks from the Mission on Second Avenue, hoping to warn her of possible tails as well. She wasn't picking up. Park surmised she was probably already on her way back to Virginia.

When Park got off on the thirteenth floor and walked into the office, Deputy Ambassador Kwon Woo-Shik was standing in the main hallway, staring him down as though he had been waiting there all day. As soon as he saw Park, he turned around and headed for the Faraday cage – a signal to Park that he should follow him.

As soon as Park closed the door to the cage, the transistor radio that was kept there went silent. The air inside always tasted different to Park – acidic, as though he were tasting particles of copper coming off the mesh.

"Events have taken a troublesome turn, deputy ambassador," Park said.

"Yes?" Kwon said, his tone unsettlingly friendly.

Park told him where Han was, and what he was doing to try to get him out. Kwon was unperturbed.

"You trust this woman of yours?" Kwon asked.

"As much as you can trust anyone with mercenary motives."

"From all you've told me, that doesn't seem to be her primary reason. She likes you, right? No matter. It works to your advantage. The question is whether we should be relying on her to solve our problems."

"It's the cleanest way," Park said. "It gives us some cover."

"No, Consul Park. The cleanest way to solve a problem is to get to the root of it. What would you say is the root of *this* problem?"

Park wished it wasn't so quiet in the cage. He could hear himself breathe as he searched for an answer.

"That would be comrade Han's wife," Park said finally.

"I agree. This woman of yours – she told you where Dr. Han's wife is in Virginia, yes?"

Park nodded.

"Perhaps you should get to the root of the problem yourself then," Kwon said.

"Deputy ambassador, there could be another problem," Park said.

Kwon looked at Park incredulously. Park wished he could hide somewhere. "I can't be one hundred percent sure, but I think I might have been followed by someone when I went to Ryu Jin-Hee's home."

Kwon got out of his chair and stood in front of Park. Without warning, he slapped Park hard across the face. Park noted how the sound did not echo at all in the cage, despite how firm the strike had been.

"Enough of this toying around! Comrade Han and his family are as good as dead anyway. Clean up this mess, now!" Kwon said and walked out of the cage.

Chapter 20

The courthouse where Han Chol-Soo was being arraigned was a prim, red-brick building with white gables and a white steeple. It seemed more like a church to Jenny. Lush lawns and bushes framed the building, and a prosperous dogwood arched toward the diminutive colonnade facing the quiet, two-lane street. A sweet scent of flowers drifted on the air. It seemed strange to Jenny that such an idyllic place would even need a courthouse.

The receptionist was bizarrely friendly, even as she seemed to be suffering from an allergy that made her cheeks and nose rise with a rosy glow. But her cheerfulness came too late to lift Jenny's sour mood. It was her first sustained entanglement with the American legal system and she was feeling worn down by it. She had taxed the limits of her English while navigating the unfamiliar bureaucracy between the sheriff's office, the court and the public defender's office, located in an adjacent town. She had taken a detour to the circuit court, further down Main Street, just to learn she was in the wrong place, and was redirected to the district court. At each stage, she feared she also would become ensnared by this byzantine world for her own illicit role.

When a bailiff finally walked Han into the courtroom late in the afternoon, Jenny's eyes welled up with tears of relief. Han nodded to her. The hardwood floor echoed under the bailiff's booted footfalls.

The judge, the prosecutor, the public defender, and the clerk all seemed to be ignoring one another for the most part, doing their own thing, sometimes quietly chatting with other people even as one or the other took turns speaking out. To Jenny, it was a confusing dance of people tuned into different music. The only one who seemed to be paying attention was the court stenographer kneading the mute keyboard.

When the clerk called out for Kwang-Il Kim, the bailiff led Han by the elbow and stood him next to a lectern where the public defender was standing.

The prosecutor, a woman with a pen stuck through a bun in her hair, read out a list of charges: Disorderly conduct, resisting arrest, aggravated assault, two counts. She asked the judge to set the bail at $50,000.

The public defender shifted his weight from foot to foot, flexing his free ankle each time as though he were nursing some injury.

"Resisting arrest? Really, Your Honor," he said, shaking his head. "The People are overreaching, Judge, again. May I remind the court of Monday's case? My client did not resist. He merely had difficulty understanding the deputy's instructions because of a language barrier."

The judge smiled, though he never took his eyes off his desk.

"Judge. Mr. Kim is a foreign national here on a business visa," the prosecutor said.

Before the public defender had a chance to chime in, the judge interjected. "Then he should know the value of money," he said. "Bail set at twenty thousand."

Jenny noted the prosecutor didn't seem perturbed at all. She drew the pen from her hair, made a mark in the folder, handed it over to the clerk, and then picked up another folder.

When Han was released into the hallway where Jenny was waiting, he seemed unsure of where to place his eyes, and he kept on looking at his feet.

"Live long enough and who knows what you'll see," Han said, managing a strained smile. "Well, at least it's over."

"Not quite, I'm afraid," Jenny said. Her hand was shaking.

Han's smile evaporated. "What do you mean?"

"I called Jun-Young *oppa* to let him know you were being released. Then he told me that someone might have followed me here."

"Who?"

Jenny led Han to one of the windows looking out onto the parking lot, making sure they stood behind the wall. "Do you see the black car at the far end? I think it followed me from New York."

Han peered around the edge of the window. He saw a man in the car. There was a scowl etched into his face. It seemed the act of waiting hours upon hours did not agree with him. The layer of air in contact with the hood shimmered in the late Virginia sun.

Han retreated and pressed his back against the cool wall. "It's mountain after mountain, isn't it?" he said, using a saying that described how obstacles besiege the already put-upon.

"What are we going to do?"

"Where's your car?"

"It's in the middle of the lot. He's looking right at it. I think there's another guy at the front entrance as well."

"Are you *sure* they followed you?"

"No. Maybe. I don't know," Jenny said, frowning. "I'm not sure about anything anymore."

A woman walked by them in the hallway. She gave a sympathetic nod, as though she understood Jenny's anguish implicitly, and then politely averted her gaze. The hallway was full of whispering voices. Han took Jenny's shoulders and took her to a quiet corner.

"There's only one way to find out," Han said. "Why don't you drive away and see if they follow you. Then double back here. If they're not following you any more, then you can pick me up."

"What if they are?"

"Then just leave me here. I'll find a way to get back by myself."

Han got a wad of cash from Jenny and sent her on her way. Just as he was about to lose sight of her around the corner, she turned around and stood there a moment. Then she said matter-of-factly, "I should think this will be the last time I'll see you."

Han was momentarily stunned by her adieu. Before he could muster a response, she turned away as abruptly as she had faced him and disappeared around the corner. He wanted to call her back, but he did not. Moments later, he watched her get into her rental car. She didn't even have to drive away for Han to know that the man in the black car was indeed following her. He perked up in his seat when he saw her, the scowl on his face briefly gone. Then another man hurriedly walked to the car and got in. They took off after her.

Mountain after mountain, he said to himself. There was no point waiting for Jenny's return.

* * *

It was no fault of the agents that they didn't apprehend Han. They had no reason to. They didn't even know what business this woman Jenny Ryu had at a courthouse in some podunk town in rural Virginia, let alone who Han Chol-Soo was. They had been given instructions simply to follow Jenny and not to lose her. That's what they did. So it was a surprise to them when they radioed in to the New York office to give an update that they ended up getting chewed out by the special agent in charge. They were at the tail end of the command chain, so they were working blind. They couldn't have known that the gears of the bureaucracy were winding up, with mid-level functionaries in half-a-dozen agencies all busily staking out their turf.

The special agent in charge screamed at them, "Jesus Christ! Why the hell didn't you check what she was doing in the courthouse?" He told them to bring Jenny in.

When they pulled Jenny over on the side of Route 29, she was a savage little thing – all fight and no reason. A thunderstorm had rolled in from nowhere. By the time the two agents subdued the writhing, kicking beast and got her into the back of their car, all three of them were soaked through. She looked like a feral cat plucked from the verge of drowning, eyes aglow through her dripping hair.

Chapter 21

James Avery could see that Jenny, disheveled as she now was and overtaken by sadness, was a pretty girl. If she had been wearing any makeup, it had been wiped away while drying herself off with the towel now crumpled in her lap. What remained was a mess of damp hair and bare arms, translucent under the bright lights and drooping at her sides like the branches of weeping willows.

Avery sat in the corner of the conference room, watching and listening to the FBI agents grilling her with the help of an interpreter. They lingered on her every word. Much of casual speech is inconsistent even when a speaker is not under duress. Jenny's was malformed even further by hostile scrutiny and the subtleties lost in translation. Her eyes met Avery's occasionally. They were full of frustration. It didn't take him long to see that hers was a fragile beauty, susceptible to the whims of angles and lighting, and the thoughts that emerged unfiltered onto her face. He looked down at the floor now and again, displeased with the translations he was hearing, yet he refrained from butting in.

As the agents grew testier, she volunteered less information. She was naturally inclined to helpfulness, but when her foibles were met with rebuke rather than good humor, as she was used to among drunken clients at the room salon, what leaning she had felt to cooperate disappeared. When they threatened her with deportation, she turned mute and her arms stiffened like damp rope.

Avery tapped the senior agent on the elbow and casually invited him out of the room for a chat. They spoke out of earshot and out of view of the conference room, near a window with a slim view of the Potomac.

"Mind if I have a go?" Avery asked good-naturedly. "I speak the language."

The agent glanced at the conference room and his expression said it all: This interrogation had run out of steam. "Knock yourself out," he said.

Avery walked down the hall to a vending machine and bought two bottles of water. He returned to the conference room and put one on the table in front of Jenny.

"You must be thirsty," Avery said in Korean and pushed the bottle toward her. He used the mild honorific speech of strangers who could potentially be friends – polite, yet casual.

Jenny gave him the same surprised look that Ambassador Jang Sung-Gil had given him that day in Cairo when they had met in the SUV. Jenny reached for the water.

"Where did you learn Korean?" Jenny asked after taking a sip.

Avery gave her his spiel – the condensed version of his early life. He had it down to a routine, including a few self-deprecating jokes for good measure.

"It's a little bit disconcerting," Jenny said.

It was a sentiment whispered by many Koreans when they encountered him speaking their language so fluently. This was the first time anyone had actually expressed it to him so early into a conversation.

"You're very frank," Avery said.

"Too much for my own good," she said.

"You have to live with the face you're given, right?" Avery said, using a catchphrase popularized by a Korean comedian.

Jenny cracked a smile.

Humor seemed to make her more malleable. Avery introduced himself, emphasizing he was not a cop and not with the FBI or any other law enforcement agency, and explained the situation she was in.

"What's that saying? 'A fight between whales breaks the shrimp's back,'" Avery said. "I'm afraid you're the shrimp in this proverb, Ms.

Ryu Jin-Hee." He remained polite. Humor and reason. "It's not *you* they want. You've just gotten tangled up in something that has very high stakes for some powerful people."

"I was just trying to help," she said. "If I'd known I'd end up like this, I would never have agreed to do it."

"Agree to do what?"

Jenny stared into the bottle of water as though it were bottomless. She finally said: "I came to America to make a clean start, but I can't seem to catch a break. There's nothing for me in Korea, except bad memories. I can't bear the thought of going back. Can you understand that?"

Avery thought of Kyunghee and remembered the urge to run away after she died. At first it was enough to escape that hospital room where her last exhale lingered. Then he could not bear even being near the hospital, then that neighborhood. His grief kept claiming wider territory. He took circuitous routes to avoid it, like a bullied child takes the long way home.

"As a matter of fact, I can," Avery said. "My fiancée died of cancer in Seoul a few months before we were supposed to get married. I couldn't quite bring myself to settle down there. I think I'm doomed to roam around the world."

Avery and Jenny looked at one another in silence for a while, each examining the other's face.

"Are you over it now?" she asked.

Avery shrugged. "Quite honestly, I don't know."

"I was engaged too, you know," Jenny said. "In fact, that's why I left Seoul. I guess you and I both didn't have much luck with marriage. Though in my case it wasn't an illness that took away my fiancé but his meddling mother."

"What happened?"

"He was from a good family, pretty rich, too, and she didn't think I lived up to what her son deserved. She thought I was beneath her family. I mean, we're all just human beings, right? She said she'd sooner die than let us get married. And being a good boy, he buckled."

"So you came to America."

"What better place to reinvent yourself. And now I'm here," she said, eyeballing the conference room that now encased her fate. She then looked into Avery's eyes, probing for the measure of the man, searching for something that would speak of his trustworthiness. In the end, it wasn't some halo of enlightenment around Avery's head that convinced Jenny of his integrity. Of all the people she had encountered this day, he had been the kindest to her and she surmised her odds of meeting anyone kinder were quickly dwindling.

"Look, I'll tell you what I know, but I want something in return," Jenny said. "I want to stay in the United States and I don't want to go to jail. Is that possible?"

"I'll find out," Avery said and excused himself from the room with the agent in charge. When he returned, he told Jenny that she had a deal, as long as she told them everything and didn't hold back.

Jenny nodded.

"So what is it that you agreed to do?" Avery asked.

She explained without reservation the details of what Park Jun-Young had asked of her – beginning with how she drove Dr. Han to Virginia in search of his wife and newborn son. For Avery, it was as if a fever had broken, and the mind was suddenly clear to make sense of the confused dreams. He felt elated. His heart began pounding. He wished Detective Finister could have been there. He would have appreciated the dots finally being connected.

"You drove Dr. Han Chol-Soo to Virginia?" Avery asked, trying to mask his excitement. "When?"

"Yesterday. That's the first time I met him."

"Why would you stick your neck out for a stranger like that?"

"Because Jun-Young *oppa* asked me to."

"So Consul Park is trying to help Dr. Han get his wife and son back?"

"Yes."

Avery felt his throat suddenly get dry. He took a sip of water. He had known that something wasn't quite adding up with the scenarios he and Jack Finister were coming up with. This was a possibility that had completely eluded them. It was like one of those brain twisters that required you to shift your perspective to attain the answer – once you knew the solution, it was obvious.

"Tell me step by step what happened, starting from when you met Dr. Han yesterday," Avery said.

As Jenny recounted the last day and a half, Avery stopped her occasionally, waiting for the interpreter to translate to the others in the room. When she got to the part about bailing him out of jail with a fake passport, the special agent in charge groaned audibly and then muttered, "Jesus H. Christ. He was right there!"

"So where is Dr. Han now?" Avery asked.

"I don't know. I left him at the courthouse. I imagine he's trying to get back to New York somehow. He told me it was against the rules for him to travel too far from New York. He's in a lot of trouble, isn't he?"

"Do you know who Koh Jung-Sook is?"

Jenny shook her head.

"What about the Rev. Baek Sang-Min?"

She shook her head again, then immediately corrected herself. "Wait, isn't he a pastor in Fort Lee or something? I think Dr. Han was pretending to be a deacon from his church to find out where his wife was."

Avery waited for the interpreter to finish and then looked around the room to see if the implication of this had registered with the other people. Han was probably involved in at least the death of the pastor and his wife. The interpreter was whispering into the ear of the agent in charge.

"And where is Han's wife?"

"In Virginia, at a house near a town called Charlotte or something."

"Charlotte? You mean in North Carolina?"

"No. It's definitely in Virginia. It's something like Charlotte, but not exactly."

"Charlottesville?"

Jenny clapped once. "Yes! That's it. I have the address written down somewhere. I think it's at my apartment in New York."

The agent in charge told one of the other agents in the room to have her apartment searched.

"Do you really think Dr. Han would return to New York without his wife?" the agent in charge asked Avery.

Avery pondered the question. His face changed several times, like time-lapse footage of a landscape brightening then darkening under shifting light and clouds.

"I really don't know," he said. "I don't know the man well enough to know what's going through his head. He's screwed either way. He won't have a pot to piss in when he gets back to Pyongyang. The question is does *he* know it?"

"So what do you do when a diplomat goes off the reservation like this?" the agent in charge asked.

"Office of Foreign Missions – they're the ones who would handle an expulsion. Or our Inspector General's office."

"Well, sounds like this Dr. Han's AWOL trip to Charlottesville has earned him a one-way ticket to Shitsville instead."

"Maybe, maybe not. This guy is too valuable," Avery said grimly. "We've *got* to turn him. We've got to get him to defect."

Chapter 22

Han Chol-Soo approached the farmhouse from the eastern woods, through a profound darkness – dusk made deeper by the shade of thriving oak and linden. The canopy was so dense in spots that the only light there came horizontally, in faint splinters through the tree trunks up ahead. The ground was plush with years of fallen leaves, fecund with the smell of unrelenting dampness.

"You sure you wanna get off here?" the cab driver had asked when Han told him to let him off at the main road. He was a chatty man. When Han had failed to engage him in small talk, he supplied his own running commentary of every landmark he saw along the way, including a local bed and breakfast that had a hand-painted sign hung underneath the street number declaring "Faulkner Slept Here."

When Han assured the cabbie that he would be fine, the cabbie said, "Suit yourself," as though he felt aggrieved, and left in a hurry with a quick burst of squealing tires.

It was only when Han reached the clearing beyond the woods that he saw the farmhouse, luminous against the tobacco fields that were dark and undulating in the breeze and failing light.

Someone on the edge of the fields was burning a pile of vegetation. The blue smoke rose in a column, reaching as high as the rooftop, and then spread into turbulent swirls that crept across the valley. It suffused the plantation with the scent of honeysuckle and acacia.

It reminded Han of the scent that lingered in his clothes as a child, long after he returned from working the fields with his comrades. The boy smelled the fields again as he took off his shirt to wash himself in the icy well water that his mother had poured into a basin set down in his home's dirt courtyard.

"Don't forget to wash the back of your neck," his mother had told him.

He is a boy, so he does not like to wash. But he listens to his mother and does more than she asks. He lathers up his prickly hair with a bar of soap and, with his eyes closed tight against the stinging, calls to his mother to pour out the basin over his head to rinse off. He's on his hands and feet, his rump high. She starts with the head, then pours the rest of the water over his bare back. He gasps for air against the bracing water and then screams. His mother laughs. He chases her, shaking the water off his head to spray her. He sleeps well that night.

Han paused at the edge of the woods, wondering for a moment what his mother would say if she knew his predicament now. He circled around to the south to put the house between himself and the man silhouetted against the pyre. Han climbed over a hip-high stone wall that seemed but a winter or two away from crumbling into rubble. Then he crossed the open field toward the house in a casual gait so as not to arouse suspicion if someone should spot him. In the meadow, he immediately felt a rise in temperature compared to the dank woods. The farmhouse was larger than it seemed from afar. It was a two-story, wood clapboard structure, with an ample porch that wrapped around two sides.

He climbed the stairs to the porch, taking care to avoid creaky boards. He peered through the windows, half expecting his wife to be in plain view, playing with their son. He saw no one, just the warm glow of lights.

When Han went around to the back of the house, he came upon the hatch that led to the cellar. This would be his entry into the house. He pulled back the bolt, trying as best he could to mask the rusty squeaks. The cellar door was heavy and he almost lost his grip on it as he flipped it open.

Han took two steps down, then he heard a solid, mechanical click behind him. He turned around and found himself staring down the broad muzzle of a double-barreled shotgun. He heard another firm click as the man pointing the shotgun pulled back the second hammer.

"Dr. Han, I presume?" the man said, grinning.

* * *

For someone who had moments before leveled a weapon at an intruder, the man seemed strangely absent of ill will or even agitation. He had a way about him, a preternatural air of calm. He escorted Han into the house and offered him a seat in the study.

"My name is Lawrence Ray Whitaker. Welcome to Janus Farms, Dr. Han," he said as he took the shells out of the shotgun.

Han unintentionally looked at the door, sensing this could be his one chance of escape.

"Don't bother running," Whitaker said, reading Han's intentions. "It's five miles to the nearest town, and they all know me there. One phone call and you'll be in the county jail."

Whitaker leaned the shotgun into the corner of the room. The study was adorned with mementos from all over the world – an Indonesian ebony carving, a pair of Plains Indian moccasins, a Russian nesting doll. And among the knickknacks, a framed black-and-white photo of a much younger version of himself in fatigues, his arm slung around another soldier who looked to be greener still. Whitaker was grinning wide and on the younger man's lips a smile was just beginning to emerge, as if the photographer had pressed the shutter just as a punch line had impressed one and begun to register with the other.

Noticing Han's gaze at his bookshelf, Whitaker said, "Vietnam."

Han nodded and stepped in for a closer look. "He is still a friend?"

"No. He was killed three weeks after that picture was taken," Whitaker said matter-of-factly.

Han meant to express his sympathy and regret. He just ended up clearing his throat and grunting.

Whitaker walked over to a desk and put the shotgun shells into the center drawer. From the same drawer, he took out a pouch of tobacco and a pipe. He donned a pair of reading glasses and took his time loading the shredded leaves, gauging the fill with his thumb several times. He struck a match and began breathing life into the embers. The silver in his hair and beard picked up the glow. Wrinkles on his forehead suggested an angry youth. There was a hint of discontent in his eyes, softened by age.

"Mr. Whitaker. Where is my wife, please?" Han asked.

"She'll be here shortly. She stayed at my sister's place last night. That's a good-looking boy you got, by the way. Very bright."

Han felt like a weight had been lifted off his chest. He was ecstatic and deflated at the same time. Han took in a sharp breath of air. He swallowed hard to choke back the emotions.

"How did you find out they were here?" Whitaker asked.

"Long story. Not easy," Han said.

Whitaker chuckled and said, "I bet it wasn't."

"How did you know who I am?"

"Now, that *was* easy. I don't get too many Asian men trying to sneak into my cellar. I was expecting a visit yesterday from a Deacon Lee from New Jersey, but he won't be coming after all. Apparently someone was impersonating him. And something's happened to the pastor at his church. Something quite terrible," Whitaker said, and took a long puff from his pipe. "You wouldn't happen to know anything about that, would you?"

Han looked down at his feet. "Mr. Whitaker, some day I tell you everything I know."

"Larry. Call me Larry."

"Larry," Han said grudgingly, wondering why Americans felt compelled toward informality. "Most important right now – my wife and son must come back with me to New York. If I don't go back with them, it is very difficult for my family, very dangerous."

When Whitaker peered over his reading glasses, there was no malice or judgment, just the quizzical eyes of a man who wanted to know what was being asked of him.

"It's not up to me, Dr. Han. Besides, we can't do anything until your wife gets here," Whitaker said. "I tell you what – let me give you a quick tour of the farm. She should be back by then. Have you been on a tobacco farm before?"

His tranquil indulgence was maddening. Han tried to say something but Whitaker cut him off.

"C'mon, walk with me," Whitaker said and patted Han on the back amiably. He led him out of the study and down the creaky hallway to the front porch, where Whitaker offered Han some tea that had been left there to clear in the sun. Han refused at first, but upon hearing the ice in a glass brought by one of the farmhands, he realized how thirsty he was.

The encroaching night had stricken color from the land. What remained were mere shades and shapes, save for the brightest hues in the highest reaches: the white trim on the sunward gable of the barn, the youngest shoots on the poplars. The tobacco fields murmured like heavy cloth in the wind, swaying reluctantly.

Han and Whitaker walked the fields a while in silence, the darkness deepening around them. Whitaker would pause every now and then, feeling the broad leaves, smelling them. Han mimicked him. They were moist and pungent. Whitaker spoke of his labor without need to embellish it. The work was straightforward though by no means easy. The only easy thing was the abundance of the farm itself – a fertility long since unfamiliar to Han, an abundance unaided by a corps of conscripted boys or desperate intervention against an unkind nature. The land here seemed less inclined to test a farmer's resolve or industry.

For Workers' Party elites living in exclusive compounds in North Korea, news of the privation that lurked outside the cities came sparingly and it came muted because the messengers rightly feared they would be blamed for the unrelenting bad news. It was purely by chance that Han heard the story of a couple who had been found dead in their home in a farming village, surprisingly, not too far from Pyongyang. No one had stirred in their house for days, so the story went. Perhaps it was a function of the villagers' fatigue – chronic hunger has a way of dulling the mind – that no one bothered to check until it became obvious that something had gone terribly awry. When the villagers finally ventured into the house, they found the husband and wife both dead, tidily tucked side by side under a thick blanket, as though they were warding off the cold, even though it was the middle of summer. Those dying of starvation often complained of feeling chills even in the hottest weather.

What they would have given for even a fraction of the fertility of Janus Farms. In the barn, hogshead casks, each one soon to hold a long ton of tobacco, were neatly stacked in preparation for the harvest. A squat addition to the barn was built around a lathe, a drill press, and a band saw. The workshop was well lit, bright enough to make Han squint when he first entered. Han noticed firmness under his feet and saw that, unlike the rest of the barn, he was standing on a solid concrete floor.

Whitaker explained he became a machinist when he left the Army, retiring as a captain.

"You did not like the military?"

"I left the Army not because I wasn't a good soldier. On the contrary, because I was too good at killing," Whitaker said. "I got too used to seeing the dead, and not really minding. I began to worry for my soul."

He picked up a pencil at a workbench and began to sharpen it freehand with attention to the point. The utility knife was so sharp and his control of the blade so steady that the shavings peeled off in translucent wisps.

"There was a Union general in the Civil War by the name of James Garfield. He later became our twentieth president." Whitaker said. "I read something about what the war did to him, as a human being, that is. The description stuck with me. The writer said Garfield lost the sense of the sanctity of life and the deep prohibition against taking it. I was afraid that was happening to me."

Befitting a man whose work measured tolerances in thousandths of inches, Whitaker moved with quiet assuredness and few superfluous movements. "I can't stand dull tools and dull pencils," Whitaker said. He blew the last shaving off the tip and admired his handiwork.

"Why did you become a farmer?" Han asked.

"The eyes – not what they used to be, you know," Whitaker said. "Truth be told, I inherited the farm from my uncle. He didn't have kids of his own. He wanted to keep it in the family. I remember coming here as a boy and playing hide and seek in the fields with my sister. When I returned from the war the farm was a refuge for me. I didn't like being around people much. Not a lot made sense back then, except making things and growing things – that made sense to me. And you? Why did you decide to become a diplomat? Your wife tells me you used to be a physicist."

"My brain – not what it used to be," Han said, pointing to his head.

Whitaker smiled. Han smiled back, embarrassed a little.

"May I ask, Mr. Whitaker ..."

"Larry."

"Yes, Larry." Han still found it awkward to call a man significantly older than himself by his first name, even an American. "May I ask, Larry, why do you help the Korean Christians?"

"Quite simply, I am sympathetic to their cause."

"Cause?"

"I believe in what they are doing."

"They are against my country. They are hurting my family."

"I think they would say they're trying to *help* your countrymen, and your wife and son."

"Do you know we have a daughter in Pyongyang? If my wife does not come back with me, my daughter's life – it's finished."

Whitaker nodded. "Yes, your wife told me about it the first night she arrived here. She cried terribly. It's heartbreaking. I can't even imagine."

Han was grasping for words. His mouth moved, but no words came out. He finally said: "I can't believe what she has done."

"Why do you think she ran away?" Whitaker asked. It was an earnest question.

"I have asked myself that," Han said. "That is all I think about for the last two days. I want to know myself."

Han ran his hand across the lathe. It was an old machine, but the silkiness of its surfaces suggested it was in good working order. The chip pan was swept clean. This Whitaker was a fastidious man. Perhaps it was this nature that had attracted him to being a machinist, or perhaps that job brought out that quality in him.

"If you tell me you had nothing to do with that nasty business up in Fort Lee, I'll believe you," Whitaker said. "Did you kill that minster?"

"No," Han said, and looking Whitaker in the eye, he added gravely, "but I am responsible for it."

It felt good not having to lie. Lying required so much concentration, so much energy, especially when there were so many of them to keep track of. One must invent lies to cover other lies. It felt safe to confide in a stranger. It helped that it was dark outside, heavy, like a blanket.

"I appreciate your candor," Whitaker said. "As I said, I'm helping out the church group because I'm sympathetic to their cause, but I'm not a zealot. And I sure would hate to think I played a part in breaking up a man's family. I've done a lot of stupid things in my time. I reckon I don't want to add family-wrecker to that list. I really hope you and your wife can work something out."

He was a man at ease with his body and at ease with his past. He was a man at ease with his intellect as only someone who had discovered the joys of it late in life could be. He was learned without the authoritarian streak that made some academics prickly in defense of their own narrow expertise.

When Han and Whitaker came out of the barn, the night was full and coarse. Han looked up at the sky and was struck by how many stars he could see in spite of the humid air that clung and pressed into him. The chorus of insects and the rustle of the leaves enveloped him, coming as much from the heavens as the darkness that lay beyond the reach of the house lights. The stars themselves were singing in the firmament, oscillating in sympathy through the ripples of a churning summer atmosphere with the plaintive calls and mechanical chirps of life lurking in the undergrowth.

Through that, a light came shining through– headlights of a vehicle coming down the dirt road toward the farmhouse.

Chapter 23

In the two days that Han Chol-Soo had not seen his wife, she had changed her hairstyle radically. She had lopped off her ponytail and now she had a bob, full and layered. It made her look younger, or perhaps it was that she seemed less tired. Han had to study her face for a moment when she stepped out of the pickup truck before he was sure it was her. At the mere sight of her his face returned to its habitual expressions of worry and guilt. She froze when she saw him. She was clutching a blanket-swaddled bundle. Han saw a baby's hand reach up and flex its fingers.

After Han was posted to the U.N. and his wife joined him in New York shortly thereafter, she had gone through a phase of experimenting with her hair, presumably inspired by the daily parade of examples she saw on the streets and abetted by the endless choices of cosmetics and beauty products newly available to her. The ones she could afford were from the brightly lit aisles of the neighborhood drug stores; the ones she looked at only were arrayed in the counters at Saks, illuminated with indirect lighting that elevated them to the status of art objects. She was like a teenage girl who had just discovered boys and the influence of her appearance on them. Only when she changed her hairstyle for the third time in as many weeks did Han let on that he noticed, and not to compliment her, but to caution her against conspicuous changes, lest the other diplomats' wives at the Mission start gossiping about how she was deviating from the officially approved styles spelled out by Pyongyang. He had interpreted her silence at the time as obedient acquiescence. However, the silence was just her way of exerting her own will. It wasn't the first time a man had been blinded by his own ego. As Han stood by the farmhouse, facing his wife going through the latest stage of her metamorphosis, he finally recognized the seeds of her defiance in that calm stare.

"It's me. It's Won-Sook's dad," Han said, using the Korean convention of referring to oneself through one's familial relationships. In this case, he used his daughter's name. Perhaps it would remind his wife of whom she was putting in jeopardy.

"Very clever of you to have tracked me down," she said, squeezing the blanket bundle closer into her bosom. The boy began to squirm and fuss.

"How's Won-Kyu?" Han asked.

"He's fine. He's been crying in the car. He's sleepy."

"How are *you*?"

She was momentarily stumped. It was the first time he'd asked that in a long while. "It's a bit late to be asking me that, don't you think?" she said. "Why are you here?"

A porch light came on behind Han, and for a moment he saw his wife's eyes sparkle, possibly with tears, before she looked down at the baby.

"What do you mean, 'Why are you here?' What kind of question is that? I'm here for you and Won-Kyu, of course," Han said. "It's still not too late. We'll probably have to return to Pyongyang. At least we'll be together as a family."

She looked over to where Whitaker was standing, appealing to him, as it were, to end this uncomfortable standoff. Won-kyu began crying.

"Look, why don't you let her put him to bed. Then we can sit and talk about this," Whitaker said. He took her elbow and walked her into the house, passing between Han and his wife.

* * *

Whitaker asked Han to wait in the room across the hall from where his wife was putting Won-Kyu to sleep. Han sat on the edge of a bed, staring at the door and listening to the muted sounds through it – his son's crying, slowly diminishing in urgency; casual footsteps echoing up and down the hallway; the shifting of an aging house in the wind.

Out of the corner of his eye, he saw a bright patch on the floor next to the bed, and he first thought there was a spotlight shining into the room. He looked out the window for the source and saw that it was actually the moon – waxing gibbous so brightly that it cast jagged shadows all across the landscape. He couldn't remember the last time he had looked at the moon – really looked at it. It rivaled those luminous moons over Pyongyang when the electric grid was powered down for the night. He extended his hand into the ghostly beam of light and noticed the veins stood dark like tree branches against a leaden winter sky.

It was then, beyond his hand, that he noticed the suitcase on the bed. He recognized it as his wife's. On top of the clothes and toiletries, there was a Playbill, its yellow banner peeking out from under a blouse. Han leafed through it. It was from a New York City Ballet performance they had once attended with the ambassador. The black ink on the cover had a palm print on it from her moist hands clutching it through the performance. Han wondered why, of all things, she had chosen *this* as a memento of her old life.

He realized someone was standing behind him. He turned around and saw his wife in the doorway.

"That was the happiest day of my life," she said. "Do you remember it? Do you remember how I held your hand and squeezed it?"

In all honesty, Han did not remember it that well, even though he felt he should – such expressions of physical affection between them being rather rare. To him it was just another work function he attended, chaperoning the ambassador and his wife to show their hosts that, yes, we can adopt your norms of culture when we need to.

"Those ballerinas, they were so beautiful. They floated like herons," she said.

Han looked at the cover and tried desperately to recall details of the performance. The only thing of that night he remembered distinctly was the logistical juggling he was forced to do when the ambassador's limo was late.

"Is that really what makes you happy – the trappings of a decadent society?"

The expression on his wife's face turned bitter. "Do you think so little of me? You really don't understand, do you? That was the happiest day of my life because I was so proud to be your wife. I was proud that your hard work and your talent had allowed us to be in a place where we could witness such beauty, not because I thought that it afforded us a decadent luxury."

"Myung-Ae, why did you run away? Have I been so bad to you?" Han asked.

It was so seldom that he used her name; perhaps half a dozen times since they were married. He had a clear memory of one occasion, before their children were born, not long after they had moved into a newly built apartment in Pyongyang for Workers' Party officials. They were lying in bed, still aglow with the euphoria of lovemaking. He whispered her name as he caressed her back and noted how her skin felt like paper – the cool inside pages of a thick book – crisp and supple at the same time.

Han asked her probing questions, as would a clinician to determine whether she had relapsed into depression.

"I do believe I've gone a little mad in some way," she said.

"Your family needs you," Han said. "Please, we *must* go back."

"I can't. I can't live half asleep any more. I won't."

"What about our daughter? If you don't go back, what will happen to Won-Sook?"

"I have to save at least one of them," she said, looking over her shoulder toward the room where Won-Kyu slept. "Did I ever tell you what happened the last time I saw her in Pyongyang?"

Han shook his head.

"At the airport, I told Won-Sook how much I loved her. How she was the most important thing to me in my life. You know what she said to me? 'Comrade Mother, I shouldn't be the most important thing in your life. The Dear Leader should be above all.'

"Can you believe that? A six-year-old girl chastising her own mother about indoctrination? I got goose bumps. It was terrifying to know that I had given birth to this steely thing. When I was sitting on the plane, waiting for it to take off, I was genuinely afraid that she might report me to one of her teachers."

"Why didn't you tell me?" Han said.

His wife reached out to him and smoothed out a wrinkle in his damp shirt collar. "And what would I have told you, a senior Party official?"

"Are you really going to do this? Doom your own daughter to a life as an outcast? Destroy your family? For what?"

"We can do this together. Start a new life here," she said.

"We have standing in our own country. We're a part of the elite. If we turn our backs on them, we will be nothing, we'll have nowhere to stand."

"That's not true. We can make a new life. Our South Joseon brethren do it all the time," she said, using the word *dongpo* for brethren. It literally meant "same womb."

"And do what? Eke out a living selling groceries? Or liquor to drunks? Or how about a nail salon? I'm doing something important now. I'm changing the course of history of an entire nation. Would you have me give up all of that for some material comfort? For nice clothes and a fancy car and a pretty view out the window? I saw your magazine clippings of mansions and homes in the country. Is that what you really want?"

"I'm not asking for a life of luxury. I just want to give Won-Kyu a normal life. I'm tired of being afraid all the time," she said, exasperated.

"Normal? I'm afraid normal *is* a luxury these days," Han said. "This can't be just about you and me and our family. There are people depending on me. If I don't do my duty, thousands, no, millions of people will be affected. So don't make me choose between my family and my work. That's a choice I cannot make."

She took Han's hand and stood him up. "I want you to see something," she said and led him downstairs to the porch. They sat facing the meadow that Han had crossed when he first approached the farmhouse from the woods.

"It's so peaceful here," she said. "Can we just sit for a while and talk about other things?"

His world was on fire yet she wanted to sit and chat about "other things." Han reluctantly sat on a bench and stared off into the inky darkness that murmured beyond the reach of the house lights. He felt suddenly exhausted in a way he had never felt exhausted before; in a way that he imagined one feels when one is old, when time is against you and you have achieved nothing.

"Remember when you first came to New York, you got that camera?" she asked. "You took a lot of pictures and you kept that scrapbook. You were happy then for a while, I think. *I* was happy. That's why I kept the scrapbook of my own, of those photos of houses in magazines. It wasn't that I was coveting those homes. I wanted to do something similar to what *you* were doing. I wanted to share in what gave you joy. I know that probably doesn't make sense."

Han frowned. Could it have been that he so utterly misinterpreted her? It felt as though these were memories of someone else.

"Then I saw how you behaved when we returned to Pyongyang last year. You were like a man who's come home after being at war. You went to all your usual hangouts with your old friends and colleagues but nothing seemed to give you pleasure. That wasn't just my imagination, right?"

"How is it that you remember all these details that even I barely recall?"

Han was usually a man free of regret. He believed in making choices decisively and then living with their consequences, with as little complaining as possible. He reckoned it was one of his best qualities. He expected others to do so as well, and that made him seem at times sanctimonious. He knew it, yet he could not fix it. Now, he was overwhelmed with regret, in particular for having inhabited his own life so lightly that he had to rely on his wife's memory to render it accurately.

"Yes, I remember," he said.

It was a time of trepidation; his days were filled with the unease of swimming in fathomless, murky water. Everything familiar had become tedious to him, as though someone had sucked the amusement out of everything. At the time he blamed his mood on jetlag and fatigue, and didn't think about it again until he returned to New York. Then he promptly jettisoned his hobbies, photography first among them. Even the most loyal members of the Party feel freer to indulge their secret passions – in Comrade Park's case, his vices – when on assignment away from home, and they often allow themselves to enjoy the perks their host country has to offer. But his hobbies didn't seem relevant any more after that trip back home. So much lacking; so much hypocrisy. What use was a hobby in the face of that? He had convinced himself at the time that he'd given up photography because he was too busy to pursue it further.

He was about to say something when his wife gasped. Startled, he looked at her and saw that she had one hand over her mouth and the other reaching out to the meadow. He turned to where she was pointing.

A herd of deer was emerging from the woods. They strolled through the meadow, momentarily pausing at times to graze. When an owl hooted, they looked up, their ponderous ears tilting toward the call from the darkness. As the herd moved forward, a squadron of golden-green fireflies rose from the grass where they trod, like luminescent bubbles rising up through a flute of champagne.

"Have you ever seen such a beautiful thing?" Myung-Ae said, her hand on her cheek in wonderment.

They watched the herd until their white tails disappeared into the woods on the other side of the meadow.

"I can't remember the last time I saw a firefly," Myung-Ae said. "Maybe at my grandmother's house."

The last deer Han recalled seeing as an adult was a stuffed specimen in a museum of indigenous North Korean mega-fauna. In an adjoining diorama there was an Asiatic black bear with its distinct crescent moon necklace of white fur; and in another, a rather misshapen specimen of a Korean tiger, now long extinct. The taxidermist was either just plain unskilled or perhaps unschooled about the characteristics of that sub-specie for lack of a living example. The face had been contorted to expose its fangs in what Han guessed was intended to be a fierce snarl. However, with the added idiosyncrasy of one eye being clearly larger than the other, it ended up looking like the animal was in pain. One front paw was turned upward to an unnatural degree to expose its claws. It was as though the tiger had escaped a trap and remained disfigured in a constant state of angry vigilance. Most of the species on display there were gone from North Korea, except maybe from the remotest parts of the mountainous, northern provinces.

"When we returned from Pyongyang last year, I couldn't sleep very well," Han said.

"You were having nightmares – bad ones," his wife said. "You talked in your sleep. You never did that before that trip to Pyongyang. I figured you were under a lot of stress."

"What did I say in my sleep?"

"Nothing that made much sense. Sometimes you called out Won-Sook's name. It was upsetting to see you struggling in your sleep, so I woke you up. What was it that was troubling you so much?"

"I don't think I quite understood it myself," Han said. "Did you venture outside of central Pyongyang much when we were there that time?"

"A little. I went to see my parents, remember?"

"Did you happen to notice there were a lot more people on the streets looking gaunt and ragged?"

"Yes. The famine – it was a hard time for everyone."

"Well, not *everyone*," Han said knowingly. "Those Party gatherings I went to, they were pretty lavish, considering the circumstances. The cognac didn't go down too well. At the time I thought it was just me being morose. Then this one night, late into the gathering, one of the hostess girls started crying during a song. We thought she was just pouring her emotions into her performance, but she kept crying even after the music ended. You could feel the merriment bleeding out of the room. People weren't in the mood to enjoy themselves after that. They started shuffling out. It was pitch black outside. The nightly blackout was already in effect."

"Did you find out what she was crying about?" Myung-Ae asked.

Han shook his head. "She just looked so…" Han dropped his gaze to the porch floor in search of the right words. "…so, *defeated*."

If some alien taxidermist from another world were to drop into Pyongyang and abduct one of its gaunt denizens as its only specimen of humankind, would its fellow alien beings back home think of all humanity as wiry, distorted creatures? Fierceness was no defense against extinction, as the tiger had so aptly proven. Han envisioned himself in a glass box on some alien world, misshapen, defeated, and in a constant state of angry vigilance.

"Our country is in ruin," Myung-Ae said, using the Korean word *pe-huh*, used to describe landscapes laid waste and spoiled, as in the aftermath of a war. "If we return home, our lives will also be in ruin. That's what I fear."

Han felt overcome with fatigue. He could not distinguish the stars from the fireflies.

"I can't think straight. I need to close my eyes for a bit," he said and walked into the house in search of Whitaker.

Whitaker was standing at the kitchen counter, squinting through his pipe smoke to read a newspaper spread out before him. Han asked him if there was somewhere he could lay down for a bit. Whitaker showed him to the bedroom across the hall from where Han's son was sleeping. Han crawled onto the bed and prostrated himself on top of the covers. He was unconscious by his third breath.

"The ghosts of our own still linger here. Did you see that stone wall at the edge of the forest as you were coming toward the house?"

The wall that seemed more like a pile of loose slate. Han nodded.

"Local lore has it that a whole company of Confederate soldiers – down to the last man – was wiped out on these fields, just about where this house now stands. Union infantrymen were lined up cheek by jowl behind that wall and they tore the Confederates to shreds. And they weren't slaughtered for lack of shooting back. I still find musket balls in that wall from time to time, more than a hundred years later. The men buried in these fields were lucky if they got a blanket to shield them from the dirt. And it's a good bet they barely got a tender word spoken over their pit, let alone a prayer. Townsfolk here are said to have buried the Confederates in shallow trenches, only after they could no long endure the stench of their rotting bodies."

What is it that compels people to cover or box their dead for burial, Han wondered. Is it the insult of dirt touching bare skin or infiltrating the cavities that were once the body's doorways to life? Or is it that a body buried bare resembles too much a fallen beast?

Burials back home in North Korea nowadays did not offer any better refuge from the indignities those soldiers endured. The last funeral Han had attended, for a maternal uncle who lived two hours outside of Pyongyang, was a grimly austere affair. To bury him in a pine box would have been an egregious waste of wood that could otherwise have been used for fuel. There were hardly any pines remaining of sufficient girth anyway. Even the quality of hemp, the customary burial shroud, was so diminished that Han could see clearly through the porous cloth that bound his uncle's bony remains; so slight, so spare, it was hard to imagine it was once inhabited by a mind of substance. When his tightly bound remains were laid in the tired, grey earth, the bundle looked more like a swathed bundle of branches rather than a body. Han recalled that his uncle's wife wept, but lacked the energy to cry out loud, as was expected at traditional burials.

"Sometimes in the winter I swear I hear the soldiers' voices when the wind blows through the house – a kind of mournful wailing," Whitaker said. "Took a while to make peace with 'em. I reckon they're not the only aggrieved spirits here. There were the Saponi Indians before them – all long routed from their homeland or diseased out of existence by the time the first Confederate spilled his blood here. Those soldiers, and the Indians before them, heaped upon the fields, their blood nourishing the earth and the plants that grow on it. Their souls have long gone beyond, but every time someone lights up the tobacco from here, a piece of their body ascends and rejoins them, I'd like to think, making them whole again."

"Koreans, we know about invasion, too," Han said. "We have survived more than a thousand invasions into the Korean Peninsula."

They had fended off all but two – the Mongols in the thirteenth century and the Japanese in the twentieth. Even under those two occupations, Koreans had managed to stay intact as a people.

"Maybe that is why we are so nationalist," Han said of the streak, expressed nowadays as armies of rabid soccer fans in South Korea, or in North Korea, the ideology of self-reliance.

"No country with a history long enough is completely innocent," Han said.

Whitaker stopped in mid-sip and put down his shot glass. He nodded.

Whitaker looked like he was about to continue speaking when Han noticed that he was looking intently through the windowpanes. Han turned around and saw one of Whitaker's farmhands at the door. Whitaker went to him and they whispered to each other. The farmhand was a stout Latino fellow, barely five feet tall, with square shoulders and a solid trunk shaped by enduring labor. His face was smooth and the color of damp red clay, except for the uppermost part of his forehead, sheltered by the brim of a hat. There, the flesh was as pale as the sky before a snowfall. Whitaker sent the farmhand on his way and turned to Han.

"Well, *this* is interesting. I don't think I've ever had this many uninvited guests to my farm since my neighbors crashed a party back in '84. It seems you have a visitor, Dr. Han."

"Visitor? For me?"

Whitaker nodded. "He asked for you by name, I'm told. A man named James Avery? Ring a bell?"

Han broke out into a cold sweat. The only person who could conceivably know his whereabouts was Comrade Park.

There was a knock at the kitchen door. Han stood up and balanced himself as though he were readying himself to bolt in any direction should the need arise. Whitaker opened the door and there stood Avery, in a white shirt rumpled with sweat, sleeves rolled up, tie loosened. He wasn't wearing a jacket. He showed both of his palms as if to say he came unarmed.

"You've led us on quite a chase, Dr. Han," Avery said in Korean. "My name is James Avery. I'm with the U.S. State Department."

Han went pale.

Avery repeated himself in English for Whitaker's benefit and then continued in Korean. "Look, I'm here alone because I convinced my colleagues that there would be less trouble from you this way."

For Han, this was one of those bad dreams in which you awoke, only to find yourself still in a dream. Each twist led him further and further from where he wanted to be, and now this man he had never met before had tracked him down to a farmhouse in the middle of nowhere in rural Virginia, speaking to him as if he knew him, in Korean no less.

"Let's sit and talk for a bit, shall we?" Avery said. "I guarantee you that you'll want to hear what I have to say."

Whitaker leaned against the door as if to guard it as Avery and Han sat themselves down at the kitchen table.

Avery turned to Whitaker and said, "Would you mind if I had a chance to speak to Dr. Han alone?"

"Certainly," Whitaker said.

"Perhaps we should have Mrs. Han join us?" Avery said.

Whitaker fetched her. She entered the kitchen with the sheepish look of a schoolgirl who had been called to the principal's office. She had a bad case of bed-head; her hair was bushy on one side and flattened on the other where it had, until moments before, been laid on a pillow in a fitful sleep. The baby was asleep in her arms.

Avery turned to Han and told him what he knew of Han's predicament, inviting him to correct him if his version of events diverged at all from the truth. Han and his wife sat mute. Han in particular seemed dismayed to learn that Avery's understanding was not only correct but thorough.

"I'm sorry to put it in such stark terms. Here are your options as I see them," Avery said. "You have violated the terms of your diplomatic privilege. At a minimum, you would be expelled from the United States."

"With my wife and son?"

"That depends on your wife's intentions."

Han looked at her. She didn't lift her head and she said nothing. He could not be sure that she was even listening.

Avery continued. "If you return to Pyongyang, with or without your family, what do you think will happen to you? The Party will know exactly what transpired here. You, and most likely your extended family, will spend the rest of your lives in a labor camp. With the famine the way it is now, you'll be lucky if you don't starve to death."

"You said I had options," Han said, looking directly into Avery's eyes. It was a Western habit that Han had had to teach himself.

Here was the endgame, being laid out before him like a feast of poisons. Han felt a fool for ever having thought that he could somehow untangle himself from this mess and walk away from it unscathed. The earth shifted under him. He had no footing in this world any more. He had been staring at the heavens too long. He felt dizzy.

"Well, yes, you do have options. I'm familiar with your work. You would be a valuable asset to the United States. I've spoken to my superiors and I've been authorized to tell you that the U.S. government would be willing to grant asylum to you and your family."

Myung-Ae looked up at Avery, then at her husband.

"You know I have a six-year-old daughter in Pyongyang," Han said.

"Yes." Avery stood up and went to the kitchen sink to pour himself a glass of water. He took several gulps and then inhaled sharply. "We have means to escort your daughter out of North Korea."

"How?"

"We would smuggle her to Beijing first."

"Beijing?" Han scoffed. "No offense, Mr. Avery, taking my daughter to Beijing doesn't really do her any good. If she is caught there, the Chinese government will send her back to North Korea. They cannot risk antagonizing Pyongyang by harboring a fugitive or even appearing to help in her escape."

"Beijing would only be an interim stop, of course. We would eventually escort her to the United States to be reunited with you."

It was preposterous. The gall of it – mapping out the what, where and how of defection to a senior member of the Workers' Party.

"No, no, no. Why are you even talking to me about this? This is impossible," Han said. "Even being in the same room with you, it's sedition."

"Being in the same room with me is the least of your problems, I should think."

Han caught a glimpse of himself reflected in the window, darkened by night, warped by aged panes rippled by gravity. He could not believe this reflection was the face of a 39-year-old.

"A life tempered by peril, crisis after crisis averted by resourcefulness and a bit of luck, and *this* is how it comes undone," Han said to no one in particular. "I've spent my life serving my country. Quite frankly, it's a little hard seeing it unravel like this."

"No one is questioning your honor, Dr. Han. I've often felt my own life coming undone in spite of my best intentions," Avery said. "But what I've come to realize is that best intentions are not enough. You also have to be standing in the right line."

Standing in the right line: It was an expression about how getting ahead in life, or falling behind, can depend on a fickle twist of fate. The phrase also had the connotation of betting on the right horse, especially in a political power struggle, from the lowliest workplace scrap to the life-or-death maneuverings that preceded dynastic upheavals.

"Are you suggesting I am on the wrong side of history?" Han said.

"Who's to say?" Avery said. "It's been a long time since I worried about something as abstract as history. However, when someone like Hwang Jang-Yop defects, it makes you wonder why he decided to stand in a different line, doesn't it?"

Chapter 25

Five days before his seventy-fourth birthday, Hwang Jang-Yop was in Beijing, returning home from an official trip to Japan. It was a bitterly cold February morning with a seamless sky, not a cloud all night to blanket the heat. The sky was blue for a change, its color blushing briefly ahead of the ashen veil of smog and dust that had yet to be churned up by the city's aspirations. Hwang told his diplomatic entourage that he was going shopping. Instead, he and an aide went straight from their hotel to the Chaoyang district, Beijing's diplomatic quarter. Around 10 o'clock, they walked into the South Korean embassy on Dong Fang Dong Road and requested asylum.

He was the most senior member of North Korea's ruling elite to defect to date. Describing him merely as a high-ranking official didn't do justice to the magnitude of his act. Hwang was the architect of North Korea's organizing ideology of *juche*. In the late 1950s and 1960s, as deputy chairman of the propaganda section of the Workers' Party, Hwang developed this philosophy of self-reliance to rally a people still depleted and despondent in the aftermath of the Korean War and to immunize the fledgling nation against the rival interests of its more prominent Communist allies – China and the Soviet Union. The call to patriotism in *juche* was an appeal for collective sacrifice, adroitly taking advantage of thousands of years of Confucian conditioning to have its people defer to authority for the greater good.

Hwang was a learned man, educated at Tokyo University and then Moscow University at a time when few had the opportunity for higher education. He, of all people, knew that the Confucian ideal of deference to authority presupposed benevolent leadership.

He either believed in earnest that Kim Il-Sung was that benevolent leader, or worked hard to make others believe it by building a cult of personality around the Great Leader with a brazen totality the likes of which had never been seen in the annals of propaganda. Those efforts propelled Hwang up through the ranks of the Workers' Party. He served as chairman of the Supreme People's Assembly in the 1970s and eventually became the chief secretary of the omnipotent Central Committee in 1980.

Hwang's defection to South Korea was beyond the wildest dreams of even the most optimistic intelligence officer. The young South Korean consul who greeted Hwang at the embassy that morning didn't know who Hwang was when he introduced himself. He just happened to be on duty on the front desk on Wednesdays and wasn't privy to the secret talks Hwang had been having with his superiors, and he certainly had no idea that Hwang would be arriving at the embassy that day.

Hwang merely said he was there to see the deputy ambassador. The young consul saw an urbane, soft-spoken man whose eyes were at first hidden behind glasses that had fogged up in the stuffy waiting room. When Hwang removed his glasses to wipe them, the consul saw that his eyes were moist. Hwang pulled out a worn notebook from his pocket and thumbed through it as he waited on a bench.

When the architect of *juche* turned his back on the regime, it was an admission of utter failure of his life's work. There was nothing left in Pyongyang for him. The moment Hwang crossed into the South Korean compound, the fate of his wife, his three daughters and his son were sealed. Hwang had tutored Kim Jong-Il when the Dear Leader was a boy. Now, his former pupil, who wronged him foremost by twisting his life's work into a grotesque system for perpetuating his own absolute rule, would no doubt consign Hwang's kin to a purgatory worse than death to atone for Hwang's treachery.

When embassy officials notified the Chinese government later in the day that Hwang was there and that he intended to defect, it sparked a tense, five-week standoff, with North Korean officials accusing Seoul of abducting Hwang. They threatened to retaliate, leading to fears that North Korean agents would infiltrate the embassy to kill Hwang. Chinese authorities surrounded the compound with troops and armored vehicles.

The diplomatic crisis continued for a month, until mid-March, when Hwang and his aide were flown to the Philippines, giving the Chinese government a diplomatic fig leaf to hide behind. They stayed there for a month before finally arriving in Seoul.

* * *

When a lover is jilted, rarely does he or she move on without some plot for revenge. Those who leave the plot merely as a fantasy to be entertained only in moments of bitterness find solace sooner. Those who carry out the plot, petty or grand, are doomed to relive the humiliation, for revenge is seldom as satisfying as the fantasy of it.

Thus it was for Hwang Jang-Yop, who, as a feted new son of the South, promptly embarked on a very public and vicious attack on his former compatriots in the North. He was defined by revenge now, and that inevitably made him a sad figure – the spurned lover determined to exact pain from the one he was so foolishly devoted to. At least that was the impression James Avery had of him when he saw him at a conference of diplomats and dreary policy types in Seoul just months after Hwang arrived in the South Korean capital to much fanfare.

After the local spooks concluded that his defection was authentic, Hwang went on the speaking circuit and at every possible turn, publicly railed against North Korea's foibles – the very ones he had so diligently enabled in his former life.

It was early August; one of those summer days in Seoul when even dawn provided little refuge from the oppressive mugginess. It would only grow heavier throughout the day. When Avery stepped into the auditorium where Hwang was giving his talk, the air conditioning had been cranked up so high that it felt as though he would instantly contract some horrible cold. It was wasteful. South Korea, for all its economic growth of late, was still a country whose nascent urge toward extravagance was kept in check by a generation who had experienced crushing poverty. Whatever private luxuries that corporate chieftains and senior government officials indulged in, at least in public they made a show of frugality, at times making a show of attending meetings in short-sleeved shirts as fans whirred in the background, with open windows declaring the lack of air conditioning.

When Avery saw Hwang, it was barely five months after Hwang had walked into the South Korean embassy in Beijing, and he was already talking the talk of a reformer who had left his position of privilege because he was disillusioned. As Avery listened to Hwang trash talk his former colleagues, he didn't quite buy the act, not least because he had been made privy to Hwang's extensive debriefings after his defection.

Hwang was a slight man with a receding hairline accentuated by a band of grey that bordered only the crown of his head. His speech was over-articulated and formal. Avery couldn't decide whether this diction was natural to him, befitting a former university president, or was the clipped speech a result of trying to wash his accent of its North Korean flavor.

Avery couldn't help but wonder what Hwang's life would be like from now on. When the hoopla over his defection died down, Hwang would adapt to a life without his minders and acolytes and sympathizers as the weight of their own lives pulled them away from the dimming limelight. He would eat his meals in solitude. Sometimes he would remember his wife's cooking and the bleak fate to which he doomed her when he left her behind, not to mention his children, their spouses, and the in-laws. Some morsels would evoke a memory, perhaps laced with remorse or at least a thought about what they might be eating. How bad did it have to get for a man to sever himself from everything and everyone he had ever known and cherished? A part of Avery felt sorry for the old man; another part was deeply disturbed by Hwang's concern for his own survival at the expense of his family.

Avery knew what it felt like to be a transplant, so he wanted to be sympathetic. He understood the disorientation that drives one to solitude and to keep one's own counsel because the landmarks of confidence have shifted. He knew what it felt like to have fallen asleep, so to speak, and awake in a stranger's house. He remembered running around outdoors with his brothers at a church cookout in New Jersey when he was perhaps seven or eight. Avery skidded on the grass with his knees and his mother got furious that he had ruined his Sunday best. She clutched his bicep and shook him as she pointed to his knees and shouted how their fellow parishioners would think she was raising a wild beast. Watching from afar, his great-uncle, a wealthy industrialist who had underwritten his family's missionary expeditions, took pity on him. When Avery's mother wasn't looking, his great-uncle, who must have been in his late seventies at the time, took the sulking boy for a walk. They came upon a steep, grassy hill. The old man, still vigorous for his age, took a running start and slid down the hill on his side, making a mess of his pants and crisp white shirt. He waved to Avery to follow. The boy took a look behind him to check for his mother.

"I'll give you a dollar if you do it," his great-uncle said from below, waving a bill.

Avery took a dive down the slope, much to the delight of the old man. He slapped that dollar bill in Avery's hand and told him, "Well done!"

After they climbed back up the hill the old man stopped Avery for a moment.

"James. Listen to me, son," he said. "You should be a good boy and listen to your mother. But at the same time you shouldn't let people take away the things that make you happy. Do you understand what I'm saying?"

The boy nodded reflexively, though he didn't really understand until many years later. When Avery's mother saw him with more stains on his clothes, she was apoplectic. His great-uncle calmed her down, lying that he had slipped down the hill and that James, the upstanding boy that he was, had acquired the stains when he came to his rescue. His mother shot the old man a suspicious look but said nothing further. James fingered the dollar bill in his pocket. Not long after that, James's parents moved the family to South Korea.

His great-uncle died in his sleep when he was eighty-five. He had returned to his home in New York from a tour of Southeast Asia two weeks before, replete with tales of his adventures and misadventures. Avery was not prone to tears at funerals yet he wept at his great-uncle's, for a reason even he could not quite fathom at the time; and not the polite tear or two dribbling from the corner of his eyes, but an unrestrained, embarrassing rivulet of tears cried by a lost child. He felt – diminished by his great-uncle's passing. Perhaps it was that when a man lives a full life, it becomes a mirror of one's own timidity. His great-uncle was the incarnation of Mark Twain's advice to live so that when you die, even the undertaker will feel sorry.

The Koreans had a saying: *shin-toh-bul-ee* – the body and the land are one. It posed an interesting question for someone like Avery – a seed, so to speak, that was planted in foreign soil. He had returned to the U.S. for college, but never really found a footing there, let alone put down roots.

Just months before the conference where Avery met Hwang, Avery returned stateside to see if there was some part of the land that still resonated with him. Only a handful of people knew that he had actually been forced to take the time off after one of his other operations to reel in a defector had gone terribly wrong.

He went hiking in the Sawtooth Mountains in Idaho. A college friend was supposed to be meeting him in a one-road town called Stanley. The friend bailed out at the last moment because of an unexpected deadline at work. Avery was faced with the option of either ditching the trip or going hiking alone. He chose the latter.

After a good fifty-minute walk over a steady incline from the trailhead, there was a wooden box on the path leading into the Sawtooth Wilderness Area where hikers are supposed to fill out and deposit a form detailing their itinerary. It seemed a good precaution, especially for a lone traveler like Avery. He hadn't encountered another person since he left his car. When he lifted up the cover of the box and peered inside, there were no forms; just a few scraps of notebook paper that some hikers had scribbled on in lieu of the forms. The most recent one was more than two weeks old. Hoping to use the back of one of those scraps, Avery rifled around the box to find a pen or pencil. There were none. A spider that had taken refuge under the paper scurried away. Avery embarked on his hike without leaving any record of it.

Through the tapering foliage at the crown of the pines, Avery could see the jagged, snow-covered peaks that gave the mountain range its name. He contemplated, only briefly, the prudence of proceeding alone without anyone knowing of his whereabouts. A journey has an inertia of its own and he was not about to turn back after less than an hour in the woods. The day before, he had asked the owner of the lodge where he was staying to recommend a long day-hike. Avery noticed her sizing him up, looking alternately between the map and him, measuring his mettle to fit the challenge. She suggested a destination called Alice Lake. Then, before Avery could respond, she breathed in deeply, indicating she had her doubts.

"The trails might be a bit muddy with all this rain we've had lately," she said.

"How many hours, do you figure?"

"A good seven, eight, round-trip," she said, furtively sizing him up one last time.

"I'll plan on getting a bit muddy then," he said and thanked her.

When he left the lodge in the morning, he didn't tell her he'd be heading to Alice Lake. If he didn't return by nightfall, perhaps she would have enough sense to put two and two together.

Avery didn't seriously contemplate turning back until he came upon an angry creek that had swelled up with rain and snowmelt. There were two logs felled across the creek that didn't quite connect into a bridge. He checked the temperature of the water from the bank. An unexpected dip would definitely be bracing, but the creek was narrow enough that it would not be life threatening. He walked the near bank in search of another footbridge. This seemed to be the only one without a significant detour. He decided to give the crossing a shot. It was June, and the sun felt warm and dry against his face. It gave him the courage to be a little reckless.

The logs weren't as slippery as they had looked. Once on the far bank, the air was markedly more still, as though he had crossed over into a different realm. He resolved to share a knowing greeting with whomever he met on the trail. He never got the chance. He didn't run into a single soul during the nearly nine hours it took to return to the trailhead.

Looking back, perhaps it was unwise of him to press on, even after he had reached Alice Lake. Perhaps it should have been enough to take in the grandeur of it all – the water still frozen in early summer, framed by the serrated ridge that diminished to the south. He had seen on the map at the parking lot that one could circumnavigate the lake and return on a different trail. He had gotten it into his mind that he would do that. What he had not counted on was how deep the snowfall was beyond the lake.

He lost the trail several times in the snow. But he pressed on and picked up the trail again when there was enough of a clearing. All the while, he eyed the opposite side of the lake warily. The terrain was so rocky that he couldn't see how the trail circumnavigating the lake could pass through the ridge without some technical climb over icy walls. He was certainly not equipped for that. He was wearing shorts and his socks had already become wet from all the snow.

When he came upon an expanse of uninterrupted snow that gave no sign of clearing all the way up to the tree line, he knew he had to turn back. Only on the return journey did he realize how thinly he had cut it; the danger he had put himself in. He lost his own footprints in the snow a few times, but found them after some backtracking.

Foolhardiness, daring, whatever it was, Avery was not in the mood for self-preservation. He *needed* to put himself in danger. This tendency to throw caution to the wind, his mother believed, was his great-uncle's influence. But what was caution when faced with the impermanence of it all? He stood at the shores of the lake, dark under the sweeps of snow across its icy surface as though its depths reached to the very foundations of the mountains that carried it. He was the only human being in the wilderness for miles. He remembered the weight of his late fiancée's hand on his forearm when they would walk together. It was the first time the memory hadn't made him wince.

That equanimity didn't last, however. What fortitude he drew from the wilderness quickly dissipated when he returned to Seoul, where he could not escape awkward expressions of sympathy from acquaintances close enough to know his fiancée had died but not close enough to offer any meaningful kind of moral support. He would have preferred if they offered to drown the pain temporarily together with booze, or even just cursed at the heavens with something profane. His friend Young-Chol had given the perfect two-fer response: "Fuck! Life fucking sucks sometimes! Let's get drunk."

There are always in-between people in one's life – not really strangers, yet not really close – and this untidy category of people kept on growing as Avery got older, and much of the attention and energy he expended in polite society had to do with keeping these in-between people at bay – giving them enough of himself not to seem stuck up, yet keeping private what he could, if not what he wanted to.

* * *

Then there were people like Hwang Jang-Yop, for whom nothing was private after his defection. There's the kind of loss of privacy from being in the public eye, but the breach into Hwang's inner sanctum once he arrived in Seoul was altogether different. For all the indignation that Princess Diana suffered from prying cameras and the infiltration of confidants by Fleet Street, at least her thoughts remained her own. Not so for Hwang. His handlers were not satisfied with knowing merely the external details of his past and present life – who his acquaintances were, what his daily routine was, how often he met with Kim Jong-Il. They demanded to know even what he was thinking, now and especially in the months and weeks that led up to his appearance at the South Korean embassy in Beijing.

By the time Avery met him, Hwang had become so accustomed to prying questions into every corner of his mind that he found the man to be oddly compliant, almost to a disconcerting degree, like a prison inmate who had been broken of any will to preserve his privacy.

The Korean Central Intelligence Agency was very protective of Hwang but one of Avery's contacts there arranged a "chance" meeting with him at the conference for ten minutes.

There had been rumors circulating among Avery's counterparts in the South Korean government that Hwang Jang-Yop had brought with him a list of North Korean moles who had over the years infiltrated into South Korea's ruling class.

Those rumors turned out to be much inflated, as became apparent after those ten minutes of conversation with Hwang. What also became apparent to Avery was that Hwang wasn't as big a fish as everyone had made him out to be. Many supposed that the defection of such a senior official signaled the imminent implosion of Kim Jong-Il's regime. However, Hwang was already on the downward slope, and his defection may have had more to do with his falling favor with the Dear Leader rather than being a prescient and daring leap off a sinking ship.

"I relinquished the chairmanship of the Supreme People's Assembly in 1983," Hwang told Avery matter-of-factly as a form of self-effacing introduction when Avery started asking him questions about the country's nuclear program. "Since then, it's been a bit of a downhill slide."

By the mid-1990s, Hwang's influence was an echo of its former self, he explained, especially after Kim Il-Sung, the Great Leader, died in July 1994.

Then, at what was to be a routine cabinet meeting two years later, almost to the day, Hwang's standing with Kim Jong-Il took a perilous turn.

"You know, Kim Jong-Il and I, we'd barely spoken since his father's funeral," Hwang said, and then he paused and inexplicably searched around him, taking off his glasses to wipe them down, as though he needed clean lenses to recall the past clearly.

"That's when I made some off-handed remark about China's market-oriented reforms. The Dear Leader didn't appreciate that," Hwang said.

"That's when he screamed at me, 'You're taking too keen an interest in what your neighbors are doing instead of getting your own house in order!'" Hwang recalled. "Then he berated me in front of all the cabinet members for making serious doctrinal errors in a speech about *juche* that I'd given in Moscow months before."

"He says to me, '*Juche* is an evolution of Marxism-Leninism. It's my father's original ideology. And what is this fascination of yours with Chinese capitalism? It's treachery!'"

"That was it. That was the end of the road for me," Hwang told Avery, his gaze falling downward as if those boxy gold-rimmed glasses that he favored were suddenly too heavy. Avery felt a twinge of pity for him. He seemed a broken man.

It was an ignominious end to an illustrious career. One does not incur the ire of the Dear Leader and blithely shrug it off. Everyone in that cabinet meeting that day – and, by extension, everyone linked to everyone in that room – knew that from then on, Hwang was a drowning man who might drag you under with him.

The Dear Leader was not a forgiving man, to put it mildly. There was a well-known anecdote about him that succinctly underscored both Kim's penchant for debauchery and ruthlessness. At one of his notoriously opulent parties, Kim was said to have made his troupe of female dancers strip naked. Kim ordered them to dance with his guests and then forbade anyone but himself from groping them. When one of the guests in attendance told his wife about the incident, the wife, a Party loyalist, wrote a letter to Kim Il-Sung, who was still alive at the time. She asked the Great Leader how he could condone such behavior in the future commander-in-chief. Word got around to Kim Jong-Il, who ordered her to be executed. In what passed for benevolence in Kim Jong-Il's world, the Dear Leader was said to have allowed the woman's husband to pull the trigger to save his own skin.

After the disastrous cabinet meeting, Hwang himself saw the writing on the wall. He wrote a secret letter in November 1996 to a confidant of his outside of the country.

"I expect personal changes here," he wrote, also hinting that he and his allies in the North Korean elite were in danger of being purged. "If I lose my job, I will be unable to travel abroad," he wrote to the confidant, who helped pave the way for his defection the following February.

Alas, Hwang Jang-Yop didn't bring with him the details that most concerned Avery and many of his colleagues in the American intelligence community – details about North Korea's nuclear program.

"I've been a bit out of the loop on that matter," Hwang told Avery.

He had a vague sense that the country had some nuclear capacity even before Pyongyang signed its 1994 agreement with the Clinton Administration to halt its nuclear weapons program in exchange for U.S. economic aid.

"I'm sorry to disappoint you, Mr. Avery," Hwang said in parting.

The nagging question remained – were the Americans getting their money's worth? That is, what really were North Korea's capabilities and was the regime keeping its word to stop working on nukes? No one seemed to know for sure. And it became clear to Avery that Hwang wasn't going to be much help in this realm.

Just a couple of weeks after Avery met Hwang in Seoul, Avery went to Cairo to seal the deal on the simultaneous defection of Jang Sung-Gil, North Korea's ambassador to Egypt, and his brother, Jang Sung-Ho, a trade attaché in Paris.

With the ongoing famine and a parade of elite officials heading for the exit, it might have seemed to the untrained eye that the regime was on the verge of collapse. But even things that appear fragile can be quite stubborn when you expect them to give out completely. There was a silent cadre of worker bees who were dutifully doing their part to keep the regime afloat – not because of any abiding loyalty to the Dear Leader, but because that is what they do; they work for the group. It is as much programming as it is character. And Han Chol-Soo was among them.

When all the high-level defections failed to yield the nuclear intelligence that the Americans were seeking, Avery began to widen his circle of interest, and that was when he first became aware of Han's existence.

"Here's a worker bee in the middle of the hive," Avery said to himself when he came across Han's appallingly thin dossier. But like trying to distinguish one drone from another, Han proved infuriatingly elusive, save for some tantalizing tidbits gleaned from his time outside of North Korea, such as his schooling in Moscow.

Avery had to set the file aside. There was too little known about Han for him to even begin trying to unravel the man's life. He was a shadow in a dark room. For days after he set aside the file, Avery was in a funk, and he didn't quite know why. It was as though he had seen a long-held prize in a dream, only to awake to the disheartening knowledge that it was unattainable. It was not in his nature to give up. That was his great-uncle's gift to him, and his curse.

Avery could not have known at the time that the shadow in the dark room would take form, and that form would traverse his life.

PART III

Chapter 26

Han Chol-Soo felt as though he was mired in one of those dreams he used to have in school where he would read the same passage in a book over and over, unable to move on yet unable to comprehend what he was reading; or puzzling out some mathematical equation for which the solution should have been rudimentary yet remained inexplicably elusive. In those feverish dreams the sense of urgency grows with the impenetrability of the task. It's only when you awaken that you realize how futile the effort was, and having gathered your wits, you soak in the sense of relief to know that it was only a dream.

Han wished he could awaken like that from this quandary. He scanned the faces of those assembled in the farmhouse kitchen, and knew he was beyond that. He could not hope to be miraculously plucked out of the situation.

"I know you must have apprehensions, Dr. Han," James Avery said. "But few people get the opportunity to start over with a clean slate. This is your chance to stand in a different line."

He said it with such a plainspoken openness that Han could not imagine subterfuge behind it.

"Why?" Han asked of no one in particular, then he turned to his wife. "My life's work has been to build scarecrows. My scarecrows keep birds like Mr. Avery here away from our hard-earned crops."

Avery, suddenly conscious of himself, straightened out his sweat-wrinkled collar.

Han continued: "At first, the birds kept coming, so I had to build better scarecrows. I've gotten so good at building them, in fact, that I thought I'd chased all the birds away. It seems now I didn't notice that the birds stopped coming because there were no crops to eat anymore."

Han's wife reached out and laid her hand on his forearm. It was the first time in years that she had initiated a touch. He looked at her with a bit of surprise. He dared not put his hand on hers, lest she pull away.

Han turned to Avery: "When can we be reunited with our daughter?"

Avery nodded as though acknowledging the most routine of decisions. If he was excited he did not show it. He believed just enough in karma – and the cycle of victory flowing from defeat flowing from victory – that incandescent enthusiasm seemed unbecoming. He walked over to the phone on the kitchen wall and called his superiors.

"It's done," Avery said. He answered, "yes" a few more times. Then added, "You can come pick us up now."

Han's wife began to weep and buried her head in the crook of Han's neck. With one arm she clutched the baby close to her and with the other she embraced her husband, grabbing a fistful of his damp shirt. Han assumed it was a gesture of her relief, or perhaps it was an attempt at tenderness, out of practice as it was. The baby woke up and began to cry.

Avery turned away and looked at their reflection in the darkened window – Perseus avoiding not the monstrosity that would turn him to stone, instead granting space to a husband and wife for whom such displays of affection were still to be done in private. They were a dislocated pair, from their homeland and from their privileged yet oddly impoverished class. If they had boarded a time machine and traveled here from a century ago they would be about as well equipped for this new life they were about to embark upon. That the axis of their lives would turn so acutely here of all places – a backwater tobacco farm in Virginia – made sense to Avery only when measured against the absurdity of the lives they had lived so far.

Avery didn't hear her sobbing, but he could see in the reflection that her back was heaving in silent convulsions, though it took a moment for him to discern that is was indeed her body moving and not an illusion caused by the uneven glass.

Old houses, especially those remote outposts in the woods, have a spooky presence about them. It's as though their loneliness conjures spirits to keep them company. Avery could have sworn he saw an apparition lurking outside the window, standing in the mirror-image kitchen projected above the meadow beyond the porch. The image seemed so real that Avery turned to look into the room thinking perhaps that Whitaker had returned. When Avery looked back at the reflection, the ghostly figure was still there. In fact, it moved and extended one arm forlornly toward Avery as if beckoning to him. He felt his scalp tense and he had to remind himself he did not believe in ghosts. He cupped his hands against the glass to get a better look outside.

It was not his imagination and it was not an apparition beseeching him. It was Han's erstwhile comrade, Park Jun-Young, standing on the porch and pointing a gun toward the kitchen window.

Avery recoiled, falling back just as Park fired his first shot. The round shattered a windowpane and rained shards of glass onto him, brittle and light. As he fell, Avery smashed his head hard against a counter. The pain blinded him for a moment. He wasn't sure if he'd just gotten the wind knocked out of him or been shot. He couldn't quite remember the layout of the room he was in as he lay there stunned.

Park walked up to the window and fired off several more rounds into the kitchen, avoiding the rabbets between the panes. Han's wife screamed as Han pushed her and the baby down under the table for cover. Avery tried to stand up but lost his footing on something slippery on the linoleum floor and fell face down. When he tried to push himself up, he slipped again. It was then that he realized he was gliding on a pool of his own blood. He then tasted it in his mouth – the tang of rust. He didn't know whether it was welling up from his throat or flowing in from outside. He could still breathe without difficulty, so he assumed the latter.

There was a pause in the gunfire. Avery turned and saw Park at the window, looking down at his hands with cold indifference. Avery couldn't see Park's hands; presumably he was re-loading. There was the faintest knot of agitation on his brow. Avery needed to move away from the window. Rather than fight the slipperiness, he would use it. He dropped down on his belly and pushed off against a cabinet and slid across the floor, leaving a scarlet streak behind him where once there had been a dark puddle. When he reached the table under which Han and his wife were taking refuge, he pulled the legs to flip the table on its side, creating a shield for them.

Park began firing again. The rounds tore through the tabletop. Avery felt the splinters on him, cascading down through the shockwaves that pounded his organs. It smelled like fresh sawdust kicked up by a hot blade, infused with the smell of burning resin. Avery dragged the overturned table sideways toward the door leading to the interior hallway of the house. He yelled at Han to do the same. Mrs. Han was sandwiched between them, her body draped over the baby boy. They inched their way across the floor as the shots kept coming. Avery slipped again on his own blood and strangely, in that moment when peril distorts time, found himself questioning the convention of putting linoleum on the floor of one of the few rooms in the house with running water. Avery heard a yelp and then a scream.

"I'm hit!" Han said.

"Keep moving!" Avery screamed back.

Then Avery heard what sounded like a cough or a grunt and then he felt the toppled table become stubbornly anchored to the floor even though it had been infuriatingly slick until then.

"I said keep moving!" Avery said.

There was another pause in the gunfire. Reload. This time there were footsteps on the porch. Park was coming around to the door.

"Hallway! Go into the hallway!" Avery yelled at Han.

Han got on his feet, clutching his wife's forearm with one hand and pressing the other against his own shoulder where blood was beginning to seep through his shirt. She made a feeble attempt to stand and immediately fell, slumping over the baby as she called out Won-Kyu's name as she would to coax him to feed.

"Get up! Get up!" Han said.

She didn't move. Avery grabbed her other arm and the two tried to lift her. The limpness of her body defied a proper handhold. Avery lost his grip and she fell on her back. Bright scarlet bubbled from her nose. Park kicked opened the kitchen door and planted his feet to prevent the door from rebounding into him. He squinted against the brightness of the room before lining up his sights – the muzzle rising from the floor, up the length of Avery and then beyond, settling on Han's torso. Park aimed with his arm extended straight out to the side to reduce his forward profile as he was trained to do in the army, unlike the square stance of someone used to wearing body armor or a flak jacket. Such protection was virtually non-existent in North Korea. Han stood there still tugging at his wife's arm, his eyes fixed on Park's face. Park's murderous impulse was the final act of defiance of the vanquished. If I can't have you, no one can.

Han was overcome by deep regret, from betrayal, from a life too hard yet so little accomplished. After all the effort of his days, Han was not prepared for it to end, least of all at the hands of someone he had for so long considered a confidant if not a close friend. Perhaps it was this expression on Han's face that unraveled the knot of concentration on Park's brows for the briefest moment. His face said to him, 'One day you will be hurt like this, too.' Park understood it. The hesitation lasted long enough for Avery to take two steps toward Park.

Then a gunshot.

Avery felt a pressure wave travel through his head. Then he was enveloped in a cottony deafness, pierced soon after by a pure tone that emanated from inside his skull as his eardrums and aural nerves rebounded from the percussive spike. The silence deepened. It felt as though his eyesight was also dimming. He couldn't quite make sense of what he was looking at. Even in his disorientation Avery was quite sure that Park had fired his gun.

Now Park himself seemed to be engulfed in a haze and convulsed violently. Avery thought perhaps his gun had misfired and exploded in his hand. Park staggered into the kitchen and clutched his right shoulder. His hair, which had been neat moments before, was now disheveled, and the collar of his suit was tattered and fuzzy. A man who had until then been carried by his unbreakable resolve, seemed all of a sudden tired and unsure. When Park tried to raise his pistol again he was unable to lift his arm beyond a feeble slope and he knew his shoulder had been badly mangled. The injury – the mechanical damage rather than the pain – prevented him from properly aiming. It was like trying to control someone else's arm. It would not listen to him. Park switched the pistol to his left hand.

Muffled voices emerged through Avery's deafness. He heard very faintly someone say, "drop it." Park raised his muzzle instead and aimed at Han again. There was another gunshot – one that sounded to Avery like the dull thud of a toppling plastic garbage can. Simultaneously, Park was again shrouded in a haze and it was only then that Avery realized that the haze was in fact a spray of tiny wood shards splintering off the kitchen doorframe. This time, Park fell to his knees. When he regained his wits he aimed again, his hand now shaking noticeably. Before Park had a chance to pull off a round, Whitaker ran up and clocked him with the butt of his double-barreled shotgun. Park went limp and slumped onto the floor.

"Don't move," Whitaker said as he stood over Park.

He discarded the smoking spent cartridges and re-loaded without haste, barely taking his eyes off Park, who was writhing on the floor.

Whitaker stepped on the pistol lying at Park's side and dragged it with his foot across the linoleum. He surveyed the carnage in his kitchen. One of the drapes was on fire.

"I've got half a mind to put you out of your misery, you son of a bitch," Whitaker said as he pointed the barrels at Park.

As the ringing in Avery's ears died down, he heard a yelping behind him. Han was calling out something unintelligible as he held Won-Kyu in one arm and clutched his wife's collar with his other hand. The baby's limbs dangled over his arm. His wife tried to speak. The only thing escaping from her lips was a wet cough of pink bubbles.

"*Yohbo, yohbo*," Han kept saying to his wife, using that anonymous term of endearment used among spouses. Then he started calling her name. "Myung-Ae!"

She tried to mouth something to him. Han couldn't make it out. "What? What is it?" he asked.

Whitaker handed off the shotgun to Avery and told him to feel free to shoot the bastard should he try to get up. Whitaker tore down the drapes on fire and stomped it out, then knelt down beside Myung-Ae and pressed his hand just under her collarbone. Blood oozed from between his fingers.

"Hold on," Whitaker said. "Help's on the way."

She grasped the gold crucifix around her neck and blinked at Whitaker. He began reciting Psalm 23. He had found out just yesterday that it was her favorite passage. "The Lord is my shepherd; I shall not want." When Whitaker got to "my cup runneth over" she tried again to speak and managed a sibilant jet of air through the gooey bubbles of blood. "Soo," she said a couple of times, then finally "Sook."

"Won-Sook?" her husband asked. "Won-Sook?"

If she had indeed been trying to call out their daughter's name, she was unable to confirm it – not with a nod or a blink. The effort of uttering those last syllables drained her of the ability to even close her eyes. They focused beyond him and all that remained was the vacant stare of a doll, inanimate and distant. Whitaker recited the sixth and last verse. "Surely goodness and mercy shall follow me all the days of my life: and I will dwell in the house of the Lord forever."

The chorus of insects outside the farmhouse began to rise again from its startled silence. From beyond the stirring meadow chimed in sympathy the sound of distant sirens.

The only thing more alarming than a baby wailing inconsolably is one that is hushed altogether. Avery stood over the dead bodies of Han's wife and son. In escaping this life they left a vacuum in the room that forced all other life to pause and catch its breath. Han could not breathe for want of life in his arms. The moment before he lost consciousness, it occurred to him, like an ominous premonition, that he had in fact been happy at one time but that he would never again be.

Chapter 27

In the middle of the night in Pyongyang, a six-year-old girl was woken up in her tidy dormitory room. The girl rubbed her eyes for a good minute, confused and disoriented, before she sat up on her futon, one of ten in the room – five on each side of a central aisle – a practical if Spartan layout copied from the thousands of military barracks across the country. It was early fall. There was already a chill in the unheated room and many of her classmates covered themselves to their cheeks with their blankets, their tiny noses protruding like periscopes. Cotton sheets were sewn onto the underside of the blankets, as was customary with traditional bedding. The sheets had once been white. Most of them, after years of use, had taken on the color of sand for need of a good washing in lye and boiling water, both of which were in short supply.

Someone shined a flashlight in the girl's eyes and she blinked at it without trying to avoid it, unsure in her grogginess what to do.

"Wake up, Han Won-Sook, and get your wits about you," a woman whispered.

The girl recognized the voice of one of her teachers. Won-Sook got up and, out of habit, began to make her bed.

"Leave it," the teacher said. "Just put on your clothes and bring your coat."

"Where are we going, Comrade Teacher?"

"You're going home for a few days. Your parents are back in Pyongyang."

The teacher escorted Won-Sook to the school gate and handed her off to a woman there with a face weathered dark and gaunt.

"Why couldn't they wait until tomorrow morning?" the teacher asked the woman as she passed Won-Sook's supple fingers over to her grasp.

"That's what *I'd* like to know. Two o'clock in the morning. Ridiculous," the woman said. "I suppose they're anxious to see their precious little princess after a stint overseas."

Won-Sook was falling asleep on her feet. The woman tugged at the girl's hand to move her forward as though she were shaking the reins of a horse. Won-Sook woke up momentarily then stuttered forward with her eyes closed, her bare feet squeaking in her black rubber *gomu-shin* shoes with each step into the night.

* * *

It was a short, exceedingly uncomfortable stroll for the young consuls escorting their boss from the North Korean Mission on Second Avenue to United Nations Plaza. Deputy Ambassador Kwon Woo-Shik was prickly even on the best of days. His misanthropy was in particularly fine form this morning. He had kicked off the day by yelling at his assistant for not having his appointment book open to the correct date. Now that he was actually en route to the United States Mission, he was more sullen than crabby. He barely spoke a word to his underlings as he plodded along yet still managed to register his displeasure; with his head bowed, deep in thought, like a schoolboy contemplating his punishment on his forced march to the principal's office.

Once he arrived at the U.S. Mission, they kept him waiting in the lobby for twenty minutes, asking for his ID twice. Then he waited another twenty minutes in a conference room that was spectacularly bright even with no windows.

"It's just like the Americans to wall off a million-dollar view," Kwon said in a whisper to one of his consuls while staring at the wall that, if it hadn't been blocked off due to security concerns, would have offered an unobstructed vista of the United Nations compound framed by the East River and the industrial waterfront of Queens. The consul felt obliged to nod in agreement.

The oblong conference table was too large for the room. Kwon had to suck in his stomach to fit between the chair and the edge of the table. He knew this delay was deliberate; that's why it irked him so much. He pictured his hosts lounging around in another room, drinking coffee or reading newspapers. He slammed his fist on the table and his two consuls sat up in their chairs, startled to attention. Just then an entourage poured through the door. There must have been a good dozen of them. In the middle of the pack was Bill Richardson, the U.N. ambassador, a barrel-chested man with a mane of thick dark hair. The entourage formed a semi-circle around one end of the table. None of them bothered sitting down.

"Deputy Ambassador Kwon, I regret to inform you that your consul," Richardson said and then looked down at a sheet of paper in his hand, "Han Chol-Soo, is dead. So are his wife and his son – six months old."

Richardson looked down at the paper again as if to confirm the age of the son. Kwon inhaled and felt the conference room table squeeze him against the wall.

"I also regret to inform you that another one of your consuls," Richardson continued, "a Park Jun-Young, is currently being detained by federal agents at the University of Virginia Medical Center in Charlottesville, where he's being treated for various injuries."

Kwon tried to stand up but found he was trapped in his seat by the edge of the table. His consuls had to pry his seat sideways before he could get up.

"How?" Kwon asked. "How did this happen?"

"That," Richardson said, glaring at Kwon, "is a question that *I* would like to ask *you*. What were two consuls from the Democratic People's Republic of Korea doing in Virginia in violation of their travel restrictions? And why did one of your consuls murder the other and his family? Can you answer me that Mr. Deputy Ambassador?"

Kwon stuttered for a moment then whispered something into the ears of one of his consuls. "We demand to speak to Consul Park immediately," Kwon said.

"You are not in a position to *demand* anything!" Richardson barked. The room fell silent. "Your diplomats have provoked an international incident here. In his murderous rampage, Consul Park also wounded innocent bystanders – U.S. citizens."

Richardson took one more look at the folded sheet of paper then tucked it into his jacket pocket. "The injuries to Consul Park do not appear to be life-threatening."

One of the North Korean consuls tried to whisper into Kwon's ear. Kwon shooed him away.

"I do not need to remind you," Richardson said, "that both of your consuls were in violation of their diplomatic privilege. We'll file a formal complaint with Pyongyang on this matter."

Kwon waited a moment to see if Richardson was done speaking, then asked, "When can we meet with Consul Park?"

Richardson looked at the man standing at the end of the semi-circle. "Mr. Deputy Ambassador, this is Detective Jack Finister from the New York City Police Department."

Finister took a half step forward.

"We have reason to believe that Mr. Park is responsible for the murder of an elderly Korean-American couple in Flushing a few days ago. We also believe he's responsible for the murder of a Korean-American pastor and his wife in Fort Lee, New Jersey, the same night."

"This doesn't make sense," Kwon said. "Why would he kill these people?"

"Why indeed?" said Richardson.

"It is beside the point. Consul Park has diplomatic immunity."

"Beside the point? Your man," Richardson said, pointing a finger at Kwon, "is the prime suspect in the murder of four United States citizens. As soon as Consul Park is well enough to travel, he will be expelled from the United States. We will arrange for your Mission personnel to meet with him at the earliest convenient date. Good day, Deputy Ambassador."

The member of the entourage closest to the door opened it and waited for Richardson to pass through. One of the young North Korean consuls tugged at Kwon's sleeve forcefully and spoke into his ear.

"Wait, Mr. Ambassador," Kwon said. "The bodies? The bodies of Consul Han and his wife and son. We must arrange for return."

Richardson stopped and turned back into the room. One of his aides spoke to him in a hushed tone for a while.

"We will arrange for the return of the bodies of Mrs. Han and the baby," Richardson said. "However, Consul Han's body was unfortunately burned to a crisp in a house fire that was started by Consul Park. You are welcome to his ashes if you wish." Richardson left the room followed by his entourage.

Finister lingered at the door for a moment and looked at Kwon. He took in a short breath as though he would say something; instead he just shook his head and walked out with the rest of the entourage.

* * *

When James Avery tried to stand up straight it felt like someone was jabbing a needle into his spine. He flinched each time. Also, his head was still pounding, especially around the spot where he had cracked open his scalp on the kitchen counter. Under the dressing, the bump on his skull felt like a hideous protrusion worthy of the Elephant Man. His hair covered most of the roiling bruise; only a sliver of purple peeked out from under his hairline on his forehead. He wished he were back in New York so he could soak in the scorching hot tub at his favorite sauna in Koreatown. He flinched again when he extended his arm to show his ID to the agent standing guard outside Park Jun-Young's hospital room.

Park's eyes were closed when Avery walked into the room. He opened them in a start when the door closed loudly behind Avery. His face was covered with red dots where he'd been sprayed by Whitaker's shotgun pellets.

"Consul Park Jun-Young," Avery said and then introduced himself.

Park squinted as though unsure of what he was seeing. He tried to raise his right hand but it was handcuffed to the bedside rail. He winced as his mangled shoulder pulled against the restraints. He put his left hand over the cast as if to protect it.

"Do you think they're going to give you a medal for what you did when you return to Pyongyang?" Avery said, standing at the foot of Park's bed.

Park raised his head for a moment to look at Avery then rested it back down on the pillow. "Do you serve your country for medals?" Park said to the ceiling, using the word "*dang-shin*" – a very rude way to say "you."

"No. Then again I don't murder my friends to serve my country either," Avery said, avoiding any honorifics now that Park had opened the door by dispensing with such niceties with a stranger.

It took a few seconds for Park to overcome the grogginess of the painkillers and the offense of being spoken to in such a tone – no less by his imperialist captor – before the contents of what Avery had said registered with him.

"Consul Han is dead?" Park lifted his head again.

"You're the one who shot him. Don't you have confidence in your own aim?"

Park studied Avery's face for a moment and then he lay back, exhausted at the effort. He alternated between staring at the ceiling tiles and closing his eyes, trying to piece together the moments before he lost consciousness. Park made a gurgling noise that Avery figured was the beginnings of a coughing spell. Instead, Park chuckled. "You almost had me. You American bastards – you lie as often as you eat. Han Chol-Soo isn't dead, as much as he should be."

"I'm here to tell you that he is, and so are his wife and his son."

"My government will demand his return."

"Even if he were alive, would you really want to return to Pyongyang and admit that you didn't achieve your mission *and* that you got caught? Of course, Ambassador Kim will burn for this, and Deputy Ambassador Kwon, too. Since you're the hero who managed to punish the traitor, *you* might still get a pat on the back from the Party, only if the Dear Leader's in the right mood, of course."

Trauma devours memory, invading and wiping away even those moments well in advance of when consciousness slips away. People who are hit by cars often say they have no memory of the minutes leading up to the accident, let alone the accident itself. Park was now not so confident of what he had and had not managed to do before he blacked out. Perhaps it was more convenient that he did not recall.

"Dr. Han turned his back on his country," Park said.

"He was just trying to get back his wife and son."

"That was the seed of his misfortune, wasn't it? I did try to help him, believe it or not. Tell me, mister …"

"Avery."

"Mr. Avery, have you ever been mountain climbing?"

Avery wondered whether his solo trek through the Sawtooth Mountains qualified as mountain climbing. "No."

"We have a lot of rugged mountains in North Joseon. Let's say you're in a team of men roped together and one of them falls off a cliff. You can't pull him up and he can't pull himself up either. And your team keeps slipping toward the edge. What do you do?"

"So Consul Han is the one dangling over the cliff, dragging the team down in this scenario?"

"What do you do?" Park insisted.

It occurred to Avery that this was the first time he had been in a hospital room since the death of his late fiancée, Kyunghee. He recalled one of the last times she smiled in her hospital bed, trying to cheer him up, as the ill sometimes do in the strength they muster for the ones they love.

That morning Kyunghee died, she took one last deep breath and sighed as if settling in for a good night's sleep. Her mother shook her with growing desperation when she didn't awake, calling out her name over and over again. Her father sternly forbade her to do so, saying, "Don't call back her spirit. She's suffered enough in this world."

After a long night of labored, shallow breathing, she looked at peace, even though Avery hardly recognized her wan, distended face. Kyunghee's parents were also devout Christians. Yet at the moment of their greatest trial, they reverted back to the Daoist instincts of their forebears. *Don't call back her spirit. She's suffered enough in this world.* As Kyunghee's disease took its course, her parent's prayers grew ever more desperate. In those final days, their normally gracious tone faded, especially from the pleas of Kyunghee's mother. Her words increasingly took on shades of anger and resentment. She would ask, "Why are you letting this happen, when she is your humble servant?" Her daughter was withering away, and she was helpless before it, despite their faith. Avery consoled Kyunghee's parents when he could. At other times, he gave their growing anger a wide berth.

When the moment came, a serene resignation replaced the heaviness on her father's face. The last that Avery had heard, Kyunghee's father was still attending church regularly, while her mother had stopped going altogether.

When Avery didn't answer Park's question immediately, Park chimed in: "You cut the rope to save the team."

Avery nodded. "Of course. But do you cut the rope as soon as he falls over the edge?"

"I wish we had the luxury of time, Mr. Avery. Luxury is something you Americans understand well. One of the things you *don't* seem to understand is how close to the edge we're forced to walk every day. You think I'm heartless for what I've done, I know. I merely did what I had to. I eliminate the dead weight of our society – traitors like Han Chol-Soo and Jang Sung-Ho."

Avery froze for a moment, hit with a bolt of recognition. "What did you say?"

"You heard me," Park said.

"You're the one who was in London. You're the one who assassinated Jang Sung-Ho."

Park lifted his head again and stared at Avery for a few seconds before sinking back into the pillow.

Avery felt a murderous urge as he had not felt before. He wanted to take that pillow and smother the life out of him. Did Park know that he was the one who had arranged the Jang brothers' defection? Avery steadied his nerves and told himself Park would get his comeuppance soon enough. This man who lay before him was wounded and defeated yet still defiant. *Remorse – wasn't that a luxury, too?* When Avery ventured to judge the health of Park's society as a whole from the conduct of its elite, his estimation oscillated from contempt to awe. He wondered, was it privation that created such defiance, or was it privilege? As much as he wanted to believe that Park was a harbinger of his Party's destined failure, the thread between depravity and damnation was tenuous at best.

"Perhaps it's better that Dr. Han isn't alive," Avery said finally. "I don't know too many men who could recover from that kind of loss, and that kind of betrayal. Too bad about his daughter. It's not an easy thing to grow up an orphan."

"He told you about his little girl, did he?"

"I'm sure she'll be well taken care of through the benevolence of the Dear Leader."

"Did you come here just to provoke me or are you here in an official capacity?"

"Very well," Avery said and took out a letter from his pocket. "Consul Park Jun-Young, by authority of the State Department you are ordered to leave the United States for abusing your privilege of residence by engaging in activities deemed harmful to the United States."

Avery tossed the letter onto Park's hospital bed. "When the doctors here say you can be discharged, you'll be escorted to New York. From there, you'll be put on a plane to Beijing. If and how you return to Pyongyang is up to you."

Park picked up the letter with his free hand and tossed it on the side table. It was only after Avery left the room that he read it. He braced himself against the bed railing as though fighting a bout of vertigo.

Chapter 28

Won-Sook woke up to a rocking sensation and the sun in her eyes. She smelled fish. The scent was floating up from under her. She sat up and saw that she had been lying on a pile of netting. She looked up and realized then that she was on a boat, cruising along to the rhythmic puttering of the engine. Trailing from the boat's stern was a small rowboat, periodically bucking and swerving on the waves like an untamed pony.

"Awake, are we?" The voice came from an old man whose face was so wrinkled and tan that it was more like bark than skin. His hair was a wiry mess that would have been impossible to untangle with a comb without causing much agony. "Are you hungry?"

Won-Sook nodded and then asked, "Who are you, comrade?"

The old man smiled and his teeth were a shocking strip of white against his dark face. "I'm not your comrade, girly. I'm a friend of your father's. Just call me ahjuhshi," he said. *Ahjuhshi* is what a Korean child would call any unrelated adult man. He unwrapped a cloth and handed Won-Sook a plump hemisphere of white dough called a *ho-pang.* "It's got red bean paste in it. Do you like red bean paste?"

Won-Sook nodded. "Thank you, comra-, I mean, ahjuhshi."

Something stirred from under a blanket sitting at the old man's feet. A woman got up and tidied her hair. It was a different woman than the one who took her away from the school gate in the middle of the night.

"And who are *you*, comrade?"

The woman glanced at Won-Sook and then at the old man and said, "She's a spunky one, isn't she?"

"This is a friend of your father's too," the man said.

"Are you a fisherman, comrade? I mean, ahjuhshi?" Won-Sook asked.

"I've never met a fisherman before," Won-Sook said. "Where are we going?"

"We're going to see your father," the man said.

Won-Sook took a bite so large out of the ho-pang that she could barely chew it.

"Eat it slowly," the woman said, shaking her head in disapproval and concern.

It took a minute or two before she managed to swallow the mouthful. Then she said, "I've never been on a boat before," and took another over-sized bite.

The man looked at her with a bemused smile. "Aren't you afraid, Won-Sook?"

"Of what?" she said, barely comprehensible with her mouth full.

"Of us."

"Why?"

"Because you don't know us."

"You're my father's friends."

The man smiled. "Right you are. Good girl."

* * *

There were a number of reasons why it was decided that of all the foreign diplomatic outposts in Beijing, Won-Sook should be taken to the Spanish Embassy. First of all, it was on Sanlitun Road, home to a thriving bar district that prospered with the influx of foreign embassies moving from Beijing's former diplomatic center, Legation Quarter, near Tiananmen Square. Being a booze alley *and* a diplomatic hub, Sanlitun had its share of riffraff mingling among foreigners. There wouldn't be as many tourists now that the weather was getting cooler but it would still provide some cover for Won-Sook and her escort.

Secondly, going to the South Korean Embassy was out of the question. When Hwang Jang-Yop unexpectedly showed up there seeking asylum earlier in the year, it triggered a blockade by Chinese troops for five tense weeks. Several months later, there was still a stifling police presence there on Dong Fang Dong Road. Won-Sook and her escort would get eyeballed all the way down the street; and if they were to be stopped for questioning, their journey would come to an abrupt end. Even if they did make it into the embassy, it was improbable that the South Korean government would endure the diplomatic strains with Beijing yet again, and not even over a prized defection like that of Hwang but over the six-year-old daughter of an obscure diplomat. The embassy of a relatively neutral country was preferable. That meant a country with weaker ties to Beijing, with less to lose in a diplomatic row. That ruled out the United States, Japan and Russia.

The final, and possibly the most compelling reason to attempt the Spanish Embassy was that the front gate there was usually kept wide open – essentially presenting an unguarded border to a foreign territory beyond the reach of pursuing Chinese authorities.

Sound as the reasoning was, however, it didn't take into account the wrench thrown into the works when a vigilant teacher at Won-Sook's school made inquiries as to when the girl would be returning from her visit with her parents. It didn't take long for the teacher to discover that the girl's parents were in fact not in Pyongyang. At first, school officials suspected that Won-Sook had been kidnapped for ransom. There had been rumors of such kidnappings before. There was no way to say how prevalent such crimes were – or crimes of any kind, for that matter – because such depravity existed in North Korea only as a dystopian threat that would visit upon the society in the absence of the beatific harmony maintained by the Dear Leader. Crime was a capitalist malady – one that addled not only the West, but also the pitiable brethren in South Joseon as a consequence of its greed and servitude to the West.

Once news of the diplomatic debacle in New York reached the Workers' Party headquarters, two things became clear: One, Won-Sook's disappearance was not a kidnapping for ransom; and two, her father was still alive, contrary to the report from New York, otherwise there would be no reason for the Americans to risk so much to smuggle a child out of North Korea. They needed her to make her father pliant to their bidding.

Frantic calls went out from Pyongyang to all the brigades that guarded the borders and ports. Weary soldiers, whose only ambition for the day had been to secure their promised food rations, were instead miffed to find themselves being mustered – in another pointless drill, for all they knew – into a human fence around the country.

By the time the first of the sentries were beginning to climb their guard towers, Won-Sook and her elderly handler had long since boarded the little row boat they had towed behind them and waded ashore to a small Chinese fishing village on the Shandong Peninsula, which juts out into the Yellow Sea toward North Korea. On the bus trip to Beijing, Won-Sook pressed her nose against the window for most of the trip, once in a while turning to point out some unusual sight to the old woman, until sleep overwhelmed her curiosity.

She awoke in the old woman's lap with her black hair matted against her sweaty white forehead as though awaking from a feverish dream. "It's okay. We're almost there," the woman said as she wiped Won-Sook's brow with her hand. Her own leathery skin that was a record of the ravages of time and hardships she had endured stood in stark contrast to Won-Sook's unblemished forehead as her hand traveled across it. The woman didn't know whether to pity this little girl for the peril she faced or to envy her chance to escape to a new life.

* * *

Early in the morning the following day, when the old woman handed off Won-Sook to the local contact in Beijing, she expected the girl to be as nonchalant about being put into the care of a stranger as she had been about waking up on an unfamiliar boat and meeting her and her fisherman husband. But this time was different. She seemed to sense that something serious was afoot and when adults become serious, children get frightened. Won-Sook didn't want to let go of the old woman's hand. "I want to stay with you, Comrade *ahjumma*," she said, coming up with her own hybrid honorific to call out to this woman whose name she didn't know. Children often did not know the name of adults, even their closest relatives, because by tradition adults rarely used names to refer to one another, using instead their job titles or familial titles.

It took some convincing, some bribing with candy, for the girl to uncoil her tender fingers from the old woman's hand. As short as their time had been together, it pained the woman to see Won-Sook go off with another stranger. She was surprised by how little of a fight Won-Sook put up in the end and marveled for a moment at the stout obedience. Knowing what the girl and her escort were about to attempt, she worried for Won-Sook on her behalf, as much as the girl could not comprehend the circumstances to worry for herself.

The local contact, the escort who would walk Won-Sook across the threshold of the Spanish Embassy, was a South Korean Christian missionary by the name of Yoon Hae-Jung. While her faith may have emboldened her to take on this task, her citizenship did not necessarily protect her from a stint in a Chinese prison if things went awry. Unlike a Chinese national, however, eventual deportation would offer some definitive relief from indefinite imprisonment. She was a younger, better-groomed version of the old woman, about the same height, built more solidly through her torso by dint of youth and better nourishment.

"Whatever this lady tells you, you listen to her, alright?" the old woman told Won-Sook. "You do exactly as she tells you, and you'll see your mother and father soon. Do you understand?"

Tears welled up in Won-Sook's eyes and perched precariously on her lashes. She wiped them away with her sleeve before they fell. The old woman felt a faint soreness in her heart akin to remorse as she watched the little girl walk away hand-in-hand with Yoon. Won-Sook's footsteps squeaked in her rubber shoes and she stole glances behind her until they disappeared behind a building. The old woman lingered for a moment, half expecting the little girl to come running around the corner.

* * *

The day was still too early for government offices to be open, so Won-Sook and her escort passed the time in the quiet maze of tree-lined streets behind the German Embassy, just a block away from its Spanish counterpart. Yoon had reconnoitered the gates the day before to make sure they were wide open as usual. She avoided the temptation to check again this morning for fear of arousing suspicion from a vigilant guard, as unlikely as that was. The woman bought some cheap bread from a street vendor; she and the girl fed the pigeons as they strolled in and out of the trees' shade, appearing at one moment vivid then concealed. The mature stands of ash trees in the distance sparkled as the leaves flashed their lighter underbellies in the breeze. Before long, Yoon noticed that Won-Sook had stopped feeding the birds and was instead nibbling on the bread herself.

"Have you eaten breakfast?" she asked Won-Sook.

The girl became embarrassed and began feeding the birds again. A squadron of sparrows swooped in to join the pigeons and pecked away at the smaller pieces. Yoon bought some more bread and patiently fed it to the girl.

"Do you have any brothers or sisters, Won-Sook?" she asked.

"I have a younger brother," the girl said through bulging cheeks.

"Do you like playing with him?"

"He's just a baby still. I haven't seen him. He was born in America."

"You'll see him soon," Yoon said and felt her pulse quicken in anticipation of what she was about to attempt.

* * *

When the top officials at the Workers' Party in Pyongyang figured out that there was a non-negligible chance that Han Chol-Soo's daughter had slipped beyond the borders, they swallowed their pride and sent a message to Beijing to be on the lookout for a North Korean fugitive heading their way in case she intended to seek asylum at one of the foreign embassies there. For China, being allies with North Korea was like having a delinquent nephew who would disappear for months doing God knows what, only to call in the middle of the night asking to be bailed out of jail. Sometimes you wished you could leave him there to teach him a lesson, but this nephew knows where you live, and if you leave him there to sort things out on his own and fend for himself, sooner or later there would be repercussions.

Fatigue and annoyance – those were the two feelings that overcame the police chief in charge of the Chaoyang district when he got the call from his superiors that he should cancel all leave for his men and dispatch them to be on the lookout for a possible North Korean defector. The chief was a methodical if somewhat indolent man by the name of Cai Li-Tang. He felt his blood pressure rise as he thought back to the sleepless nights he endured during the blockade of the South Korean Embassy in February when Hwang Jang-Yop was holed up there. Perhaps it was that Cai was agitated, or perhaps it was that his superiors weren't entirely clear when they communicated the mission, but the pertinent piece of information that Cai missed was that the fugitive they were looking for was a six-year-old. Cai's order to his own underlings was to look out for a North Korean woman.

That's why when one of his men saw Won-Sook and Yoon

feeding the birds near the German Embassy, it didn't even occur to him to question them. The policeman gave them a cursory glance and walked on by, their significance lost on him in plain sight for want of clearer orders. At the end of that day, he would have no memory of them, and hence no cause for regret.

To Won-Sook's escort, however, the policeman's fleeting glance felt as though it lingered, probing for their identity, and when he moved on, she wondered whether he was off to call for reinforcements. She said a quick prayer to calm herself.

"It's time to go, Won-Sook," she said, and took the girl's hand. It was encrusted with breadcrumbs.

As she and Won-Sook approached the corner of Dongzhimen Street and Sanlitun Road, she noticed a platoon of uniformed soldiers lining up in formation. It took all of her will and faith not to quicken her strides. It was still a few hundred meters to the Spanish Embassy. She thought of her husband, a fellow Christian missionary, dropping off their own daughter at school. Would he be proud of her or cross that she put herself in such jeopardy? She didn't have the chance to tell him of her task, as swiftly as it came to her from her pastor, with admonitions of absolute secrecy. She prayed he would understand, and that this would not force him to further defend her against his parents, who never quite shared the religious zeal of their son and daughter-in-law. When she told them that she was going to China to do missionary work, they refused to see her any more. She hadn't spoken to them since.

It was only as the police chief was delivering an update to his superiors that it became clear the fugitive they were seeking was a little girl. During the phone call, Cai did not let on that this was a surprise to him, his indolence working in his favor. As soon as he ended that call, he sent word to his men clarifying what they should be looking for.

Yoon and Won-Sook turned the corner onto Sanlitun. The embassy was less than a hundred meters away. Yoon's heart sank when she saw two soldiers strolling side by side down the street, casually talking to one another. She began thinking of how, if she got arrested, she would defend herself against her in-laws' spiteful accusations that she was an irresponsible mother. Won-Sook looked up at her when she began mumbling something to herself and clutched the girl's hand tighter. *Lord, protect us from these unbelievers. By Your grace, make us small in their eyes. Let us pass unhindered so that I may deliver this girl into Your arms.*

Yoon continued to walk toward the embassy. She felt her knees weaken a little and was afraid the soldiers could see them trembling. Feeling that the woman's hands were shaking, Won-Sook asked her, "Are you alright?"

She lied and told Won-Sook that she was feeling cold.

Forty meters. A breeze carried the fragrance of chrysanthemums over a wall. Mums were funeral flowers in Korea, a scent that would pierce the blanket of incense, a clear bell through the murmuring of mourners. God was sending a message to Yoon, by way of an industrious gardener, to not be afraid, for if the worst she feared was death, then He would greet her at the gates. *Suffer little children, and forbid them not, to come unto me: for of such is the kingdom of heaven.*

Thirty meters. Yoon heard someone call out from behind. She dared not turn around. He called out again, more forcefully. The two soldiers who were walking ahead of her turned around. There was some shouting back and forth between them and the people behind her, then one of the soldiers, a slight man who still looked to be a teenager barely filling out his uniform, pointed directly at Yoon and Won-Sook. Yoon turned around and saw two policemen trotting toward them, one of them speaking into his walkie-talkie. There's a time to play it cool and a time for urgency, and Yoon recognized instantly that this was the latter. She tugged at Won-Sook's hand to get her attention and said, "Are you a good runner? Let's see who can run faster to that gate!" Yoon gave Won-Sook a little push and she started running after her.

Twenty meters. There was shouting all around and the two soldiers sprinted toward them on an intercept. Yoon could not feel her legs. It was as though she were floating above the ground. She looked down to make sure that Won-Sook was still with her. All her senses were dulled. She feared she was losing consciousness. She could only hear the squeaking of Won-Sook's bare feet in her little rubber shoes.

Five meters. One of the soldiers grabbed Yoon by the sleeve of her coat. The force of the interrupted momentum spun her around, but in doing so she shed her coat neatly and began to move forward again.

Two meters. The other soldier latched on to her belt. This time she couldn't break free. She leaned forward, dragging the soldier behind her and pushing Won-Sook ahead of her. They were now at the threshold of the Spanish Embassy's gate. By now both soldiers had grabbed on to Yoon. She lost her balance and fell on top of Won-Sook, then she rolled over onto her back and shoved the girl through the gate into the arms of a bewildered Spanish guard. The last thing that left Yoon's grasp was the girl's icy feet when her shoes popped off, and even in the desperate commotion of being dragged on the ground Yoon regretted not having paid more attention to the girl's comfort and wondered why Won-Sook hadn't complained of being cold.

When the Chinese policemen finally joined the soldiers at the gate, they tried to walk through, but two other Spanish guards showed up and pushed them back. In the stillness after the storm, Yoon Hae-Jung's blunted senses trickled back to her. Before she was dragged away, she saw the little girl for the last time, crying and barefoot in the arms of a young Spanish soldier who was humming a tune to her and brushing away the tears from her flushed cheeks with his finger. She wondered what they would do to keep her feet warm.

Chapter 29

It was an unseasonably warm October morning, with an odor of summer, redolent of heated pavement recently cooled by a passing thunderstorm, masked as it was by that distinct smell of airports – jet exhaust, fumes from idling cars, and a whiff of the flat cabin air that clung to weary passengers whose nights were now days. A parade of humanity walked into the arrivals lobby at Terminal 4 at John F. Kennedy International Airport. Some were greeted with exuberant hugs and kisses, others with feeble bouquets bought as an afterthought on the way to the airport. Dour business travelers were met by chauffeurs holding up their names, often misspelled, on a card covering their hearts.

Even standing together, Han Chol-Soo and James Avery were not out of place here. They sported a complementary set of injuries; Han's arm was in a sling. Avery had a large Band-Aid on his forehead, still surrounded by remnants of his nasty bruise.

Han noticed the hum of the airport anew, though he had been here on many occasions, both passing through himself and greeting his countrymen – more accurately, *former* countrymen. North Korea was no longer his home, neither in a practical sense nor in principle. He glanced at Avery and Avery looked back. Without prompting, Avery proffered a word of encouragement.

"Don't worry, Dr. Han. This is a good day," he said.

Han tried to smile but instead ended up with something like a scowl. His nationality – it was beyond his worry now. The hard summer had burned all ambition out of him, save the desire to see his daughter again. When he woke up in the morning nowadays, he didn't bother making his bed.

"I was waiting for a taxi the other day in Manhattan. Sometimes it's hard to find an empty one, especially during rush hour," Han said to Avery while keeping an eye on the exit from customs. "Then this one cab swerved a few lanes and slammed on the brakes to stop right next to me even though the light on top was off. Guess who was in the taxi."

"Who?"

"Jenny Ryu."

"Seriously?"

Han nodded. "She said through the window, 'I saw you from afar and at first I didn't know it was you. I thought that man looks so sad.' I guess I was lost in thought. Is it really written on my face like that?" Han turned to Avery as if presenting his visage for inspection.

Avery didn't answer, so Han knew it must be true.

"They say a man is responsible for his own face after the age of forty," Han said. "I don't want my face to evoke pity from others."

Avery looked away from Han and back at the exit from customs. People were beginning to dribble out, some with giant stacks of luggage portending a new start.

"I don't think anyone wants to wear their personal tragedies on their face, even though perhaps some people have a right to," Avery said. "It's one thing for your country to turn its back on you, despite years of distinguished service. I'm sure that cuts deep. It's an entirely different kind of insult for that country to try to extinguish you. It's the kind of thing that makes you lose faith."

Han looked at the floor, and his eyes lost focus, as if he were looking into the past.

"I thought I was doing something important. It turns out I was just one mistake from being expendable," Han said. "Now, I'm an enemy of the state, even though treason was the furthest thing from my mind when I went looking for my wife and son." Then he added, "It's not so much the betrayal that bothers me. I just feel like I've been …" Han grappled for the right words, "… duped for having been so loyal all these years."

"So did Jenny say what she's doing these days?" Avery asked, changing the topic to brighten the dark turn the conversation had taken.

"She said she's going back to school," Han said. "She reached out the window of the cab and squeezed my hand before she said goodbye. I think she was crying."

"Why was *she* crying?" Avery asked.

"I guess it was my face," Han said, apologetically.

Avery had told Han about his last encounter with Park Jung-Young – how he had left Park's hospital room after telling him that Han was dead. Soon after that day, a spokesman for the State Department issued a statement: "Two officials at the Democratic People's Republic of Korea's Mission to the United Nations have been expelled by the State Department because they were involved in activities deemed harmful to the United States. The expulsions resulted from an investigation by the State Department in conjunction with the national security division of the F.B.I."

Park would have figured out by now that Han's death was a ruse. Han wondered where Park was now – whether he had returned to Pyongyang to face the consequences or had disappeared into his netherworld of spooks. When Han was in Manhattan recently, in a car driving up Third Avenue, near his old haunt, he saw a red neon sign that read "PARK," with a curved arrow pointing toward a garage on East 43rd Street. Behind the sign, in the background, were the blue-green windows of the U.N. Secretariat building, rising up beyond the end of the block. The neon sign taunted him, as if saying that Park Jun-Young was there, waiting for him. But of course he was long gone.

Knowing Park, it was more than likely that he had stashes of currency awaiting him in places like the Sociedade de Jogos de Macao. He may have to live out his days looking behind his back to escape the retribution of the Dear Leader, but he would never suffer the hunger of his compatriots. He would be at home there, as long as he didn't provoke the triads on the island. Gang killings were so common there that a police official had recently tried to soothe jittery visitors with the curious assurance that the city had "professional killers who don't miss their targets."

Park Jun-Young would be at home there.

"Did you hear that Deputy Ambassador Kwon Woo-Shik has also been recalled to Pyongyang?" Avery said.

Han nodded and said, "The deputy ambassador is a survivor. I suspect he'll make it through this scandal, perhaps diminished, but intact. He's blessed by a lack of imagination and ambition, except to acquire the next job title above his. He's probably not in danger of being sent to a gulag, but it's not beyond the realm of possibility that he'll end up in some dead-end diplomatic post."

"I'm sure it'll make him sick with envy to see his old classmates outpace him," Avery said.

There was an old Korean saying that served as a warning to would-be despots: *The will of the people is the will of heaven.* Tyrant kings were overthrown with such rallying cries. Han wondered whether the rulers had so lost the favor of their people that even heaven, nature itself, had turned against them, decimating the landscape, bringing this famine upon them.

"You know, on the drive over here, I noticed for the first time there was all this tall grass in the marshes surrounding the airport, growing wild, untended yet green and flourishing," Han said. "It occurred to me that even that grass could be harvested for food in my home country right now. The hunger there is quite desperate, isn't it, James?"

Avery nodded.

Han felt suddenly ashamed. "What was it exactly that I was trying to protect?" Han asked no one in particular. It was a question that had plagued him since that day at the farmhouse. "That question pops into my mind in those early morning hours, and I can't get back to sleep again. The more I mulled it over, the less clear the answer is," Han said. "I have to get out of bed to shake off the thought."

Avery tapped Han on the arm to get his attention. It looked like passengers from the flight from Manila had made it through customs. He pointed to the door where people were now streaming out. Through the crowd, a woman emerged holding the hand of a little girl dressed in clothes so bright that she seemed surrounded by a halo of light. Han squinted through it and saw that it was Won-Sook.

He was suddenly afraid that some catastrophe might befall her in the few steps remaining between them. He pushed through the crowd – the exuberant huggers, the ones holding bouquets, and the listless chauffeurs – in his need to shorten the distance between them. Won-Sook spotted him, and there was a flash of recognition on her face, yet she did not run to him. She walked slowly, and Han saw that her shoes flashed with tiny lights with each step. He dropped to his knees and opened his one good arm, beckoning an embrace. The woman escorting Won-Sook let go of her hand and thrust her toward her father.

Han squeezed her. Instead of melting into him, she resisted ever so slightly, putting her two fern-like hands against his chest. The gesture stung him, but he understood her reluctance was of his own making. He had done nothing over the years to accustom her to the physical affection of her own parents. Han caught a glimpse of why his wife had become estranged of her own daughter.

Traits both physical and mental have a habit of skipping a generation, leading to those fond alliances between grandparents and their progeny when they recognize themselves in one another, much more so than they ever did in their child or parent who stubbornly refused to understand them. Han wondered whether he might one day find redemption in Won-Sook's children.

The gunshot wound in Han's shoulder began throbbing. He rubbed it with his palm and adjusted his sling.

"Are you alright, Dr. Han?" Avery asked.

Han looked at Avery and suddenly felt grateful for his little kindnesses. "I'm alright. I'll be alright," Han said. "Thank you. Thank you for everything."

Now that his daughter was with him, Han felt responsible for her as he had never felt before. His wife was gone, and he was beyond the aid of every person he had called friend or kin, as well as his erstwhile Party and country. Han had never thought of himself as a particularly gregarious person, but it dawned on him in that moment, when he realized that he and he alone would be responsible for his daughter's future, how much of a social animal he really was. He felt as though he were on the high desert of New Mexico again. Craning his neck up toward the heavens and listening, like those gargantuan radio telescopes, for the voice of the universe to tell him that somewhere in the vastness there was a place for him. The atoms of his body yearned to hear the echo of the firmament beckoning him home. Eons from now, when the sun is extinguished, and the scattered iron and carbon that once anchored his blood and bones are reassembled, he wondered if perhaps they would be reunited with an atom or two of his wife's, or his son's, or anyone he loved and loved him back.

Han was truly afraid for the first time in his life, more so than when his own life was in jeopardy. When one is visited by tragedy, the world seems a scarier place, full of malice.

"They will pay for this," Han said to no one in particular.

"Say again?" Avery asked.

"They will pay for all of this suffering," Han said, wiping the bangs clear from his daughter's eyes.

Avery concurred immediately. "Yes, some day there will be a thorough accounting of all that's been done."

"No. Not an accounting. There's a word for it in English," Han said, and blinked for a few moments to recall it. "Reckoning."

Avery tried to imagine a clockwork universe in which sins were met inevitably with punishment, the cardinal ones with damnation. "If only it were so," Avery said.

Han stared at his daughter. Feeling his gaze upon her, she looked back, with curiosity, then looked back down at her shoes, shuffling her feet a couple of times to activate the lights again.

He must commit his life to her – what meager half of it was left. That is all he knows.

The End

About the Author:

Paul H.B. Shin's debut novel follows a career as an award-winning journalist for more than 20 years, most recently for ABC News. He previously wrote for the New York Daily News. He was born in South Korea and lived in London during his childhood. He now lives in Brooklyn, New York.

CPSIA information can be obtained
at www.ICGtesting.com
Printed in the USA
LVOW12s2352130917
548683LV00001B/43/P